Banjo Lessons

By

Jack B. Hood

authorHOUSE™

1663 LIBERTY DRIVE, SUITE 200
BLOOMINGTON, INDIANA 47403
(800) 839-8640
WWW.AUTHORHOUSE.COM

First published by AuthorHouse 11/18/04

ISBN: 1-4184-9742-8 (sc)

Library of Congress Control Number: 2004097026

Printed in the United States of America
Bloomington, Indiana

This book is printed on acid-free paper.

Dedication

To my wife, Patricia Christine Perry Hood

<u>Biblical Translator 1</u>- "Here is the translation of *DEUTERONOMY* **25:11-12** as I see it:"

If two men are fighting and the wife of one tries to save her husband from his opponent by reaching out with her hand and seizing him by the testicles, one must cut off her hand and show her no pity.

<u>Biblical Translator 2</u>- "Whose testicles has the wife seized--those of the opponent or those of the husband?"

Many of my life's lessons were learned around playing the banjo.

Anonymous

Introduction

Sam Stone, Esquire
Birmingham, Alabama

No banjo was ever placed on his knee from the age of four like several bluegrass pickers he had met, and he did not have one tattooed on his knee like some Army types he had run across from Alabama while in the Air Force stationed in the Panama Canal Zone. As with most 5-string banjo players, Sam Stone did not have formal music training, and he was not a professional. He had enjoyed playing since the age of sixteen, even though he had not improved his performance much since the age of nineteen. Banjo players were likable sorts as a general rule, and over the years banjo playing had created for him some unique social opportunities and experiences. Sam was now fifty-six, and he was on his fourth banjo, and his last wife, in his mind. He didn't know it, but his first one wanted him back. Sam did understand, however, that his current wife and boss at the U.S. Attorney's Office wanted to fire and divorce him. She also wanted to inflict maximum pain during the process.

In the meantime, Sam sometimes taught banjo, and played it to maintain some sanity in a seemingly insane world.

Chapter 1

Birmingham, Alabama
Sam Stone's Apartment on Southside
Thursday, June 5, 2003
6:00 p.m.

As Sam hauled the well worn 5-string banjo case out from under his bed in anticipation of a student's visit for his first lessons, the phone rang. The caller I.D. displayed a 731 prefix. This usually meant the U.S. Attorney's office was on the line. Sam had an unlisted number, and he answered with his full name, "Sam Stone.".

Official business got conducted more efficiently on the phone if all parties knew exactly who they were dealing with from the get go, in Sam's view. If the government caller was not recognizable by voice, and did not in the first sentence tell Sam his or her name, he asked immediately. Too many times screw-ups had occurred because you did not get the name of the person or agent calling with some critical information about an arrest warrant, killing, or some other crisis.

Sam only used only a cordless phone at his apartment. He also had his own cellular and a beeper that had been issued by the U.S. Attorney's Office. Cordless and cellular phones give greater mobility, and you can safely talk over the phone during a lightning storm. Technology was such that criminals, terrorists, and law enforcement personnel could be tracked as long their cell phones were turned on. Phone records solved crimes and put away bad guys every day.

Sam also knew that it was easy for people to snoop on phone conversations despite all precautions. For this reason, Sam tried to keep business conversations brief over any phone, and if sensitive matters came up he changed the subject or suggested to the persons on the other end that they have a face-to-face conference somewhere. Serious business should never be conducted over the phone lines or airwaves according to Sam. He subscribed to the theory that just because you are paranoid it does not mean that there aren't people out there who are really trying to do you harm.

"Sam, this is Linda. I heard that Judge Crowell, in Pickering case, Rule Twenty-nined your ass. That case was a lay-up. I've decided to reassign you."

"Wait a minute," Sam said. "I don't want to move out of the Organized Crime and Racketeering section. I've been there 7 years, and one case does not a prosecutor make or break. After all, where would you send me, to Child Exploitation and Obscenity?"

She knew Sam's dislike for that area. Maybe she was thinking Narcotic and Dangerous Drug section. That was pretty bad too, because it was so repetitive. One crack cocaine case after another got boring for prosecutors, judges and probation officers, but they kept a lid on local crime and the case statistics up for budgeting purposes. She knew Sam did not like that section either.

As cold as ice, she said, "Today is Thursday, and tomorrow you will become the newest Assistant U.S. Attorney in the Civil Division."

Sam was speechless. Sam heard the phone go click on the other end. He thought to himself that she had been rude and crude. The sorry wench did not even give him a chance to call her an appropriate epithet.

Sam Stone was 56 years old and had a full head of graying dark brown hair. He still moved his 6-foot frame with good athletic agility for his age. Arthritis had not taken over his fingers like it had with some old banjo pickers that he had met. He hoped that day would never come. His brown eyes needed glasses these days, but the rest of his body had held together rather well. He attributed much of this to playing football and baseball at Woodlawn High in Birmingham while he was growing up.

His parents had always encouraged physical activities as well as good grades. Sam had gone to grammar school in Hoke's Bluff in northeast Alabama before his father took a job as a salesman at Sears in downtown Birmingham. Sam was smart enough that he started the first grade at four years of age and then skipped the third grade.

Sam's father, John Henry Stone, was from a farming family near the Coosa River in eastern Etowah County, and his mother was from an Italian immigrant family in Ensley that worked in the steel mills. Both had been killed in a car accident near Fruithurst on Highway 78 just after Sam had graduated from high school. A lawsuit was filed for their wrongful deaths, but the jury found for the defense.

In a wrongful death suit in Alabama, then and now, the only measure of damages is punitive for ordinary negligence. Alabama is the only state or jurisdiction in the world that developed and retained such a wrongful death statute. The wealth or needs of the survivors are irrelevant and inadmissible. Furthermore, contributory negligence bars any claims. This means that if the deceased's own negligent conduct in any way contributed to the cause of the accident, then recovery can be barred.

The defense lawyer argued contributory negligence successfully, in part, because some whiskey bottles were found in the car with Georgia tax stamps, and the trooper had reported that the radio in his parent's car was still on and playing loud rock and roll music when he arrived at the scene of the head on collision. An Alabama jury in those days did not like these facts, and disallowed any recovery for Sam's benefit.

The lawsuit was Sam's first introduction to the law and how it worked in real life. Fortunately, a small insurance policy helped him get through college and law school. Despite this first disappointing encounter with the legal system, Sam generally remained fascinated with the practice of law, especially in the U.S. Attorney's Office. In the Organized Crime and Racketeering section something new and different happened with just about each case he handled, and in Sam's mind, each new one was almost as fun and interesting as learning a new banjo tune.

Sam never joined a political party because the extreme ends of the Democratic and Republican parties turned him off. He told everyone that he was a "practical pedestrian" if asked about his political affiliations. Sam voted for individuals, not parties.

Linda Lott, Sam's wife and soon to be ex-wife, was five years his junior. She had bleached blond hair on a shapely 5 foot 10 inch body that included breasts enhanced by plastic surgery. She was also the U.S. Attorney for the Northern District of Alabama, and therefore his boss.

Sam first became romantically involved with Linda in 1991 while attending a LECC (Law Enforcement Coordinating Committee) meeting in Gulf Shores, Alabama. Linda had been an Assistant U.S. Attorney in the Middle District of Alabama in Montgomery since 1986, and in 1989, she joined the office in Birmingham in the OCDETF (Organized Crime Drug Enforcement Task Force) section when her husband moved his dental practice to North Shelby County, just south of town. This was the fastest growing metropolitan area in the state. Linda did not want children, and she divorced her husband who did.

After the end of the first day's LECC program, Linda bought Sam a drink at the Holiday Inn bar, saying, "You know, if I wasn't a fed, I'd spend the next three nights here at the beach like the locals, smoking dope, snorting coke, and fucking till my eyes rolled back."

Sam suggested in reply, "How about we experiment with your idea by substituting illicit drugs with single malt scotch and imported beers?"

Linda said, "You're on. Let's do it."

In a flash, they were off to the booze store and the relationship races.

By the time Sam and Linda got back to Birmingham, each was an item of intense office gossip. Despite Sam's reservations stemming from a first failed marriage in the 1970's, within a year Linda and Sam were wed.

As Linda often said, "Fucking and fighting crime, what a high."

Linda was born and raised around Anniston, Alabama. Her father was a local construction contractor who got his share of government contracts with the U.S. Army's Ft. McClelland and the Anniston Army Depot, the later being a place where tons of nerve gas and the like were stored. Her mother taught high school math and was the financial advisor for the construction business.

Linda studied finance and accounting at Tulane in undergraduate school and then got her law degree at Alabama. She was political and driven to succeed, probably due to the influence of her parents. Her father saw to it that she learned to hunt and fish like a boy when she was growing up, and her mother steered her towards tax and accounting, seeing to it that Linda took over a part of the bookkeeping responsibilities for her father's construction company while Linda was still in high school.

She was smart, aggressive and, at times, ruthless. She bragged to Sam once how she had used her "feminine skills" to persuade a law professor to give her an A rather than a C on her first year torts exam, insuring that she would get placed on law review. Linda did not like dogs or kids and told Sam that she would have neither. She also did not like modern art. As she said, "I think those kinds of artists are trying to trick me."

Prior to working for the U.S. Attorney's Office, Linda worked for a reasonably prominent plaintiff's firm that got most of its business from referrals from other lawyers. In Alabama, an attorney typically signed a client to a 50 per cent contingent fee contract in plaintiff cases and then referred the case to a prominent plaintiffs' firm on a one-third, two-thirds split of any settlement or recovery.

For example, on a $150,000 settlement in a malpractice case, the client got $75,000, the referring attorney got $25,000, and the prominent plaintiffs' firm that actually handled the case got $50,000. The referring attorney did not have to do any work on the case except for signing up the client.

One might wonder why someone would sign a 50 per cent contingency fee contract, but Linda had a good routine for closing the deal with prospective personal injury clients which she had learned from a senior partner.

She would look a potential client in the eye and say, "Look, these cases are difficult, high risk, and very expensive. It will take lots of legal research and the hiring of highly paid experts which will cost a ton of money. Despite the risks and the high costs, the firm and I are willing to take your case. We will do all the work, pay for all costs and expenses, and if we recover anything, then we will split it with you. Does that sound fair?"

Invariably, the prospective client would say "Yes, splitting things even sounds fair."

Forthwith, Linda would have the client sign a contract with a 50 per cent contingency arraignment. Of course any expenses were also billed against the client's recovery.

Linda had a falling out with the senior partners after almost 8 years of work because she had started billing some unusual expenses against client recoveries. Some of the expenses included clothes, jewelry, concert tickets, and trips to the beach. She was invited to leave.

At the age of 32, she joined the U.S. Attorney's Office in Montgomery, initially in the civil section, but after 9 months she switched to the criminal side. If one was politically ambitious, that was where the action lay, and that's what Linda wanted. She eventually became a good prosecutor.

After her move to Birmingham, divorce, and marriage to Sam, she sought only the most high profile of cases. She learned a lot from Sam, and made sure that she capitalized on Sam's community and agency contacts. Linda soon made quite a name for herself taking on the redneck mafia, crooked bankers, assorted bank robbers, fraudfeasors, and swindlers.

In 2001, she was made the First Assistant, which is the position just below the U.S. Attorney.

About this same time Sam and Linda drifted apart. She spent a lot of time attending meetings and no longer tried cases. They saw each other only briefly, and she did not to want to be close anymore, physically or otherwise. Linda certainly made no attempt to pursue the physical relationship that had started off the marriage.

She seemed driven to make a name for herself and gain some unknown goal of legal respect.

Sam did not care for this change in her attitude and ambitions, and he told her bluntly, "Your ambitious shift in attitude and direction is ruining our marriage. It will lead to no good and bring you down if you're not careful."

Linda acidly replied, "Get out of my way and out of my life. You are holding me back, and I won't stand for it another minute. Get your banjo and your other shit together and leave."

Sam left. Linda filed for divorce.

Around the U.S. Attorney's Office, Linda seemed embarrassed by the breakup, and said very little about it to the other attorneys and staff members. They, in turn, were afraid to bring up the topic and kept the gossip mill to a minimum for fear that Linda would lash out, given her temperament.

Linda decided to distance herself further from Sam by getting rid of him at the office if she could. When she moved up to U.S. Attorney, Linda started to scheme in earnest in this direction.

The First Assistant becomes the Acting U.S. Attorney on a temporary basis if for some reason the U.S. Attorney is incapacitated or out of the jurisdiction. A good First Assistant runs the office and does all of the crappy work for the U.S. Attorney, including personnel management matters where the hatchet is called for.

It was generally conceded in the U.S. Attorney's Office that Linda had been a fairly good prosecutor but that she was hell on wheels as a manager. She devoted her full time to the job; however, she ignored any suggestions that Sam or others might have had, and generally let her ambitions lead her life.

The President appoints the U.S. Attorneys. It is a political decision by the party in office. There are 93 U.S. Attorneys in the districts of the United States, the Virgin Islands, Guam, Puerto Rico, and the Northern Mariana Islands. They wield enormous power and influence. A U.S. Attorney is more powerful than a U.S. District Judge because only the U.S. Attorney has the ability to indict. That power trumps federal judicial power every time. Just ask any federal judge that has been indicted.

If the U.S. Attorney dies, resigns, or becomes disabled, then the Attorney General of the United States may appoint the U.S. Attorney for a period of 120 days. If the President has not chosen a new U.S. Attorney within that period, then the U.S. District Court for the district may appoint the U.S. Attorney to serve until the President makes an appointment.

Carson Blaylock, the former U.S. Attorney in the Northern District, and moderate Republican, resigned because his wife came down with breast cancer. Linda got the Attorney General's 120 day appointment, and she was working the federal district judges to get the court's appointment. She had Democratic baggage from her days as a plaintiff's attorney and was having trouble convincing the Republican power players that she should get a permanent Presidential nod. In the words of a Republican congressman, "Linda has too much Democratic dust on her shoes to suit me."

In Linda's view, Sam's loss of a high profile criminal case made her look bad and lessened her chances with the court and with any Presidential appointment. The Pickering criminal case had gotten too much press for her likes. There was supposedly an office pool going on as to how many months Sam had before Linda terminated his employment as an Assistant U.S. Attorney. Linda knew that she had to be careful in how she ran Sam off, but she was clever, devious and determined. The Pickering case gave her the first opening.

Chapter 2

Birmingham, Alabama
Sam Stone's Apartment on Southside
Thursday, June 5, 2003
6:05 p.m.

Sam stared out the window of his apartment as he reflected on the loss of his first criminal trial in years.

Troy Pickering was an Anniston businessman who helped certain contractors obtain road construction and maintenance contracts with the state highway department. His associates also managed to obtain favorable leases from certain state agencies. He paid state agency decision makers bribes, and he received moneys from the contractors that he assisted. He got kickbacks and extorted money from the contractors to the tune of $5.3 million over a three-year period.

Pickering attended state agency office retreats, and he actually sat in on official meetings from time to time and "guided them", even though he was just a private citizen. Sam charged him under the federal RICO (Racketeer

Influenced Corrupt Organizations) Act in an indictment that accused Pickering of running a criminal enterprise that engaged in a pattern of racketeering activity. It included structuring monetary transactions, extortion, bribery, money laundering, wire fraud, mail fraud, and tax fraud.

Somehow the case jumped the tracks and wrecked, yet Sam could not understand why. He thought he knew and practiced the basics as well as anyone.

In fact, one semester a year, for the past 6 years, Sam taught a criminal trial practice seminar as an adjunct professor at Samford University's Cumberland School of Law in the Homewood area of town. It helped him keep a proper focus and perspective on his job as a federal prosecutor, which required a constant review of the basics.

Sam liked to give a series of mini lectures to his law students and encourage questions.

Typically, his first lecture included: "People generally understand that in a federal or state criminal case, the prosecution must prove its case beyond a reasonable doubt. This is called the burden of proof. Lawyers argue about what it means all the time. Beyond a reasonable doubt does not mean that all doubts must be resolved, only reasonable ones. It is frequently contrasted with the lesser civil case burden of proof that only requires proof by a preponderance of the evidence. How do lawyers explain these burdens to juries?"

Most of the time, no one from the class would answer, so after a pause, Sam would continue: "Some trial attorneys in Alabama courts use analogies to explain these burdens and their differences. As might be expected, the most popular analogies involve football in this state. In a typical civil case, one might hear some version of the following from a plaintiff's attorney: 'Ladies and gentlemen, this is a civil case, and Mr. Smith's claim that the defendant negligently drove his vehicle causing personal injuries to Mr. Smith only needs to be proven by a preponderance of the evidence. Pretend it's a football game, and the plaintiff Mr. Smith has the ball on offense. He doesn't need to score a touchdown with his proof; he only needs to cross the 50 yard line to prove his case.'"

This usually drew some student laughter, and Sam would say: "Now, in a criminal case, by contrast, one might hear from a defense lawyer: 'The proof the prosecution needs to show is proof beyond a reasonable doubt, and in football talk that means the prosecutor has to carry his proof close to the goal line. In this case, it was the government agent's word against the defendant's word, and therefore, we stopped the government at the 50-yard marker. That means you have to acquit.'"

At this point a student would raise a hand and ask, "What's a prosecutor's response to that?"

Sam would smile and say, "I tell a jury, 'Using the football analogy of the burden of proof, the prosecution only needs to cross the 50 and get into decent field goal range.'"

From this point of departure Sam would launch into the presumption of innocence, the right of an accused to remain silent and testimonial issues: "The accused in a criminal case is presumed innocent until proven guilty, and a jury of 12 generally decides guilt or innocence. An accused does not have to take the stand and possibly incriminate himself, and a prosecutor cannot comment on an accused's silence if he chooses not to testify. Does anyone know what the old unsworn statement practice was or where it came from?"

Invariably, no one would volunteer an answer and Sam would continue: "Under the old English common law, a person accused of a crime was legally incompetent to testify at all, the theory being that anyone formally accused of a crime, even if innocent, would be unable to tell the complete truth. Because this situation left large gaps in the stories of what happened, the common law courts eventually developed a fiction that allowed an accused to give an unsworn statement. One accused of a crime did not place his hand on the Bible and swear to tell the truth, but rather, he simply told the jury his story. This was usually done without the aid of his lawyer asking any questions."

"Was this ever the practice in this country?" a student would ask.

"The practice was in fact imported into the United States, and some states developed unusual rules for its use. Less than 50 years ago in Georgia, an accused could elect to give an unsworn statement instead of testifying under oath, and the prosecution was not allowed to comment on the fact that the accused's statement was not made under oath or cross examine the accused in any way. For the most part, these old practices have been supplanted in all state and federal courts by allowing an accused to take the stand and testify under oath like other witnesses. The modern theory is that the penalty of perjury should be sufficient to make everyone, including those accused of crimes, want to tell the truth."

A law student would usually ask at this point, "What does a lawyer do about a lying client?"

Sam's response included: "A lawyer's duty of candor to the court prevents him or her from placing false evidence or testimony before the court. If a client wishes to lie on the stand, and if the lawyer cannot withdraw from representation, or talk the client out of giving false testimony, then in many jurisdictions, the lawyer is allowed to put the client on the stand. The client presents testimony in a narrative form without the assistance of the lawyer's questioning. It has the look and feel of the old unsworn statement practice, but it is under oath, and sometimes the client picks up a charge of perjury for his or her efforts."

Another law student then would ask, "What standards or measures does a prosecutor use to indict and present cases?"

Sam usually responded with: "A good prosecutor does not generally indict a case unless he is 95 per cent certain that the evidence is strong enough for a conviction. We at our office have a system of indictment reviews, and evidence issues are thoroughly hashed out before any get to court, with some rare exceptions."

"Do you worry about 'jury nullification' very much?" another student would ask.

"Not much," was Sam's answer. "Jury nullification happens when a jury disregards the law, despite clear evidence of guilt beyond a reasonable doubt, and sets a criminal defendant free with a not guilty verdict."

A student would ask, "Can a defense lawyer argue nullification to a jury?"

Sam's response was: "By ethical rules, a defendant's lawyer cannot expressly urge a jury to disregard the law. However, lawyers have been known to argue that the prosecution's burden of proof has not been met or that the police or FBI investigation and testimony was biased and not credible and worthy of belief because of animosity towards the defendant's political views. The legal system in the United States, in both state and federal courts, gives juries the power of nullification. Juries are instructed to accept and follow the law as they are given it at the end of each case by the trial judge. The judge decides the law and the jury the facts."

"Is that true everywhere?" a law student would ask.

"Two states, Maryland and Indiana, are different. They have special constitutional provisions indicating that the juries in those states have the right and authority to determine the law as well as the facts. There must have been a significant distrust of judges in those states at the time those special provisions were adopted. Most courts have rejected attempts to have jury instructions that tell the jurors that they have a right to nullification."

"Can you give us a concrete example of nullification?" someone would ask.

Sam would respond: "One of the most famous cases in which a jury exercised the power to nullify came out of a Massachusetts federal court in 1851. Abolitionists in Boston stormed a federal court and took a slave whom they spirited off to Canada in order to prevent the authorities from returning the person to Virginia pursuant to the Fugitive Slave Law. The abolitionists were indicted and tried for aiding and abetting the slave to escape. The federal jury acquitted them all."

"Has jury nullification ever happened in one of your cases?" another law student would always ask.

Sam's reply was, "No. Please remember that if a criminal case is properly chosen, prepared, and tried, this should never occur in my opinion."

Sometimes, however, cases went south for reasons one could not readily explain. Sam called this aberration "having a ghost walking in your case." The happenstance was usually associated with the judge and politics of the case. He did not give mini lectures on this topic to his students because it was too difficult to articulate in a rational fashion.

Sam kept staring out the window as he thought back through his mini lecture basics. He had chosen and prepared the Pickering case well. Sam thought he had tried it well. He wondered, however, if he would ever identify the ghost that had walked through the case.

Chapter 3

Birmingham, Alabama
Sam Stone's Apartment on Southside
Thursday, June 5, 2003
6:10 p.m.

In federal criminal trials, a prosecutor's worst nightmare can be found in Rule 29 of the Federal Rules of Criminal Procedure. The Federal Rules are the procedural rules that govern all federal criminal trials throughout the United States. Under Rule 29, the federal trial judge, after the close of the prosecution's case, can enter a judgment of acquittal on one or more of the offenses charged in the indictment, and there is damned little that the prosecution can do about it.

In the old days this used to be called "directing the verdict." In the usual circumstance today, a defense lawyer usually makes a motion for judgment of acquittal, instead of a motion for a directed verdict, after the prosecution rests. The trial judge frequently reserves ruling on the motion until after the defendant has had an opportunity to present any evidence and the jury has reached a verdict. It is very unusual for the court to grant a judgment of acquittal on its own motion after the prosecution has rested, but it happens from time to time. The Federal Rules of Criminal Procedure authorize such a dismissal in Rule 29.

Judge Nathan Bedford Crowell had been on the federal bench in the Northern District of Alabama for 10 years. He was not from a prominent Birmingham family, but he lived in a mansion on Red Mountain overlooking the city. He had donated large sums to the Democratic Party over the years, and the Clinton administration had rewarded that financial loyalty with a federal judgeship.

Judge Crowell was about Sam's age. He had gone to undergraduate school at Washington and Lee, and then to Yale law school. After law school he bounced around from small firm to small firm handling what appeared to be mostly minor business planning matters and a few state court personal injury cases which he always referred to prominent plaintiffs' firms. Prior to going on the federal bench he had never tried a criminal or civil case in federal court. No one was really sure what kind of law he had practiced over the years, but he was obviously successful financially.

He bragged that his family was originally from England and named "Cromwell". But, because of the dislike for Oliver Cromwell in general, and in particular by the Scots and Irish, the Judge's ancestors, on their voyage to America in the mid 1700's, decided to change the name to "Crowell".

The family supposedly had a ceremony on the ship in which the "m" was cut out of the name in the family bible and cast into the Atlantic. The Judge claimed to be a legal historian, and frequently told the family name story. He always insisted that his ancestry could be in fact traced to the famous Oliver Cromwell, Lord Protector of the Realm, who died in 1658 and was buried in Westminster Abbey.

History shows that Cromwell was so disliked that by 1661, Parliament ordered his exhumation and posthumous execution by hanging and beheading. The headless body was lost, but Cromwell's head, which was displayed on a pike for years and also lost, became a collector's item.

In 1960, it was bequeathed to Cromwell's school, Sidney Sussex College at the University of Cambridge, where it was buried at an undisclosed location. There was a real fear that someone would dig it up and desecrate it, so hated even today was his memory by some.

Judge Crowell's extremely arrogant attitude was such that many people referred to him behind his back as "Lord Crowell." As a federal district court judge, he frequently let his temper loose on lawyers and litigants that appeared before him. As a former past president of the Birmingham Bar Association said of him, "Judge Crowell is one of those federal judges, that at his swearing in ceremony, he was sprinkled with a generous portion of shit-ass dust."

As an Article III (of the U.S. Constitution) judge he was appointed for life, and there was little anyone could do to curb his judicial temperament. He was not the gentleman or gentlewoman which was the pattern for all of the other federal judges and magistrates in the Northern District. In most criminal cases he had been fairly tough on the accused. In other criminal cases that Sam had tried before him, Judge Crowell handed out stiff sentences with stern law and order lectures to the convicted. Ordinarily, he cut few criminal subjects any slack.

In the Pickering case, however, Judge Crowell did the unusual. After seven days of testimony and evidence from twenty-five witnesses, Sam rested the United States' case in chief. Without waiting for the motion from Pickering's defense lawyer, Judge Crowell dismissed all counts pursuant to Rule 29.

Sam was shocked, and the FBI was pissed off. Sam thought he had his 95 percent certain proof on all counts, and so did the government agents. Now, reports and evaluations of what went wrong had to be generated as soon as possible and reviewed by various supervisory attorneys up the line. This included the U.S. Attorney, and people at the U.S. Department of Justice in Washington, DC.

That same afternoon, Sam had gotten a notice that his divorce trial with Linda was set for the end of the month. This was indeed a bad day at Blackrock.

Divorce and dealing with the federal bureaucracy, what a low.

As least for Sam, playing the 5-string banjo, and giving lessons from time to time, kept his mind off the problems of divorce, his career with the feds, and his professional disappointments, like the unexplainable dismissal of the Pickering case. He had learned from an early age that you have to play the cards that life deals you as best you can.

Sam got out his banjo, tuned it, and waited for his student to arrive. He was tempted to cancel the lessons, but he knew that it was better to stay busy on non-work related pastimes. Otherwise, he would end up in a depressive state, which would cloud his judgment. Some important decisions would soon have to be made about his career because of Linda, and thinking straight was going to be essential.

Chapter 4

Birmingham, Alabama
Sam Stone's Apartment on Southside
Thursday, June 5, 2003
6:15 p.m.

"**M**r. Stone, teach me to pick just like Earl Scruggs. That's all I want to learn on the banjo."

"Well, Steven, I'll show you the basics of three finger bluegrass style, but you need to remember the first lesson. You will never play the banjo just like Mr. Scruggs or any other player. You will play only like you and no one else on this earth. I will show you the basics, but you will mostly teach yourself. Be proud of that fact, be creative and inventive in your playing, and most of all, have a good time with whatever music you generate from your two hands, five strings, and plastic head."

The phone rang. Sam went to the phone, recognized the caller I.D., and picked up the phone.

"Yeah, Paul. He's here. What's that? First lessons should not be over half an hour. Send him there when we are finished. You bet. Bye."

Sam put down the phone and turned to Steven. "Professor Redmond says you have a tutoring session with him in western philosophy this evening in about an hour. He says you did poorly on the last test, given your abilities. Are you smoking dope again?"

"No. I'm clean. Check my lab testing results t h e y make me do every week for pre-trial diversion. They also test me for the soccer team and track. I just wasn't interested in what Bertrand Russell had to say about the pursuit of happiness without religion."

Steven's major was philosophy and his minor was math.

"Well, you should be interested. Your mother tells me that you may be in line for a Gates scholarship to Cambridge. Not many kids get that chance."

Steven's mother, Karen Kemper, was a FBI agent with whom Sam had worked many cases with over the past 10 years in the Northern District of Alabama. She was 49 years old, 5 feet 7 inches tall, with short copper hair and steely blue eyes. She was smart as a whip and well trained. Two years ago, Karen had even finished her law degree from the night program at the Birmingham School of Law and had passed the Alabama bar on the first try. No criminals intimidated her. Karen had less than a year until retirement, at which point she planned to do contract work for the FBI and private investigations to supplement her retirement income. She might even pick up some legal work.

She divorced her agent husband George eight years ago when she found out that he had become involved with a young deputy U.S. Marshal while on a three month special assignment to El Paso, Texas. Absence had made his heart grow fonder of another. She tried not to be bitter.

Karen worked hard to stay in good shape, physically and mentally, and to perform her work at the highest levels. Yet, the divorce and drug situation with her children had ruined her appetite for most fun things. She buried herself in work.

Steven was so bright it was scary. He never made less than A's in grammar and high school, and he got a perfect score on his SAT's. He was also an athlete that liked soccer, and he ran on the cross-country team. Steven would graduate in another month and a half after completing four years of work in two. He could have gone to any number of colleges, but he chose to stay close to his mother and sister.

Lauren, his younger sister by four years, was struggling with drug problems. Two years earlier, she had been a happy, normal teenager in high school. Her boyfriend was killed in car crash coming back from a football game in Tuscaloosa, and she went from severe depression to drugs to more drugs. She was presently in rehab again for 30 days at the Cahaba Heights Drug Clinic.

Unfortunately for Steven, some of his friends at the Birmingham College of Christ introduced him to marijuana, and he, as they say in the South, "took to it". Within three months, he got caught with half an ounce at a Sloss Furnace concert by undercover cops in downtown Birmingham.

Because it was his first offense, and because his mother was connected to law enforcement, he was put on pretrial diversion. This was an oral deal made strictly between the local prosecutor and the defendant. Steven had to agree to regular drug testing for one year, to stay straight, and remain in school. After a year, his case would be dropped and all arrest and other records would be destroyed. If he screwed up, his original case would be ginned up, and he would be prosecuted. Pretrial diversion worked in 90 per cent of the cases, and it was a great tool for young first offenders.

The fact that he was a candidate for a Gates' scholarship also seemed to keep him on the straight and level. He really wanted to study at Cambridge, and the potential scholarship was his ticket.

Sam inquired, "Tell me some more about this Gates scholarship business that you are in the running for."

Steven looked up from his banjo and with a serious look said, "Bill Gates, who had made a fortune at Microsoft, is doing for the University of Cambridge in England what Cecil Rhodes did for Oxford University about a hundred years earlier. Gates has recently created an endowed scholarship system that attracts the best and the brightest. The comparison of Gates and Rhodes scholarships is a good topic of discussion in higher academic circles these days."

"How so?" asked Sam.

Steven explained. "Rhodes had made his fortune in South African diamond mining, and upon his death in 1902, his will left £ 6,000,000 to public service endowing 170 Oxford University scholarships for youths of the

British Empire, the United States and Germany. It took the Rhodes Trustees until 1976 to allow women applicants."

"That sounds a little late," said Sam.

Steven continued, "As of this millennium, foreign male and female students could apply for a Rhodes scholarship if they were from certain designated countries: the United States, Canada, Australia, South Africa, India, Germany, New Zealand, Commonwealth Caribbean, Zimbabwe, Bangladesh, Bermuda, Hong Kong, Jamaica, Kenya, Malaysia, Pakistan, Singapore, Uganda, and Zambia."

"How do you know all of this?" Sam inquired.

"I looked into both programs, but I liked Cambridge better than Oxford for what I want to study. Anyhow, in 2000, the Bill and Melinda Gates Foundation first announced plans to donate $210 million to the University of Cambridge in order to create an international scholarship program for graduate students from outside the United Kingdom. Unlike the Rhodes Trust, the Gates Foundation has no restriction on the student's foreign country of origin. About 100 scholars are selected each year. The first group of Cambridge Gates Scholars was chosen in 2001, and the program has been a great success ever since."

"So what does your professor say about your chances?" asked Sam.

"Professor Redmond is eager to have one of his students be one of the first Gates Scholars from Alabama. He thinks I have a better than average chance, but he has warned me that, in his words, 'immature social diversions' could derail all of his efforts in my behalf."

"The professor is right about that," said Sam.

Picking up a xeroxed photo Sam began with some fundamentals. "Let's go over the banjo, and get the names of the parts correct so we know what we are doing to do and with which. Look at this copy of a photo I found in a magazine of a custom built Panama Canal commemorative banjo that some fellow from Georgia had made about 25 years ago. I'll write some of the part names on the xerox for you and you can keep the copy. At the bottom end is the tailpiece, which anchors all 5 strings, and at the top is the peg-head, which has tuning pegs for four of the strings. The 5th string peg is a little over half way up the neck at the fifth fret. At the upper end of the fret board is the nut where the four longer strings cross onto the peg-head."

Sam went on to describe the plastic head or drumhead, brackets holding the tension hoop over the head, the bridge on the head supporting and separating the 5 strings, the heel at the base of the neck, the adjustable tension rod underneath the rim which ran into the neck, and the tone ring on top of the wooden shell just underneath the head.

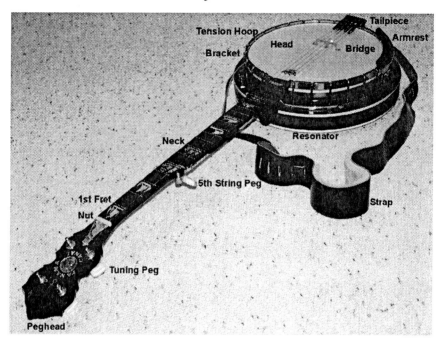

Chapter 5

Birmingham, Alabama
Sam Stone's Apartment on Southside
Thursday, June 5, 2003
6:30 p.m.

"Let's start with the banjo playing basics, Steven. We will play right handed, mostly in what is called open G tuning. The first string, which is the one closest to the bottom and having the lightest gauge, is tuned to the D just above Middle C on the piano. The next string is called the second string, a slightly heavier gauge, and it's tuned to the B just below Middle C. The third and middle string is heavier still and is tuned to the G below Middle C. The fourth string has the heaviest gauge and it is wound. It's tuned to the D below Middle C."

Steven nodded, taking everything in.

Sam paused and pointed, "The light gauged short 5th string runs only part of the way up the neck. They call it the 'drone' string. It's tuned to the G above Middle C, and it drones in the background like a bee buzzing, and gives that distinctive ringing sound as songs are played in the related G chord progressions."

Sam produced a pen and plain piece of paper. "On paper, the tuning looks like this."

He wrote down:

5th	4th	3rd	2nd	1st
G	**D**	**G**	**B**	**D**

"There are other tunings for the banjo, but it's easier to learn to play in open G to begin with. You can take up the other tunings later. I learned to play in G first, and I think it'll work fine for you."

Steven asked, "Do I need to know or learn music to play?"

Sam replied, "Not really. You can get by with knowing the names of chords, the names of keys, the notes to tune with, and the simple things. Knowing music in the classic sense could help in some instances, but many famous pickers know very little about music and perform great. The common comment among banjo players is that they know a little music but not enough to hurt their playing."

Steven laughed. "I think I'll join that group."

Sam continued, "You can always tune the banjo to itself, but it's easier these days to simply stay properly tuned. I carry a G harmonica instead of a pitch pipe, because I like to play the harmonica, and it's hard to play any music with a pitch pipe. Most importantly, I also have a $19.95 electronic tuner in my banjo case. I only use the harmonica for tuning when the batteries are out on the tuner. Remember, there is really no good excuse for being out of tune these days. Nothing sounds worse than an instrument that is off key."

Sam picked up his electronic tuner and made sure Steven's used, open back Kay banjo was in tune with his Gibson Mastertone. Sam had found the old Kay banjo for Steven in a pawnshop in Bessemer. It cost $15.00 to buy and another $45.00 to have it restored to playing at Fretted Instruments in Homewood.

Sam explained, "You can still pick up a new open back for two to three hundred dollars; a good new one costs about six hundred. Banjos with resonators covering the back tend to get pricey these days. These are the instruments of choice, however, for many bluegrass pickers. Original, pre-World War II Gibson arch top Masterstones fetch prices up to $50,000.00. This Mastertone of mine was a bow tie model from the 1960's, and it is not worth anywhere close to the pre-war models."

"Why is it called a bow tie model?" asked Steven.

"It's because of the mother of pearl inlays in the fret board that resemble white bow ties. A really good and classy resonator banjo, new or used, can be had for around three grand, including a hard-shell case, which is a must for a valuable instrument. Some of the famous brand names include: Gibson, Stelling, Ome, Deering, Bart Reiter, Wildwood, Goldtone, Mike Ramsey, Crafters of Tennessee, and Nechville. Everybody has his or her favorites."

Sam wanted to design and build his own someday. He turned and asked, "I'm curious Steven, why did you decide to learn the banjo?"

"Well, Mr. Stone, I have always liked the sound of bluegrass music. My limited research showed that the 5-string banjo is one of the few American musical instruments. It has African origins with the *banjar*, and all that, but the American creation of the five strings and styles of play make for a unique sound. In many ways, the banjo is quintessentially American. Its roots are foreign, like most Americans. It is technical and loud, like most Americans. It plays lead melody; again Americans want to lead in everything. The banjo stirs up a sense of fun in our crazy American culture."

Steven had something there. Sam asked, "Any other reasons?"

Steven continued, "I'd like to be able to travel outside the state and tell everyone that I've come from Alabama with a banjo on my knee. Besides, I have been secretly in love with Emily Robison of the Dixie Chicks for some time, and more recently with Alison Brown. Are those reasons enough?"

Sam laughed. "Yeah Steven, those are enough. I have held similar fascinations with female banjo players over the years, starting with Jackie Miller of the New Christy Minstrels. I also ran into some stellar female pickers at bluegrass festivals in the late 1970's and early 1980's, but luckily for me, they were all usually spoken for. Else I would have run off with them."

Sam recalled other female banjo players with superior talent including: Peggy Seeger, who wrote the book, *The 5-String Banjo: American Folk Styles*; and Ronnie Stoneman of the Stoneman Family bluegrass band and the Hee Haw T.V. show. In Sam's mind, Ronnie's character on T.V. looked like she could snag lightning, but she could flat play the bluegrass banjo.

Sam said, "I'm going to give you my version of '5-string banjo History 101.'" You need to appreciate where it came from and where it may be going. This will also help you talk the talk with other banjo players that you will run into."

Steven laughed and asked, "Should I take notes and will there be a test?"

"No," said Sam. "This is fun stuff, not formal instruction. Just listen up for 2 minutes to some info that I have accumulated over the years. It's like most histories, mostly right but some wrong."

Steven said, "O.K. Let's have it."

Sam began, "The history of the 5-string banjo is murky. Some say that the Middle Eastern rebec, with its skin head gourd on a stick and three stings was the centuries old ancestor, which was brought to the United States from Africa in the 1600's and 1700's by Negro slaves."

Steven asked, "Do you think it is kin to the sitar from India?"

"I don't know. Maybe," replied Sam. He continued, "In the late 1700's, Thomas Jefferson wrote that the instrument proper to the slaves was the *banjar* which they brought with them from Africa. Other names for the instrument included the *bangoe, banza,* and *banjil.* Also by the late 1700's, Caucasian banjo players first began performances in black-faced minstrel styles. It was in the 1840's, however, that the 5-string banjo achieved its first great popularity. You should note that controversy exists as to the origin of the shortened 5th string on the banjo."

"Does it matter?" asked Steven.

"Probably not," said Sam. "Anyhow, many claim that one Joel Walker Sweeny, in Virginia, around 1830, first invented the banjo which has the five strings that we typically use today. As to the shortened 5th string, who knows where it originated. Some claim that it was invented in the late 1700's on plantations in the South, while others say that the additional unique string came out of English roots. We do know that Sweeny started a minstrel show in the 1840's with his two brothers, and almost single-handedly popularized the 5-string. Banjo clubs and contests began to spring up in urban areas across America."

"A banjo cultural revolution," Steven commented.

"You could perhaps call it that," said Sam. He continued, "In the 1850's metal strings were added for the first time, and by the Civil War in the early 1860's, the 5-string banjo was well known. Dan Emmett, who wrote Dixie and the Bluetail Fly, which was, by the way, supposedly one of President Lincoln's favorite tunes, had learned to play and perform in the 1840's and 1850's."

Steven interjected, "Speaking of Lincoln, have you ever heard of an early Alabama lawyer and writer named Joseph G. Baldwin?"

"I don't believe that I have," replied Sam. "What did he have to do with Lincoln?"

"Professor Redmond told us last week that Lincoln, during his presidency, supposedly slept with a copy of Baldwin's 1853 book called *Flush Times in Alabama and Mississippi*. It kept him amused during the Civil War."

"What's that got to do with your philosophy course?" Sam inquired.

"Someone in the class had raised the issue of whether there had ever been a famous philosopher in Alabama. Apparently, according to the Professor, Mark Twain considered Baldwin to be a 'frontier philosopher' because of this early Alabama book."

"What happened to Baldwin?" asked Sam.

"He moved from Alabama after it was published and became a justice on the California Supreme Court."

"I didn't know any of that," said Sam. "Let me finish banjo History 101. In 1855, Thomas Briggs published the first banjo primer. All sorts of circuses, traveling shows, riverboat entertainers, and minstrel groups touted their banjoists."

Steven politely listened while checking out his banjo.

Sam paused and said, "You need to know some of the famous historic names in case you run across old banjos or eccentric collectors. Here's a sketch and some important names and places. William Boucher of Baltimore, beginning in the late 1830's, first manufactured banjos for sale. From the 1860's to the 1890's, the James H.

Buckbee Company of New York City became the largest manufacturer of banjos. Successors produced Orpheum and Paramount banjos, which are much sought after by collectors today.

"Around 1878, frets were added by Henry Dobson to banjos made by the Buckbee Company. He is also said to have come up with the first tone ring and resonator.

"Also in the late 1800's, A.C. Fairbanks of Boston and S.S. Stewart of Philadelphia manufactured banjos in great quantities. Fairbanks produced the first White Laydie banjo in 1901.

"Then, in 1904, Vega banjos started into production in Boston, and Vega brought out the first Tubaphone in 1909. The Gibson Company created its first banjos in 1918, and by 1921 had introduced adjustable tension rods. The first Gibson Mastertone was sold in 1925."

Steven looked up and asked, "Where does the four string banjo fit in?"

Sam replied, "The four-string, or tenor banjo, was created in the early 1900's to be played in jazz and other bands of the day. The strings were heavier than those on the 5-string, and the sound was louder in order to compete with trumpets and the like."

"I see," said Steven.

Sam continued, "The 5-string suffered a decline in popularity after the Great Depression and the stock market collapse of 1929. In remote parts of Appalachia, and on the Grand Ole Opry, broadcast from Nashville, some banjo playing was still heard; but that was about all of the popularity that remained."

"When did bluegrass picking arrive?" asked Steven.

Sam answered, "It was Earl Scruggs, in the 1940's. He invented and introduced the world to his famous three finger picking style and the modern banjo era was born. His success was immediate, and the 5-string enjoyed a brand-new popularity."

"What about the folk scene?" asked Steven.

Sam replied, "On the folk front, Pete Seeger created and popularized his long neck 5-string banjo in the early 1940's. His 1948 mimeographed manual, *How to Play the 5-string Banjo*, was instantly popular with the folk crowd, and it still available in the third edition at most instrument stores where banjos are sold."

"Were there any technological changes?"

"Well," said Sam. "The first plastic banjo heads were created in the 1950's. Prior to that time heads were made of skin, which stretched or shrunk depending on the climate for wet or dry. The plastic heads cured the lack of uniform sound problems created by the vagaries of the weather and the like."

"So everyone in the mid-1900's jumped on the banjo bandwagon?"

"You could say that," replied Sam. "The Weavers, the Kingston Trio, the Limelighters, the Chad Mitchell Trio, and others in the late 1950's and early 1960's, led the folk music revival that saw the 5-string banjo jump in sales."

"What about the pure bluegrass groups?"

"Traditional bluegrass bands, such as Bill Monroe's Bluegrass Boys, Flatt and Scruggs, the Stanley Brothers, Jim and Jesse McReynolds, the Osborne Brothers, the Lewis Family, the Dillards, the Stoneman Family, and others, with the 5-string playing the lead melodies in Scruggs style, met with widespread popularity."

"Who is your favorite bluegrass picker?" asked Steven.

"My favorite picker is Doug Dillard," Sam replied. "Other famous pickers that I like include: Bill Keith, Don Reno, Raymond Fairchild, Little Roy Lewis, John Hartford, Eric Weisberg, J.D. Crowe, Eddie Adcock, Walter Forbes, Tony Trischka, Peter Wernick, Bela Fleck, and locally, Jim Connor, Bobby Horton and Herb Trotman."

"What else do I need to know about banjo 101?" Steven asked.

"Just that an immediate best seller with banjo pickers everywhere was Earl Scruggs' book first published in 1968, entitled, *Earl Scruggs and the 5-String Banjo*. Bill Keith helped Earl Scruggs in writing the technical parts. It remains the "Bible" for most bluegrass banjo aficionados. You should also know that from the 1960's forward, Gibson and Vega began having competition from many new banjo manufacturers. Today, banjos are not in short supply."

Steven asked, "Is that it?"

Sam said, "Yep. Let's get you started playing."

Chapter 6

Birmingham, Alabama
Sam Stone's Apartment on Southside
Thursday, June 5, 2003
6:50 p.m.

Sam said to Steven, "The first playing technique I want you to learn involves simply strumming the banjo. I call it the *brush* stroke. It will help you get familiar with the instrument and allow you to play back up with other musicians for all kinds of tunes. With your right hand fingers cupped, brush down across all 5 strings with the back of your fingernail tips. The tips of your fingers should be at about a 45 degree angel to the five strings."

Sam showed Steven how to position his right hand, and then he made him watch as Sam brushed his fingernails down across the strings. Steven moved his fingernails across the five strings in a similar fashion as instructed.

"Congratulations," Sam told him, "you have just played a G chord. I'm writing the chord down for you. It's easy because all strings are open. No left hand fretting of the strings is required."

Sam wrote:

G Major Chord
(open; no fingers on any frets)

```
5th   4th   3rd   2nd   1st
 G     D     G     B     D
_____
 |     |     |     |
 |     |     |     |
 |_____|_____|_____|   1st fret
 |     |     |     |
 |     |     |     |
 |_____|_____|_____|   2nd fret
 |     |     |     |
 |     |     |     |
 |_____|_____|_____|   3rd fret
 |     |     |     |
 |     |     |     |
 |_____|_____|_____|   4th fret
 |     |     |     |
 |   |     |     |     |
 |   |_____|_____|_____|   5th fret
```

Steven asked, "What do you call these little metal spacers on the neck again?"

"These little metal spacers, as you call them, are called 'frets.' You hold strings down just above these frets with the left hand fingers to play different chords and notes."

"O.K.," said Steven.

"Now, count up from the peg head end of the banjo to the fifth fret. That's the one just at the fifth string peg. With your left hand, take your index finger and lay it across all four strings at the fifth fret, holding all strings down evenly. With your right hand brush down on all five strings like you did before. I'll write this down also. '1' stands for index finger. Throughout our lessons, I'll use numbers for the left hand fingers and letters for the right hand ones."

Sam wrote:

C Major Chord
(bar strings 1, 2, 3, & 4 at the fifth fret with left index finger)

Steven did as instructed, and produced a clear sound.

Sam said, "That great, you have just played a C chord."

Steven grinned, "Two full chords already; I like this."

Sam replied, "It gets a lot better. Now, again with your left index finger, at the seventh fret, that's two frets above where you were with the C chord, and lay your finger across strings one through four, but not touching the fifth string, and again with your right hand, brush down on all five strings."

Sam wrote again:

D Major Chord

(bar strings 1, 2, 3, & 4 at the seventh fret with left index finger)

5th	4th	3rd	2nd	1st
G	D	G	B	D

```
5th  4th  3rd  2nd  1st
 G    D    G    B    D
 |    |    |    |
 |    |    |    |
 |____|____|____|____| 1st fret
 |    |    |    |
 |    |    |    |
 |____|____|____|____| 2nd fret
 |    |    |    |
 |    |    |    |
 |____|____|____|____| 3rd fret
 |    |    |    |
 |    |    |    |
 |____|____|____|____| 4th fret
```

```
    |    |     |    |
  |    |    |    |    |
  |    |    |    |    | 5th fret
  |    |    |    |    |
  |    |    |    |    |
  |    |    |    |    | 6th fret
  |    |    |    |    |
  |  (1)  (1)    (1)   (1) (index finger)
  |    |    |    |    | 7th fret
```

"Great. You have now played a D chord."

Steven was elated.

Sam continued, "I am also writing out the following exercise on a piece of notebook paper, which in fact is an old song called 'Boil Them Cabbage Down'; it's also called 'Bile Them Cabbage Down.' You need to practice this with some other songs and exercises that I will write down as we go along. Try to make the brushing down strokes, written '*Brush↓*', even in terms of timing or tempo. Count 1, 2, 3, 4 if you prefer counting to using the words of the song. It's like all new things in life, these beginning simple exercises will help you to get that always much needed hands on experience."

He wrote:

G (open-no fingers on any frets)
Brush↓
Brush↓
Brush↓
Brush↓
"Boil them cab-bage"

C (bar strings 1, 2, 3, & 4 at the fifth fret with left index finger)

Brush↓

Brush↓

Brush↓

Brush↓

"Down boys"

G (open-no fingers on any frets)

Brush↓

Brush↓

Brush↓

Brush↓

"Turn them hoe-cakes"

D (bar strings 1, 2, 3, & 4 at the seventh fret with left index finger)

Brush↓

Brush↓

Brush↓

Brush↓

"Round"

G (open-no fingers on any frets)

Brush↓

Brush↓

Brush↓

Brush↓

"The only song that"

C (bar strings 1, 2, 3, & 4 at the fifth fret with left index finger)

Brush↓

Brush↓

Brush↓

Brush↓

"I can sing is"

G (open-no fingers on any frets)

Brush↓

Brush↓

"Boil them"

D (bar strings 1, 2, 3, & 4 at the seventh fret with left index finger)

Brush↓

Brush↓

"Cab-bage"

G (open-no fingers on any frets)

Brush↓

"Down"

Sam took Steven through the exercise five times to make sure he understood each chord change.

He then said, "That's your first set of lessons. You have played a complete song on the 5-string in the first 15 minutes of instruction. You can't beat that with a stick. Now, let's get in some more learning right quick, because I can tell you are going to be a fast study."

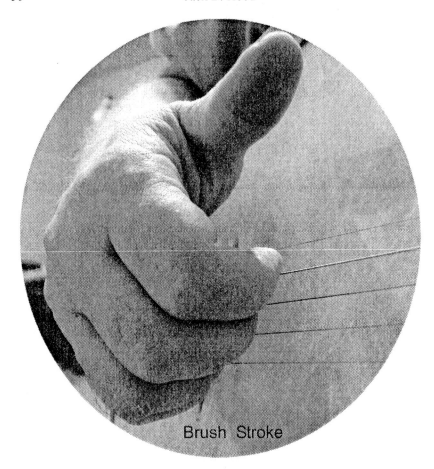

Brush Stroke

Chapter 7

Birmingham, Alabama
Sam Stone's Apartment on Southside
Thursday, June 5, 2003
7:15 p.m.

Sam turned to Steven. "Let's look at a few more banjo items to practice."

Sam adjusted Steven's banjo so that it was flat against his body. "You cannot play very well at an angle. If you develop bad habits in your banjo playing at the beginning, they are hard to drop later on. Just like the rest of life."

Steven asked, "What's next? Bluegrass?"

"No, that's a little later," Sam replied. "The next exercise involves learning an up and down strum along with one of the simple chords, as I call them. With your right hand brush down across all five stings and up across some of the strings. The down and up should be fast enough to be one beat, or one pat of the foot, if you are comfortable keeping time that way. You already know how to play the G chord by simply strumming the open strings."

Sam demonstrated on his Mastertone and said, "With you left hand, take your index finger and hold down the second string just above the first fret. At the same time with your middle finger, hold down the third string at the second fret. The 4th and first strings are open and not fretted. Now, brush down across the strings. That's called a D7th chord. On paper, remember, '1' stands for index finger of the left hand and '2' stands for the middle finger."

Sam wrote:

```
5th   4th   3rd   2nd   1st
 G     D     G     B     D
       |     |     |     |
       |     |    (1)    |
       |_____|_____|_____|  1st fret
       |     |     |     |
       |    (2)    |         |
       |_____|_____|_____|  2nd fret
       |     |     |     |
       |     |     |     |
       |_____|_____|_____|  3rd fret
       |     |     |     |
       |     |     |     |
       |_____|_____|_____|  4th fret
       |     |     |     |
  |    |     |     |     |
  |    |_____|_____|_____|  5th fret
```

Sam instructed, "Now practice that old children's song 'Skip To My Lou', and I'll also write it down for you."

He wrote:

G (open-no fingers on any frets)
Brush↓↑
Brush↓↑
Brush↓↑
Brush↓↑
"Lou, Lou, skip to my Lou"
D7th   (3rd string index finger (1) at 2nd fret;
        2nd string middle finger (2) at 1st fret)
Brush↓↑
Brush↓↑
Brush↓↑
Brush↓↑
"Lou, Lou, skip to my Lou"
G (open-no fingers on any frets)
Brush↓↑
Brush↓↑
Brush↓↑
Brush↓↑
"Lou, Lou, skip to my Lou"
D7th   (3rd string index finger (1) at 2nd fret;
        2nd tring middle finger (2) at 1st fret)
Brush↓↑
Brush↓↑
"Skip to my Lou my"
G (open-no fingers on any frets)
Brush↓↑
"Darling"

Sam said, "Some other 'two-chord' songs to practice like this are 'Way Down Yonder in the Paw Paw Patch',

'Hush Little Baby', and any number of the versions of 'Tom Dooley.' I should also mention that beginning banjo players, and seasoned ones for that matter, can be annoying to others who are in the house while you are practicing the 5-string. To muffle the sound while you practice, take an old towel or some old T-shirts and stuff them in the back of the banjo up against the head. Respect the rights of others around you at all times."

The doorbell rang. Sam looked out the window of his apartment, and he saw a white panel truck driving away. Sam went to the door, opened it, and saw a brown package tied up with string on the doorstep. It had his name and address, but there was no return address. That was odd because most non-U.S. Postal deliveries showed a receipt or some identifying return address for the shipper.

The package was about 10 inches high and 36 inches square with a heavy string over the brown packaging paper. Being a federal prosecutor in Birmingham, where some famous bombing cases had occurred over the years, made Sam suspicious and very cautious. While the situation probably did not call for panic, it did call for an expert opinion.

Chapter 8

Birmingham, Alabama
Sam Stone's Apartment on Southside
Thursday, June 5, 2003
7:20 p.m.

Fortunately, Sam had an expert staying in his apartment with him named Holmes.

He was in the bathroom because he did not care for Sam's banjo playing. Sam went to get him. Holmes was Sam's black Labrador retriever that he had rescued from an arson investigator's outfit in Huntsville. It was about the time that Linda had split the sheets and filed for divorce. With Sam moving out, Sam needed Holmes' company as much as the dog needed Sam to get completely healed back up from a bad injury that had ended his arson dog activities.

He was the smartest dog Sam had ever seen. Holmes had made the news in his earlier career because he had survived an actual cross-examination by Johnny "Robert

E. Lee" Brown, one of the most famous defense lawyers in north Alabama.

The FBI and the U.S. Attorney's Office had brought a criminal RICO case to clean up an arson ring headed by Brown's client, Joe B. Crain. The scheme was simple. Crain would loan money to small businesses teetering on the brink of bankruptcy, take out fire insurance, and then send around his two sons and sometimes-other "family" members to torch the establishments. Crain would then collect the insurance moneys. Sam was the prosecutor and Karen Kemper was the FBI agent responsible for the case.

Holmes was originally trained as an attack-guard dog, but he was so smart that the arson unit picked him out for special schooling. He was the best dog anyone in the business had ever encountered. Holmes was not afraid of anyone, including members of the legal profession.

Arson dogs are trained to detect hydrocarbons after a fire, and Holmes had alerted on the hydrocarbon remains in some ruins after one of Crain's fires at Billie's Beauty and Tanning Salon near Hytop, Alabama. This was good evidence of arson when coupled with other fire origin testimony from the investigators.

In a show of arrogance, Johnny Brown told Judge Nathan Bedford Crowell, "That the dog could not possibly detect hydrocarbons in the manner described by the investigator. I hereby move to cross examine Holmes by having the handler place small drops of hydrocarbons at three places in the courtroom for the dog to find in front of the jury."

This was a grandstand play in open court, and if it worked, the case against Brown's client would be considerably weakened.

As a federal prosecutor, Sam suspected something was about to go wrong. He knew that a good defense lawyer does not usually make such a big play or show with a jury unless he is certain of the result.

Sam called the arson investigators aside and asked, "Can Holmes really perform and survive an examination in a crowded courtroom?"

The arson canine handler said, "Yes. Holmes is the best animal we have ever had, and we have trained him to put on demonstrations in front of others, indoors and out. We aren't afraid of any defense lawyer on Holmes' account."

Sam said, "O.K. Let's put on a good show." He was still concerned and suspicious of Brown's tactic. He wondered what tricks Brown might have up his sleeve.

The courtroom was cleared, and Holmes was brought into the courtroom to sniff around and make sure the room was free from contaminants. He was then taken outside, and the arson team went in and placed three small drops of hydrocarbon fluid on the carpet: one drop at each end of the jury box and one just below the front of the judge's bench.

Just as Johnny and his defense entourage were about to enter the courtroom, they passed close to Holmes and his handlers. Holmes made a lunge for Johnny's shoes and those of his associates that were with him. He went into an alert posture. Sam saw this and told the deputy U.S. Marshal not to let anyone into the courtroom with shoes on until he had spoken with Judge Crowell.

Sam sent for the Judge and explained that Holmes had alerted on the shoes worn by Brown and his associates. Sam said that they were obviously trying to contaminate the courtroom to throw off the dog's demonstration.

Johnny denied to the Judge that he or his defense group had any contaminating substances on their shoes, but he did acknowledge that they may have walked through some oil in the parking lot while on the break just prior to the demonstration. At Sam's suggestion, Judge Crowell ordered all shoes off in the courtroom while the dog's examination was in progress.

With the jury and parties assembled, and everyone in the courtroom shoeless, Holmes was brought in. The arson team released him, and with little fanfare, Holmes went over to the carpet below the jury box and alerted on the first point, by being motionless over the first sample on the carpet. He resembled a bird dog doing a frozen point.

The jurors leaned forward in fascination and started nodding their heads with approval. They liked this dog.

On command, Holmes left that position and immediately alerted on the second point at the other end of the jury box.

The jury members nodded more vigorously in affirmation of the demonstration. Clearly things were going well for the prosecution and badly for the defense.

On final command, Holmes went to the third spot directly below the judge's bench. Judge Crowell, who was standing, leaning forward, and watching closely, forgot to turn off his microphone. As Holmes alerted, and with plenty of amplification, the Judge said, "Well, I'll be a son of a bitch."

Laughter erupted, and Sam could swear he saw Holmes grin. His kind of dog.

In any event, Crain plead out later in the day because the jury was clearly won over to the prosecution side by Holmes' abilities.

Three years later, Holmes snapped a leg and had a bad compound fracture while exploring a difficult fire scene in Muscle Shoals. He was to be "retired," and Sam asked for him when he found out about his condition. Sam had considered Holmes to be his partner ever since. Holmes was another reason for Sam's impending divorce from Linda. She had refused to allow Sam to take care of Holmes in the same household. As Sam's favorite living relative from North Alabama, Uncle John Stone, had said, you should never get married to a woman who hates dogs.

Sam led Holmes to the front door, and the dog immediately went over to the package. He sniffed it for all of 2 seconds and alerted on the box by being dead still. Then, Holmes uncharacteristically backed away and began barking and growling. Sam grabbed Holmes by the collar and dragged him back inside, slamming the door shut. He did not know what was in the box, but Sam was not going to take any chances. Holmes was never known to be wrong, and his behavior pointed to something unusual about the box.

Sam told Steven, "Your first lessons are over. We have a slight situation here. Grab your banjo and head for the back door now."

Sam reached for the cordless phone and began calling the FBI duty agent, as they all went out the back door and down the steps.

"What's going on?" asked Steven. He began to understand as he overheard Sam's description of Holmes' alert on the package on the front steps and request for the bomb squad and firemen.

Chapter 9

Birmingham, Alabama
Sam Stone's Apartment on Southside
Thursday, June 5, 2003
7:35 p.m.

Sam made sure that Steven was not shaken or upset and sent him on to his tutoring session with Professor Redmond. Sam waited in the street in front of his apartment for the bomb squad to arrive. He was standing behind his 2001 black Ford F-150 with Holmes when the first fire truck arrived.

The lead fireman asked, "What's the problem?"

Sam pointed at the package on his front steps. "See that brown package. My dog used to be in an arson unit and he alerted on it. It has no return address. I'm a prosecutor with the U.S. Attorney's Office and I'm a suspicious sort. That's why the bomb squad and fire and rescue were called over here."

Just then, the package moved slightly.

Sam thought he was seeing things.

The fireman said, "That's mighty strange. Bomb and incendiary packages don't usually move by themselves."

The package suddenly flipped over on one side. "It's got something alive inside, and I'm betting it's a cat or a rat," he observed.

"Why did my arson dog alert on the package then?" Sam asked.

He said, "I don't know but I'll bet you a plate of ribs from Dreamland that I'm right." Dreamland was one of the area's favorite barbecue joints, located on Birmingham's Southside. The Dreamland franchise had originated in Tuscaloosa. The original and the local restaurant were famous for pork ribs and green neon signs inside that read, "No farting."

At that moment the bomb squad arrived, and Sam and the lead fireman filled them in. A bomb squad professional in full blast protective gear cautiously approached the package. It suddenly flipped again and tumbled down the steps, where it continued to move at irregular intervals. When the bomb squad member bent down to look more closely, a hole suddenly appeared in the side of the package. Wispy white smoke started coming out of the hole, which caused the bomb squad member to jump back quickly. In less than a minute a large copperhead snake poked its head through the hole and began its slow exit.

The bomb squad member, with some relief, yelled, "Snake."

The lead fireman exclaimed, "Holy shit house mouse! Look at the size of that son of a bitch. I'll bet he's five foot."

It turned out that the copperhead was only three and one-half feet long. Snakes always appear larger than they are because people are so afraid of snakes in general. Throughout history few good things have been said about snakes. After all, a serpent was the villain in the Garden of Eden according to Genesis in the Bible. Actually, snakes like the copperhead do a great job of keeping the rodent population in check, and people should be grateful.

On the other hand, the highest numbers of venomous human snakebites in the United States each year come from the most common venomous snake, the copperhead. It is from the genus, *Agkistrodon*.

The copperhead is a pit viper, and it is a cousin to the cottonmouth water moccasin. In fact, some people refer to the copperhead as the "highland moccasin." The bites from copperheads are seldom fatal because their venom is the least toxic of the poisonous snakes in North America. Its poison is hemotoxic, which means that the venom causes a breakdown in the red blood cells of animals.

In the Southeastern United States there are two basic subspecies. First, there is the Southern Copperhead, *Agkistrodon contortrix contortrix*, which inhabits the coast and upper piedmont, which grows to a length of 3 feet, and whose body is light brown in color. Then there is the Northern Copperhead, *Agkistrodon contortrix mokasen*, which lives in the mountains and upper piedmont, which grows to 3 1/2 feet, and which is more reddish in color. Both have reddish or copper colored heads; hence the name.

The fire crew managed to capture the snake and put it in one of the bomb squad's portable containers. The packaging the snake came in was also taken so that forensics could have it inspected for evidence of the sender. It was obvious that someone did not like Sam and was sending him a not so subtle message.

Forensics called Sam later and said that they could find no latent prints or DNA on the packaging. They did find significant traces of gasoline, which, they explained, is frequently used by snake hunters to capture snakes. Also inside was a chunk of dry ice which explained the wispy smoke. It was used to cool down the snake and make it woozy and easy to handle.

Later that evening, as Sam was doing some laundry, his cell phone rang. It was Professor Redmond.

He said, "Steven had told me about the strange package emergency at your apartment."

Sam said, "Yeah. Some sick someone sent me a copperhead snake."

The Professor asked, "Goodness sakes alive. Are you safe and all right?"

Sam replied, "I'm fine. No one has been hurt including the snake. How did Steven's tutoring session go with you?"

The Professor laughed, saying, "Sometimes I think my student is tutoring me. He discussed, or rather gave me a mini-lecture on Steven Hawking's comments that the 'Big Bang' theory helps to make the case for God's existence."

"Who is Hawking?" Sam asked.

"Professor Hawking is the wheel chair bound star of the faculty at the University of Cambridge. Steven is really into Hawking and others' quest for the 'TOE,' and he just explained to me the latest research in that area. It was over my head for the most part."

Sam said, "Pardon my ignorance again, but what is the 'TOE'?"

"It's the Holy Grail of science these days. 'TOE' stands for the theory of everything. It's the unified theory of the universe. It's also a search for other dimensions. You know, humans have more perceptions of the world than a worm or a fish, so why shouldn't there be aspects or dimensions around us which humans don't readily perceive? With study and intellect we might be able to identify them."

"Does this mean that there are life forms around that man has not perceived or identified?" Sam asked.

"That's a good question. Some form of polymorphic biological parallelism I suppose," said the Professor. "I think I'll ask my students in philosophy class tomorrow."

Sam asked, "How does Birmingham College of Christ tolerate such studies? I always thought they were pretty fundamentalist. Its detractors around town refer to that place as 'Jesus Tech'. Science and God do not mix for them, or so I've been told. How did they hire an open minded professor?"

Professor Redmond paused and said, "They hired me 10 years ago supposedly because the administration liked the fact that I had done my Ph.D. thesis on Helen Keller's personal beliefs in Swedenborgian theology."

"Come again?" Sam asked.

"Emanuel Swedenborg was a Swedish scientist and philosopher who lived from about 1688 to 1772. Everyone from John 'Johnny Appleseed' Chapman to Ralph Waldo Emerson in the 1800's was influenced by Swedenborg's religious Christian mysticism. Helen Keller was born in Tuscumbia, Alabama, in 1880. She became blind and deaf before the age of two, yet she overcame these terrific handicaps and went on to graduate from Radcliff. My thesis was about how and why she wrote *My Religion* in 1929, supporting her brand of activism for the handicapped with her Christian views of Swedenborgian theology."

Sam asked, "Wasn't she also a famous speaker about which plays and movies were made?"

The Professor replied, "Yes. In fact she has been the most famous inspirational leader from Alabama in the state's history. This is of course despite what some of former Alabama Chief Justice, Roy 'Ten Commandments' Moore's supporters may think. Don't get me started. We just had a special class on the Moore business. But back to your question, the college also hired me because I was black, and the college needed a token minority professor. Recently, the administration has let it be known that they don't care to keep me around forever."

"What do you think brought all of this on?" asked Sam.

The Professor paused again and then spoke slowly with some emotion rising in his voice. "The President called me in last semester and said that I needed to add more in the way of Christian teachings to all my classes and exams. He was particularly critical of the fact that the bonus question for my Basic Philosophy 101 examination asked the students, 'Does God exist? Why or Why not?'. Equally correct answers for the extra credit were, 'Yes, because I believe,' or 'No, because I don't believe.' The President indicated strongly that here at the Birmingham College of Christ there was only one correct answer."

Sam said, "Gee, I didn't know you were having such problems. Let me know if I can be of help."

Professor Redmond said wearily, "Find me another position. Or else I might have to pray the 35th Psalm on the administration each Sunday."

"What's that?" Sam asked.

"Some of the fundamentalist Christians around town, including a few here in the college administration, think that you can put the curse and wrath of God on your enemies by praying certain Biblical passages on them at church. The 35th Psalm is a prayer to God for help against unjust enemies. I was making a bad joke. I don't believe in that sort of thing. After all, true Christians should not engage in such activities."

Sam said, "Yeah, jokes about religion, politics or football can be dangerous in this state."

"Being a federal prosecutor, you should know what my theory is about the cause of corporate greed and corruption in America," commented Professor Redmond.

"What's your theory?" asked Sam.

"It's because of college football. You train your business and corporate leaders at colleges where the icon and pinnacle of economic and social success is the football team. Everyone knows that it's a scam, but everyone ignores the situation because of the huge amounts of money involved. The players are generally not real college students. They are more like indentured servants. College students see that money trumps rules of conduct and ethics, and they apply the college football program's teachings to the business world. It's the old story of the Emperor with no clothes. We see it's a scam, but no one wants to speak out or face the truth."

Sam said, "You should be careful about letting loose with that football theory in Tuscaloosa or Auburn. Some fans would consider your analysis to be sacrilegious."

Professor Redmond laughed and said, "You are probably right. Oh, by the way, have you heard from Steven's mom? She called here and interrupted our session, asking for Steven to come home as soon as possible."

Sam suddenly felt a twinge. "I'll call her right now and see if there are any problems. Good evening and good luck with the college administration."

Both hung up, and as soon as Sam could get a dial tone, he called Karen. He knew her home phone number by heart because she had been the lead FBI agent on the Troy Pickering criminal case that had been flushed, and they had worked plenty of other cases over the years. In the Pickering case alone, they had spent a year on the indictment and trial, with huge amounts of overtime. Contact had been constant.

Karen picked up on the first ring. It was a curt, "Hello."

Sam asked, "Karen, this is Sam, what's going on?"

She said, "Oh Sam, someone came and induced Lauren out of rehab, gave her more drugs, and took her off to Winston County where she was dumped out and left alone. I had gone home for lunch, and someone called and said that if I knew what was good for my children, I would stay away from cases like Pickering's. They said Lauren was in an abandoned Gulf filling station on Highway 278 east of Addison."

Sam interrupted, "What did you do?"

"I called the local county sheriff, told him get someone over there, and meet me at the local medical clinic.

I drove like a bat out of hell. I called my supervisor on the way and told her what was going on. When I finally got to the clinic, the sheriff did not want to release Lauren, and I told him it was part of a continuing federal investigation. He said I was interfering with his official duties, that this was obviously an in state matter in which the FBI had no jurisdiction, and that I had no business in this other than as a parent."

"What a jerk," said Sam. "How did you handle it?"

"I lost it, and suggested that he stop me if he thought he was man enough. I grabbed Lauren, and walked out. I took her straight to University Hospital here in Birmingham."

"Did you tell him about the phone call?"

"Hell no. He was such a cretin. Besides, I don't know the politics up in that area."

Sam thought for a second, "Do you believe that there really is a connection to Pickering's crowd?"

She said, "I don't know but I'm going to find out, even if this is how I spend my time in retirement."

They said goodnight and made plans to pursue the investigation starting the next day. Sam forgot to tell her about his transfer and the snake. What a day.

Sam went into the kitchen and poured himself a drink of Jameson's Irish whiskey. He returned to his living room and put on a CD of the early Dillards. The Ozarks came alive, and he briefly lost the edge from some of his worries. His mind drifted back to an earlier time in his legal career.

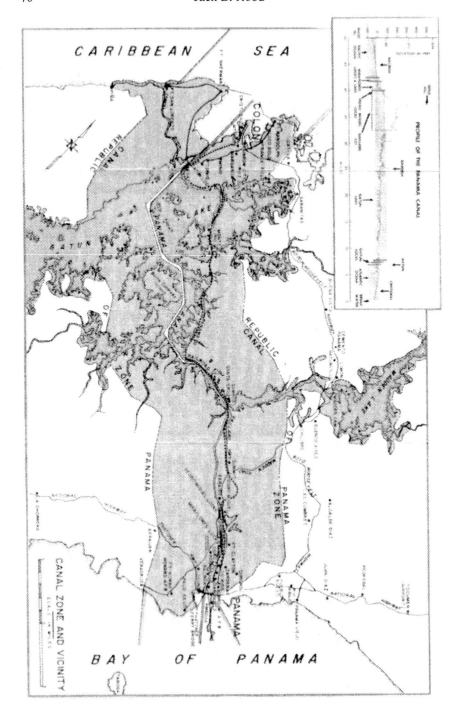

Chapter 10

Panama Canal Zone
Albrook/Howard Air Force Bases
1973

Sam joined Air Force ROTC at the University of Alabama in the late 1960's and avoided the draft that had swung into high gear due to the Vietnam conflict. Law school in Tuscaloosa was an easy choice, but hard work. As many would attest, law school in the late 1960's was real and it was fun at times, but it was never real fun. After graduation Sam wound up owing Uncle Sam four years of active duty as a lawyer. The U.S. Air Force made Sam a Captain in the Judge Advocate General branch. The service then sent him to JAG school at Maxwell AFB outside Montgomery, Alabama.

From there, a slot opened up in the Panama Canal Zone, and Sam volunteered for the assignment. It beat the hell out of being sent to some stateside training base where most of the other new Air Force JAGs were sent.

Sam held a variety of legal jobs at Howard AFB and at Albrook AFB, which were located on opposite sides of the canal. Albrook was on the Panama City side, and it was where the USAF Southern Command was headquartered.

For Sam, the Panama Canal Zone was a tropical oasis, engineering marvel of the modern world, and unique legal jurisdiction. Its critics called it America's "mini socialist colony" because any civilian head of a household had to have a job to live there, and anyone who created too much of a disturbance was made to leave. The military was there on orders and rotated in and out with typical duty reassignments. The average population was about 30,000.

There were no elections or elected officials in the Zone. A Canal Zone Governor ran the place, and he actually issued administrative regulations called "CZAR's", which stood for Canal Zone Administration & Regulations.

The Canal Zone had some strange features, including a leper colony located at Palo Seco and a mental hospital at Corozal. There was a prison at Gamboa for Panamanians convicted of crimes in the Zone. All U.S. prisoners were sent to federal prisons back in the states. The mixing of U.S. and Panamanian prisoners was viewed as a recipe for disaster.

No advertising or outdoor billboards were allowed, and each house and community was kept neat, clean and spotless. Sam thought it was like living in the United States 30 years earlier. There was a slower pace to life, and everyone had a sense of purpose. Sam liked the place a lot.

The United States had the right to act as "if it were the sovereign" in the 10 mile wide, 50 mile long strip of land called the Canal Zone, according to a 1903 Treaty with the Republic of Panama. The name "Panama" in local Indian language meant "plenty of fish."

The isthmus area has had a colorful history with visits from Christopher Columbus, who explored the mouth of the Chagres River; Vasco Núñez de Balboa, who discovered the Pacific Ocean; Sir Francis Drake, who is buried in a lead lined coffin off Portobello harbor; Sir Henry Morgan, who sacked and burned Old Panama City; and the French canal builder Ferdinand de Lesseps, who built the Suez Canal but floundered in his attempt in Panama in the late 1800's.

Panama had been a part of Columbia until the United States helped it suddenly achieve independence in 1903. The official language in Panama is Spanish, and Latin customs and manners prevail.

A group of wealthy families, or oligarchy, dominated the various governments. A dictator, or "strong man," Omar Torrijos came to power in 1968. Manuel Norreiga was his second in command.

The 1903 treaty was a constant source of political conflict with Panamanian leaders and students. The 1964 riots had been started by some Panamanian students over their attempt to raise the flag of Panama in the Zone, and those tensions were still evident in the early 1970's.

A special U.S. District Court and two U.S. Magistrate Courts were created by the U.S. Congress to enforce laws and provide legal rights and remedies for those in the Zone. All of this was established in a federal "Canal Zone Code." Appeals from the U.S. District Court went to the U.S. Court of Appeals for the Fifth Circuit, headquartered in New Orleans.

The U.S. District Court in the Zone was a "legislative court", as opposed to an "Article III" or Constitutional court. The latter was derived from Article III of the U.S. Constitution, which is source for the typical U.S. District Court in the United States. By contrast, the U.S. District Court for the Canal Zone was a creature of the United States Congress' power over territories, possessions, and the like. The Canal Zone was considered a possession of the United States.

The Canal Zone Bar Association members generally referred to the Canal Zone court as having a "bastard federal jurisdiction." No tax cases and no bankruptcies were allowed, and there were no grand juries for federal criminal prosecutions. The peculiarities did not stop there. Unlike federal district courts in the United States, the U.S. District Court for the Canal Zone handled divorces, adoptions, paternity proceedings, and decedents' estates. It also did the traditional work of federal district courts with cases involving admiralty, federal tort claims, and federal crimes.

The local contrast of legal systems was interesting to say the least for Sam. In the Canal Zone, the enforcement of criminal laws was under the typical U.S. model, with its accusatorial, jury trial, common law-type system.

Of course this system was based upon the "fight theory" of opposing sides presenting and questioning the evidence and law before a neutral fact finder, the jury, and law decider, the judge. Supposedly under this approach the truth was likely to be found from the facts, and points of law were sharpened. This in fact happened in most cases.

As in other U.S. courts, probable cause was required for searches and arrests, and accused criminals were presumed innocent. Of course one could not be forced to incriminate himself, and the Canal Zone police routinely gave *Miranda* warnings to suspects. Under U.S. laws, sentences of life in prison and death were possible. Death sentences were not given in the 1970's. They were highly questionable due to procedural issues and U.S. Supreme Court rulings. Thus, such sentences were avoided.

In Panama, on the other hand, the legal system was based upon the civil law and civil code traditions of France and Spain. Criminal laws were enforced by an inquisitorial system in which administrative law elements prevailed. The maximum sentence was 20 years, and there was no death penalty; but, very few murderers survived 20 years on Panama's prison island of Cobia. Gambling was legal in Panama, and the government regulated prostitution.

Panama had a unique economic relationship with the United States. The U.S. dollar and the Panamanian Balboa were the same. There was no exchange rate, and Panama did not print any paper money. Panamanian coins were of the same size and metal content as the U.S. coins. All were generated by the U.S. mint. The Panamanian coins were completely interchangeable with U.S. coinage.

Panama had bank secrecy laws akin to those of Switzerland or the Caymans. One could have numbered bank accounts, own bearer share corporations, operate foreign businesses, and invest moneys offshore without any tax consequences in Panama. Taxation was strictly territorial for the most part; taxing laws did not extend "offshore." Foreign branch banking offices were almost too numerous to count in Panama City.

There is a famous bar bet type question: which end of the Panama Canal is further east, the Pacific end or the

Atlantic end? Of course the answer is the Pacific end. From the Pacific entrance, the canal runs northwest. In fact, if one lived on the Pacific end of the Canal, say in Ancon, the sun arose in the Pacific Ocean each morning and set in the Atlantic.

In the Canal Zone, Sam prosecuted and defended court martial cases for the military, worked on defense of claims against the USAF, and acted as defense liaison counsel in order to get servicemen out of foreign jails from time to time.

In Panama itself, most of the arrested service personnel wound up in jail for "being in a place" where drugs were being used or found. This was a special crime under the laws of Panama. It usually came as a shock and surprise to those arrested. Many were actually unaware of any drugs being in a bar, house, or outdoor area, but would be arrested, charged, and convicted just the same.

Once arrested in Panama, one was held incommunicado until a formal "declaration" about the events of the arrest was made to the police. An arrestee could not make a phone call, contact family, friends, or even a lawyer until the "declaration" was finished. Many U.S. personnel stayed in jail longer than necessary because they thought they should exercise their right to remain silent. One could also be arrested in Panama for public indecency simply by having one's shirt off within the city limits.

Sam spent a lot of time as defense liaison counsel in and around the Carcel Modelo jail and in the Panamanian courts. He depended greatly on the U.S. military liaison personnel who were completely fluent in English and Spanish. On occasion, Sam relied upon a local Panamanian lawyer or two that were hired by the Air Force to make formal appearances for arrested service personnel.

Sam had no dull legal assignments while in the Canal Zone and Panama.

Chapter 11

Ft. Clayton, Panama Canal Zone
Building 519
1973

Sam was also assigned as the USAF's legal representative to the Armed Forces Disciplinary Control Board. Among other duties, the board investigated bars, restaurants, and houses of ill repute, and put them off limits as necessary for the health and welfare of the troops. The board was made up of Army, Navy, Air Force and Marine law enforcement, public health, medical, and legal personnel.

It was in this capacity that Sam first ran across Jefferson Duval, a Warrant Officer in the U.S. Army, assigned to the Army aviation battalion. Duval flew Huey helicopters, and had just spent two tours in Vietnam. He had grown up in a poor and broken family near Muscle Shoals, Alabama, but had been mostly influenced by his rural relatives in Winston County.

Legend had it that at the outbreak of the Civil War in the 1860's, the county decided to secede from the State of

Alabama and to declare itself the "Free State of Winston." Poverty and fierce mistrust of any government was said to be the two main traditions of Winston County. Great hardwood forested hills cut with limestone ravines and creeks made it difficult for large plantations to flourish there. From the outset, only poor small landholders settled or remained for the most part. It was a beautiful but sometimes dangerous place.

One of Duval's favorite pastimes as a kid was catching stray dogs and cats and tormenting them. He would take a corn cob dipped in turpentine and hold an animal by it tail. He would then scrape the rough cob across the animal's anus and turn it loose. There were no strays around the Duval trailer. Duval worked on cars and trucks from an early age, and showed some promise as a mechanic. Hard times and bad relatives in Winston County soon steered Duval into car theft and chop shop activities. He would have landed in jail had the draft board not sent him a notice to report to Ft. Rucker, near Dothan, Alabama for basic training. His mechanical aptitude was immediately apparent, and he was encouraged to become a helicopter pilot. These abilities were much in demand in Southeast Asia.

In Panama, Duval drove a brand new Corvette, and hung out in most of the local bars and gambling casinos. He seemingly developed a close relationship with the owner of the Broadway Bar because Duval turned up at a board meeting.

The board had issued a notice to the Broadway Bar, which was located in Panama City, just off the Fourth of July Avenue border with the Canal Zone. The notice to the bar indicated that for the second month in a row over five venereal disease contacts had been reported by servicemen being treated at sick call, and that therefore, the board intended to put the establishment off limits to all service personnel.

Servicemen were required to furnish the name of the bar and name of the woman if possible upon commencement of medical treatment. Failure to provide such information could result in adverse action being taken pursuant the Uniform Code of Military Justice in the form of non-judicial punishment or even a court martial.

Non-judicial punishment, commonly called an "Article 15", charged a military member with an offense under the Uniform Code and proposed a certain punishment. The military member had the choice of accepting the punishment, or turning it down and demanding a full court martial on the charge. If the military member was acquitted by the court martial he went free. If found he was found guilty, the service member wound up with a federal conviction. Clemenceau was probably right when he supposedly commented that military justice is to justice as military music is to music. However, the justice system in the military was designed to enforce discipline, not just to punish crimes.

Hector Gonzales, the bar owner, spoke little English, and had persuaded Duval to speak for his establishment. Hector and other similar bar owners depended on a constant flow of women from around the Caribbean and South America to entice and service soldiers and tourists transiting the canal. The profits were large.

After five minutes of telling the board what a wonderful friend Mr. Gonzales had been, Sam interrupted Duval and pointedly asked, "Do you have any evidence to refute the allegations of over five reported V.D. contacts within the past month?"

Duval turned angrily to Sam and said, "I was brought up in Alabama, and we don't normally stop another man's performance until he's finished."

Sam responded, "I'm from Alabama too, and your song and dance so far has nothing to do with the reasons for this hearing. As my Uncle John back home would say, dodgers always fiddle with the truth."

Anger flashed across Duval's face. He maintained control however, and said, "I'll cut to it. Hector Gonzales will donate Five Thousand dollars to the health, morale and welfare funds on Ft. Clayton and at Howard AFB, if the board will drop the off limits threat to his business."

Sam could not believe the audacity. Someone publicly trying to bribe his way out of trouble was unbelievable.

The board chairman intervened, "The answer is not only no, but hell no. If you don't have any other information or evidence to present, please leave."

Duval muttered something that sounded like, "church mother," and then distinctly, "*Capitan, pendejo*," as he and Gonzales left the room quickly.

The chairman turned to the secretary and said, "Make sure the notice posting the Broadway Bar as off limits to all service personnel goes out today."

Sam reflected on what had just transpired. The United States government had afforded administrative due process rights, with full notice and an opportunity to be heard, to a business that based its profits on white slavery. What a legal world.

The chairman turned to Lt. Colonel Jim Stark, a USAF fight surgeon, and a serious Southern Baptist from

Macon, Georgia, and remarked, "I can't believe that the board takes the time to hear this kind of crap. Why don't we just summarily put them off limits after one warning letter? Hearings aren't necessary."

Lt. Colonel Stark replied, "Well, I think it's because the concept of due process is as old as mankind."

A puzzled chairman then asked, "What are you talking about, due process old as mankind?"

"Well you need to look in the Bible back there in Genesis at Chapter 3, Verse 11. God asked Adam, before throwing him and Eve out of the Garden of Eden, 'Hast thou eaten of the tree, whereof I commanded thee that thou shouldest not eat?'. God gave Adam notice and an opportunity to be heard. Today we call this due process. It's the oldest tradition of Judeo-Christian ethics and Western Civilization."

Sam laughed and told the U.S. Army JAG representative, Major Crenshaw, that the Army ought to consider giving Duval an Article 15 for conduct unbecoming an officer under Article 133, or conduct discrediting the service under Article 134, of the Uniform Code of Military Justice. The Major said he would contact Duval's commander.

Sam later found out that Duval's commander refused to take any action because of Duval's good combat record in Vietnam.

Duval also knew the military legal system well. When previously threatened with discipline, he on two occasions had filed Article 138 complaints against his commanders.

Under this article of the Uniform Code, any serviceman who believed himself to have been wronged by a commanding officer, could apply in writing to the commander for a correction of the wrong. On being turned down, a review of the matter went to the commander's commander, with a copy to the Secretary of the Army, Navy or Air Force, as appropriate. His current commander did not want any hassle with Duval.

Sam later ran into a U.S. Army liaison sergeant, Juan Padilla, who had worked with him before to get servicemen out of Panamanian jails. Padilla and others with liaison duties conducted regular patrols of off limit bars and restaurants to insure that no service personnel were patronizing off-limits establishments.

Sam asked him what he knew of Duval and Gonzales. Padilla told Sam that Duval had invested money with Gonzales. No one seemed to know where Duval came by all his money; perhaps it was from bar investments and gambling. Duval also hung out with some other Army buddies from Alabama, and they were known for the strange fact that they all had blue banjos tattooed on their left knees.

The last time Sam saw Duval in Panama, Duval was coming out of the Mongolian Barbecue at the Albrook Air Force Base Officer's Club one evening.

Duval was half drunk when he spotted Sam, and yelled, "Hey *Capitan*, come on down to the Broadway Bar tonight and I'll see you get the special. Four beers and two blow jobs for twenty bucks."

Sam made no reply and turned away. There is no percentage in conversing with drunks.

Duval persisted and yelled, "I hope I catch your ass in North Alabama sometime. I will see that you get more than an Article 15."

Word of Sam's recommendation to Major Crenshaw must have leaked back to Duval.

Sam never thought he'd see him again, but he was wrong.

Thomas Jefferson once wrote that the art of life is the avoiding of pain, and anyone having future encounters adverse to Duval would have that proposition tested.

Chapter 12

Panama City, Panama
La Cresta
U.S. Ambassador's Residence
Early 1974

The bluegrass/folk group Sam played with was called, "The Professionals." The guitar player was a doctor, the fiddle and mandolin player was a dentist, the bass player was an accountant, and Sam played the 5-string banjo. They were all military officers and everyone in the group was married but Sam. The group had been asked by the U.S. Ambassador to provide traditional American entertainment for a party at the Ambassador's residence one evening during dry season. They gladly obliged. There must have been 30 guests gathered on the back patio for the performance.

Before they began to play, Sam asked the Ambassador's wife, "Where is this crowd from?"

She said, "Oh, they are ambassadors and guests from the various embassies in Panama. In all, six invitations went out to the local diplomatic corps of France, Taiwan, Spain, Great Britain, Mexico, and Brazil."

Sam said to her, "Gee, I'm not sure that this sophisticated crowd will understand or appreciate the kind of music that we are about to play."

She looked Sam in the eye and said, "If they don't like it, screw'em. Now play as you normally would."

That was all the direction that Sam needed. He told the others with him what she had said, and everyone laughed and relaxed a bit.

The group started off with "Cripple Creek" and ended the first set of songs with a comical rendition of "Oh Susannah."

During the first break, the Brazilian Ambassador came over to Sam and asked,

"After that last song, are you by any chance from Alabama?"

Sam acknowledged that he was in fact.

The Ambassador then said, "My unmarried niece is here on a visit from her home in Brazil, and I would like to introduce you to her because some of her ancestors were originally from Alabama I believe."

Sam said, "Sure."

In Brazilian Portuguese, the Ambassador called over to a throng of women, *Regina, vem aqui! Eu quero que você conheca uma pessoa. (Regina, come here, I have a person for you to meet.)*

One of the most beautiful young women Sam had ever seen in his life suddenly appeared before them in a low cut yellow dress. She had dazzling green eyes, sun streaked long hair down to her waist, lightly beach-tanned arms and face, and a terrific figure. She was three inches shorter than Sam, and he tried hard not to stare at her near perfect cleavage. She looked to be in her early twenties, and she carried herself with an air of sophistication and mischief which left Sam fascinated.

The Ambassador said, "Regina, the banjo player is from Alabama. Please introduce yourself. You and he may have some common relatives." He turned and left them staring into each other's eyes.

She held out her hand, and as Sam took it, he felt a spark fly between them.

Sam said, "Hi, my name's Sam Stone, and I've come from Alabama with a banjo on my knee just to play for you." He winked at her.

She coolly replied in perfect English with absolutely no accent, "My name is Regina Jones Oliveira, and I was born and raised in Rio de Janeiro. My father was an American businessman, but my mother's family is from a town called Americana, near Sao Paulo, in the southern part of Brazil. The Confederados, as we call them, settled Americana. The original Jones family was from Demopolis, Alabama."

Sam asked quizzically, "Confederados, who were they?"

She smiled slightly and said, "Don't you know? Surely you must if you are from Alabama. But then again, few Americans I have ever met know very much about the history of Brazil or South America."

Sam nodded slightly.

She looked Sam in the eyes, and continued, "Look, they were from all over the southern United States. They took their gold, goods, and slaves, right after your Civil War, along with other die-hard Confederate families, and moved to Brazil at the express invitation of our then beloved Emperor, Dom Pedro II."

Sam interrupted, "Do you mean that Brazil had a royal family that actually reigned from a throne?"

"Yes. From 1822 to 1889 the crowned family of Pedro I and Pedro II, with the assistance of regents, ruled the Brazilian Empire."

"So why did the migration of Southerners take place?" asked Sam.

"Dom Pedro II actually sent recruiters from Brazil to the States because he was trying desperately to promote Brazilian agriculture, especially cotton farming. Brazil had not abolished slavery and did not do so completely until 1888, when Brazil passed what is called our 'Golden Law.' Children of female slaves had been declared free in 1871, and in 1885 all slaves over the age of 60 were declared free by another law."

"What brought about the legal abolition of slavery there?" Sam asked.

She continued. "The legal changes were brought about by international political pressures. Also, Dom Pedro II had a change of attitude about slavery, and he began the sponsorship of a movement to abolish slavery. His change also doomed the monarchy in Brazil due to the opposition of large landowners. The throne in Brazil was replaced with a republic in 1889, which we have had ever since. Dom Pedro II and his family became European exiles."

"How many Southerners immigrated to Brazil?" Sam inquired.

"About 10,000 Confederados came in all, and the majority of them tried to establish plantations around Americana, their main town in the south of Brazil. They were unique because they were mostly Baptists, or protestant, in a Catholic Brazil. They also insisted on education for their female children, which was a new concept for the Brazilians in those days. Over the years, many intermarried and faded into the local populations. But, the St. Andrew's Cross is on the town crest for Americana, and sometimes banjo music can be heard at local heritage celebrations."

Sam was amazed and his mind was spinning, but he finally managed to get out, "I guess you are what I would call a real southern, Southerner. What are you doing in Panama?"

She said, "I'm an anthropologist specializing in Indian cultures throughout Central and South America. I'm here for six months studying the Choco, Guayamí, and Cuna tribes. My Uncle, the Ambassador, helped me get permission from the Panamanian government for my research."

Sam asked, "Are you a U.S. citizen?"

She said, "No, I'm Brazilian by birth. I never lived in the States, which was required by your laws to acquire citizenship through my father. I have little accent in English because my U.S. father only spoke English with me as I was growing up. He was completely bi-lingual from a Portuguese speaking family in the San Francisco, California area."

"Your father did a heck of a job. You speak better English than I do and with no accent that I can detect."

"We always had English and American friends at the house, including American Redemptorist Priests, who did their R & R visits in Rio at least once a year from their remote missions up the Amazon. They taught me a great deal of American slang."

"Your father must be very proud of your linguistic abilities," said Sam.

She replied, "I believe he was. Unfortunately, he died when I was 17, while working for an American owned mineral exploration company in the headwaters of the Amazon, near the trapezium of Leticia."

Sam said, "I am so sorry. Look, I would like to chat with you some more, but I've got to play some songs. Can I see you afterwards?"

She grinned, turned away, and looking over her shoulder, said, "Chat, huh? Sure." She winked one of those beautiful green eyes at him.

Sam could hardly wait until the playing was over. He was smitten.

She apparently felt the same about Sam because they were married six months later.

Chapter 13

Panama Canal Zone
Howard AFB Officer Housing
Late 1974

Sam called her Jonesy because it seemed a good American choice, given her Jones name and ancestors. Also, "Regina", as pronounced in Portuguese, sounded funny to Sam, like "Hey Gina". She in turn, in Portuguese, called Sam, *Nênê*, pronounced, "Nay-nang" (*Baby*).

There was never a dull moment in their marriage. They learned something new and different about each other and their cultures every day. Both savored the interplay.

She had been raised in the Catholic Church, and Sam had been raised in the Southern Baptist traditions, but both were educated enough to not let these backgrounds interfere with their relationship.

Jonesy had an almost photographic memory, and she had a facility for languages that was unrivalled by anyone Sam had ever known. In addition to English and Portuguese, she spoke fluent Spanish and French. When she was growing up, French was the official second language in Brazil, and the schools were required to teach it. The Spanish she had picked up in her South American travels. She also got by in Italian.

Jonesy and Sam talked openly with each other about religious views of God and the world. Sam told her that the Baptists believed that only by your personal belief in God could you be saved and go to Heaven instead of Hell. Jonesy told Sam in return that the Catholics simply asked, "why not believe," just to be on the safe side.

Sam explained to Jonesy that a Frenchman named de Tocqueville toured the United States in the 1800's and observed that there was no other country in the world in which the Christian religion retained a greater influence over individuals. Further, de Tocqueville found in the United States that religion directed the manners of the community, regulated domestic life, and that therefore, religion regulated the country. Both agreed that the Christian religion was still the predominant factor in American life in the 1900's.

She told Sam that in Brazil, the Catholic Church predominated, but that *macumba*, or back magic, was in vogue with all classes. People synchronized these two sets of beliefs so that they did not interfere with the other. When asked, the typical Brazilian would say that he believed in the good of the Catholics, but to keep off evil, you needed to practice *macumba*.

She chided Sam about being too much of an "anal-retentive American control freak" that needed to be in charge of the details of life around him. She continually tried to tell Sam that he needed to loosen up.

Sam's best counter had to do with the issue of personal responsibility. If he dropped his plate and broke it, he would always say, "Gee, I'm so sorry I broke the plate."

If Jonesy dropped her plate, she and the millions from the Portuguese-speaking world in her place, would simply say, *"caiu"* (*it dropped*). In Spanish cultures they would say, "se cayó" (it dropped itself).

Sam did not recall her ever saying she was sorry for anything, even in the most embarrassing moments, of which there were a few.

Language differences produced an endless discussion of topics. According to Jonesy, the further south in Brazil one goes, one finds a more distinctive the Portuguese speech pattern. The colder south of Brazil seemed to produce clipped words with a faster pace. As one heads north toward the equator and the heat of the Amazon basin, a slower speech pattern is encountered. It's similar to the differences in accents by a New Yorker and an Alabamian.

In Brazil, there are at least three distinct accents, depending upon where one is from. In the south, for example, to say "restaurant", one would say *restaurante*, which is pronounced "res-ta-rant-ay". In the Amazon region, one would hear a slow drawl or "ress—taa-rantt-aayy". Of course in Rio de Janerio, the people have their own unique accent. There one would hear "res-ta-rant-chay".

Sam's favorite language differences that he discovered were spoken animal sounds. In American English, a baby chick goes "chick, chick, chick" while in Brazilian Portuguese, it goes, *pio, pio, pio*, pronounced, "pee-o, pee-o, pee-o". A rooster goes "cock-a-doodle-doo" in English, but in Portuguese it goes *caw-cara-caw*. The list goes on.

Both had great fun with these, not to mention swear words, dirty words, and common sayings. Jonesy told Sam that he had to learn basic Brazilian Portuguese because he would be around her friends and family members from time to time, and he needed to be able to defend himself and know what was really going on. This meant, in her words, "a coarser course" in Portuguese.

She told him that a famous politician in Rio de Janeiro noted that Brazil was the only country in the world where just about every word in the language, including the word, *mãe*, or mother, could be, and frequently was, a curse or dirty word. Jonesy gave Sam quite a lesson in filthy language.

Jonesy started the course in her direct style with what she considered the most basic. "Most men are interested in one thing about a woman, her pussy or cunt, as you call it in English. In Brazil there are numerous names for this part of the anatomy, including *boceta*, *chochota*, *cona*, *xana*, *xochota*, or my favorite, *aranha*, which literally translated, means spider. The entire list of names would go on for a couple of single spaced pages if you wrote them all down."

Sam naively asked, "So what is the male member called?"

She responded, "Your dick or cock is called *cacete*, *caralho*, *pau*, *piru*, or *pinto*. Again, the entire list is quite long. Most fruits and vegetables can be used to describe male and female sex organs depending on the context. For example, holding up your fist with the right hand and crossing the right elbow with the left hand, signifies 'giving someone the banana.'"

"Are there any other signs I should be aware of?" asked Sam.

Jonesy replied, "We do not 'shoot the bird' at someone in Brazil with the middle finger. Instead, you hold up your hand with your index finger and thumb touching and the other fingers extended so that it looks like your 'O.K.' sign. It does not mean O.K. So don't do like some of your visiting American politicians have done, and hold up the 'O.K.' to the crowd. That's telling them all to get fucked."

Sam said, "Wow. I don't want to make that mistake in polite company."

Jonesy continued, "Now in Brazil, a woman's breasts are called many things, but typically *mamão* or *mamas*. Unlike you Americans, large breasts, or *lolôs*, are not desirable with Brazilian men. In fact many women go to plastic surgeons for breast reductions, so they can have small breasts, or *pitangas*."

"What part of the female anatomy is the most talked about and desired then?" Sam asked.

"Brazilian men desire a woman with small breasts and large ass, or *bunda*. You are not going to believe this, but a popular Brazilian slang word for ass or butt is *banjo*."

Sam started laughing, but he was catching on. He was starting to realize that you can learn a lot about a culture by the way they swear and by their common expressions.

Sam asked, "What's damn or darn?"

"The polite darn or such is *caramba*. For an impolite expletive we say *caralho*."

"How do you say 'son of a bitch'?", he asked.

"That's *filho da puta. Puta* is whore or slut, so it's really son of a whore. There was a famous English racehorse in the early 1800's named *Filho da Puta.* The framed print is popular in England, Portugal and Brazil. I have a copy along with the racehorse print of *Filho da Puta's* famous son, who was named *Birmingham.*"

Sam laughed again. This was really getting funny.

"*Vaca,* or cow, is used for bitch or prostitute," she continued. "A fart is a *pum* or *peido.* Shit is *merda, caca,* or *cocô.* Faggot is *bicha,* or *veado,* which also means deer. Asshole is *cú.* To fuck is *foder* and to screw is *transar.* Often you may hear *foder-se,* or 'fuck it.' But the most frequently heard expression of disgust is *porra,* which translates as semen or cum. The Brazilians are famous for dragging out and rolling the r's when saying this word."

"Great sakes. So how would I say anything that is not offensive in Brazilian Portuguese?"

She said, "As an American you will mostly be forgiven, especially if you make an effort to speak the language. The Brazilians basically like Americans, but they believe that Brazilians have a better attitude about life and love."

Sam would have to think about that. "What about more polite common expressions or sayings?" he asked.

She thought a few seconds and said, "The most common expression is probably *dar um jeito,* which translated means, 'make a way.' This expression is used in the context of getting through daily life difficulties or finding a way to deal with bureaucratic red tape."

"In Brazil, do you have expressions like 'still waters run deep', 'lie down with the dogs and get up with the fleas', or 'straw that broke the camel's back'?"

Jonesy replied, "Yes, but they are slightly different. We say *nao confie em aguas paradas*, or don't trust still waters. We also say, *dorme com gato, acorda arranhado*, or sleep with a cat, wake up scratched. We again use, *a última gota tansborda o copo,* or a last drop makes the cup overflow."

"What else could I run into?"

"Sometimes you will hear, *abre-se um olho pra comprar e dois pra vender*, or open one eye to buy and two to sell.

Sam said, "That's like the old English wine merchant saying, 'buy on apples and sell on cheese'."

She said, "Explain that one."

"Apples cleanse the palate for the taste of wine while cheese coats the tongue and covers up the taste. So if a merchant was offered wine and cheese, he knew he should not make a buy. If he was offered apple slices with the wine, then he knew he was getting an honest taste. Therefore, a merchant would buy wine if offered apples and sell wine by offering cheese. 'Buy on apples and sell on cheese' became an expression of how to conduct business. Are there any other common expressions from Brazil that I should know about?"

Jonesy thought for a moment and said, "Yes. *A oportunidade faz o ladrão*, or the opportunity makes the thief."

Sam said, "That sounds like a good one to remember. What about men's talk?"

"Men say things like, *a águia não se detém caçando moscas*, or an eagle does not hang around to hunt flies. Also, *a mulher chora antes do casamento, o homen depois*, that is, a woman cries before the wedding, the man after. Also men frequently say, *a melhor esposa e a que se comporta como dama na societdade e como uma puta na cama*, or the best wife is a lady in society who is a whore in bed."

Sam laughed and asked, "What do women say?"

She replied, "Expressions like, *amor de asno é coice e dentada*, or loving an ass is a kick and a bite. Frequently you hear, *amor, com amor se paga*, love is paid with love."

"Have you encountered many American expressions?" asked Sam.

She thought and said, "The priests from America that visited from time to time frequently would use the expression 'beauty is only skin deep'."

Sam laughed and asked, "Have you ever heard the complete version?"

Jonesy looked puzzled. "No. What do mean?"

"My Uncle John Stone back in Alabama," replied Sam, "says it this way: beauty is only skin deep, but ugly is to the bone; beauty always fades away, but ugly holds its own."

They both started laughing.

"What kind of words or sayings do you yourself personally like?" asked Sam.

She thought for a while and said, "*A palavra é como a abelha, tem mel e ferrão*, or, a word is like a bee, it has honey and a sting. I also like, *para o bom entendedor, meia palavra basta*, that is, for one good at understanding, half a word is enough. But I think my favorite is, *a felicidade não*

é um destino onde chegamos, mas uma maneira de viajar,
or, happiness is not a destination but a way of traveling."

Chapter 14

Panama Canal Zone
Albrook AFB Officers Club
Late 1974

Jonesy loved American slang and had great fun practicing curse words and odd phrases on Sam and others.

Her emotions were in Portuguese, but her English sounded solid American. She was not bashful in speaking her mind despite the fact that some of the American idioms and slang could be viewed as inappropriate. Jonesy seemed to derive pleasure out of language and out of the reactions of people to her spicy phrases. Sam never knew exactly what she might say in polite company, but he did not try to restrain her. She was too much fun to be around for him to want to curb her enthusiasm.

By their hanging around the officer's club with a bunch of Air Force pilots, she managed to overhear, and sometimes adopt, some very unique terms and slang. At a Dining Out, which was a formal gathering of officers and wives, at the officer's club, someone in Sam and Jonesy's group mentioned that he had recently met the Panamanian Colonel Norriega, who was the second in command under the strong man in charge of Panama, General Omar Torrijos. The person told the group what an ugly face Norriega had, and that his nickname was "Pineapple Face."

Jonesy allowed, "I met him once at a Brazilian Embassy function, and I agree that he is really ugly. In fact he is so ugly that if I had a face like that, I'd skin it back and pee through it."

Everybody was stunned at first, and then everyone burst out laughing.

Jonesy also played the guitar, and sang *fados*, or ballads, in Portuguese. Sam got her to play along with his banjo, and soon they had a rendition of "Going Up the Amazon", a take off on "Going Up Cripple Creek".

Sam sang:

Going up the Amazon
*   Going on the run*
Going up the Amazon
*   To have a little fun*

I've got a girl from the southern world
*   And I like to give that girl a whirl*
She's crazy for me and treats me fine
*   And wraps her legs around me*
Like a jungle vine

Then she'd sing:

Eu vou para a Amazona
*   Correndo pela barra*

Eu vou para a Amazona
Para fazer farra

After one such rendition, Jonesy asked Sam, "Do you know the origin of the name 'Amazon'?"

Sam confessed that he did not. "No, please tell me." He had gotten to where he enjoyed her little lectures.

"The word 'Amazon' is from ancient Greek, and it means 'no breast'. There was supposedly a tribe of warrior women around 8000 B.C. who burned off their right breasts in order to use bows and arrows more easily."

"So how did the name get affixed to the largest river in Brazil?" asked Sam.

"An early Spanish river explorer was attached by a tribe of Indians with strange headdresses and grass skirts. They apparently reminded him of the legendary Amazon warriors. Hence the name."

"What about the name 'Brazil'? Where does that come from? The nut?" Sam inquired.

"No, silly," Jonesy replied. "In the early 1500's, after Spain and Portugal had signed the Treaty of Tordesillas in 1494 which gave eastern South America to Portugal, Portuguese adventurers exploring the area found a red dyewood called 'brazilwood', so the they called the place 'Brazil.'"

Jonesy was also a fair athlete. She especially enjoyed making Sam play soccer with her. She would tell him tales of the great Pele' from Brazil, and she taught Sam how to kick goals soccer style by planting the left foot, keeping the head down, and sweeping the right foot sideways toward the ball. They held regular kicking contests using the local football goal posts. She generally won.

Amazingly, they agreed on many cultural things. Jonesy and Sam agreed that the macho aspects of Latin male culture were overwhelming. Any political, economic, or social issues were generally overridden by the macho egos of the males involved in any decisions. In the current spate of canal negotiations between the United States and Panama it was predicted that Panama would give up unlimited economic and social benefits for its peoples just to be able to claim sovereignty over the Panama Canal. Things were certainly headed in that direction from all accounts.

Jonesy claimed that most Brazilian men had the same blinding macho egos. Her father had always said that American businessmen that knew about this cultural feature could always out-negotiate the Brazilians every time.

Jonesy and Sam both believed that education was the key to cultural survival, and that local justice for the common man was a feature that the United States had that Latin America generally lacked.

Jonesy envied the judicial system in the United States because it was the only one in the world that was both a vehicle for social change and a mechanism for the administration of local justice to the rich and poor alike. A poor person in the United States could actually sue a rich person for breach of contract or in tort and win. That was unheard of in Brazil and in most of the world.

Chapter 15

Panama and the Canal Zone
Howard AFB Officer Housing
Late 1974

Jonesy continued her studies of the local Indian cultures. Sam took leave and traveled with her to the Volcan mountain area, in the Chiriqui Province, near the Costa Rican border to speak with and photograph the Guayamí. They flew into the Darien swamp area near the Columbian border to do the same with a Choco family unit. Their favorite trip though was out to the San Blas Islands off the North Coast of Panama, to vista the Cunas.

The Guayamí were famous for their pottery and gold *huacas* made with the lost wax process. The gold frog figure *huacas* were especially prized, and many graves of the Guayamí had been robbed in search of these and other artifacts. Sam and Jonesy also traveled to the El Valle area, where they saw ancient figures, called petroglyphs, carved into rock walls, living gold frogs, and square trees. Jonesy photographed all with glee.

Compared to the other Indians in Panama, the Guayamí were fair skinned, well clothed, and very hardworking in their small farms and fields in the mountains. They were said to be somewhat mistrustful of Spanish speakers due to maltreatment by the early Spanish explorers and colonizers. In fact, within some remote groups, outsiders were so feared by some Guayami that they set mantraps along trails to keep strangers away.

The Guayamí would talk some to tourists and sell items to people outside their tribe, but they would not tell too much about themselves. As a tribe, they were a fairly friendly and cohesive group. They were also a growing political force in Northern Panama due to their increasing numbers.

The Choco family they encountered in the Darien was very different. They were barely clothed due to the heat. A man was the head of the family, and he hunted, fished, and made love to his three wives. He wore only a loincloth.

The women did all of the work. They built the thatched-roofed, platform dwellings. They cooked, cleaned, and farmed small jungle plots with slash and burn technique. They raised the children, and they obeyed the male head of the family.

All were naked from the waist up. Other Choco families acted as similar independent units, scattered throughout the jungle, so there was little in the way of obvious cohesion among the Chocos as an overall tribe.

For Sam, the excursion to the San Blas Islands was the most fun. The Cunas lived on tiny islands in the Caribbean and created bright colored cloth artworks called *molas* that were sold around the world. These were hand sewn colorful pieces of cloth depicting the shapes of animals, fishes, or other designs, only limited by the imagination. Tourists came from all over the world to visit the Cunas, purchase their *molas*, and take photographs.

The Cunas had a matriarchal society that was very close knit. Women ruled, but they weren't showy about it, and they were very peaceful. But, they invited no one into their circle of beliefs, and they permitted no marriages with non-Cunas. A child born of a Cuna with an outsider might be killed.

The Cuna language was not akin to any other language so far as anyone knew. Missionaries and anthropologists had tried to either convert or seriously study the Cunas, and the Cunas would not cooperate with either.

Because of inbreeding, the Cunas had one of the world's highest incidences of albinism. In some societies, albino children and adults are treated as outcasts, but the Cunas treated them with special reverence. The young ones were called "moon children", and many grew up to be tribal leaders.

The Cunas always kept their beliefs within the tribe, and they held firm to their culture, warding off all outside attempts to gain any foothold in their society. They also thought the rest of the world was crazy. Sam thought that they may have something on that score.

The Cunas refused to answer any of Jonesy's serious questions about the tribal culture, and they charged her for each photograph of tribal members. She was not too happy about that fact, but she paid up each time. With her eye for quality, she bought some exquisite *molas* which she later made into a large wall hanging. Jonesy was always proud of her tapestry of Cuna art. Her talents and abilities seemed unending to Sam.

Sam never forgot the first Saturday afternoon of the week after Jonesy and he were married. Jonesy decided to introduce him to Brazilian cooking and her brand of Brazilian humor. She fixed the national dish, *feijoada*, which consisted of black beans and rice, with *chorizos* (*pork sausages*), *carne seca*, (*dried beef*), chunks of beef tenderloin, and you name it, thrown in. After the rice, beans, and meat were plated, over the top was sprinkled toasted manioc flour, along with a *piripiri* sauce made of chopped onions, tomatoes, and spicy peppers in olive oil and vinegar. *Cove*, sautéed kale, with olive oil and garlic, was served as a side dish. Fresh orange slices were also a side item.

All of this was washed down with Brazilian firewater made of sugarcane, otherwise known as *cachaça*, in a drink with fresh limejuice and sugar, called a *caipirinhia*. For desert Jonesy made *bananas com castanhas do para* (*bananas with ground Brazil nuts, berries, and peach liqueur*). What a meal, Sam thought.

After they finished, Jonesy told Sam with a smile, "I've got a really great joke to tell you later. Now you should go to bed and take a nap. I'll clean up the table and kitchen and wake you up later."

About dusk, Jonesy slipped naked into bed behind Sam and kissed his ear to awaken him. She whispered, "*Nênê*, go brush your teeth and come back to bed without any clothes."

Sam did, and when he retuned, Jonesy reached up for him and guided him into her.

She locked her legs around Sam and said, "I have a joke to tell you."

He started to pull away to hear the joke, but she said, "Don't move. I'm going to move for both of us. Listen up and pay attention."

Sam had no trouble following these orders, and he was certainly comfortable in this position inside her.

Jonesy held his head close beside hers and began, "Once there was a young bride who knew nothing of sex, so she asked her godmother what she should do on her wedding night with her husband. The godmother told her the basic mechanics of arriving in the position we are in at this very moment, and then said, once you are like this, use your hip movements, pretending that there is a nickel coin on the left side of your hips, a dime on the right, and a quarter beneath, hitting each one in turn with your *bunda* (*rear end*)."

Sam was getting more than curious as to where this was going, and his excitement was building.

Jonesy continued, "On her wedding night, she did as instructed and when she got into the very position we are in right now, she started moving as instructed whispering, 'hit the nickel'," which Jonesy demonstrated to Sam with a movement of her hips to the left.

"She then whispered, 'hit the dime'," Jonesy moved her hips to the right.

"'Hit the quarter'," moving her hips down. Her locked legs then pulled them back into their beginning positions.

Jonesy continued the story and demonstration, "The bride started slowly but then built up some speed with her *bunda* movements, whispering, 'hit the nickel, hit the dime, hit the quarter, hit the nickel, hit the dime, hit the quarter, hit the nickel, hit the dime, hit the quarter, hit the nickel, hit the dime, hit the quarter'."

Jonesy fully demonstrated as the name of each coin was said.

Sam was starting to like this story a lot.

Then Jonesy said, "After about five rounds of the coins, she suddenly exclaimed, 'screw the small change, hit the quarter, hit the quarter, hit the quarter, hit the quarter, hit the quarter, hit the quarter, hit the quarter, hit the quarter, hit the quarter, hit the quarter'...."

She made love to Sam with increasingly rapid up and down hip movements from then on, and he had his first laughing orgasm.

With a wife like this, Sam believed that nothing could go wrong. But it did.

Chapter 16

Panama Canal Zone
Howard AFB Hospital
1976

In March 1976, Jonesy got pregnant. She had switched birth control pills in February, and somehow she was with child a month later. Both Jonesy and Sam were anti-abortion but pro-choice, which is not as contradictory as it might sound. Neither believed in abortion, but both thought the decision ought to be left to the woman up to a reasonable point without any interference or regulation by the state. It should be a matter of personal responsibility and freewill. The actual thought of terminating a life created between them never came up in conversation.

They were happy, and looked forward to life's new adventure. Both discovered that there was a new type of love that they had never before experienced, that of a parent's love towards a child of their own.

All was right in heaven and earth with Jonesy and Sam until the middle of rainy season in September. A son was born prematurely at the Howard AFB hospital, and he lived 6 hours. They named him James Jones Stone. Testing was to be done to try and determine the cause.

Jonesy was devastated. She went into severe depression in the hospital. In her already depressed mood over the loss of a child, and without being told the results of any tests, she happened to be walking down the hall and was about to turn the corner by the nurses' station when she overheard a physician and three nurses laughing about the test results.

The Air Force ob-gyn physician laughed and said, "I guess Baby Stones's death certificate will have to list the race as Negro, because the autopsy showed sickle-cell disease."

The nurse giggled and said, "There must have been a nigger in the woodpile."

Someone else in the group said within Jonesy's earshot, "He was a little Brazil nut, you know, because he had little nigger toes."

Another nurse chimed in, "I recently heard that science had discovered the real cause of sickle-cell disease in the United States: it was the glue on the back of food stamps."

The groups' laughter was suddenly interrupted by a violent onslaught of Brazilian and American curse words and epithets from Jonesy. The group scattered, and Jonesy checked out of the hospital immediately without going through any hospital administration requirements.

In 1976, sickle-cell disease was the most common genetic disease in North America. The disease is a group of red blood cell disorders that is inherited. Sickle-cell disease occurs frequently in Africans and African-Americans, and is politically associated with races of darker skin color. Latin Americans, Italians, Greeks, Arabs, and peoples from India are also known nationalities in which heredity can cause the disease to appear.

The word of the sickle-cell condition of the Stones' child spread like wildfire in the Air Force base community. The gossip mongers could not keep their mouths shut due to the fact that two ostensible Caucasians like Jonesy and Sam had a child with sickle-cell disease.

The officers' wives generally shunned Jonesy, along with people Sam had considered friends. Sam tried to consol her, but she barely spoke to him. She silently turned away from Sam's approaches, and she even refused to sleep in the same room with him. Sam could not kiss or touch her. Both received stares and were whispered about at the Base Exchange and at the Officers' Clubs.

Sam spoke to his commanding officer about the situation, and he suggested that Sam should not make a federal case out of it. The officer did agree to speak to the hospital commander, and suggested that Sam and Jonesy seek family counseling. The commander said that the gossip and rumor mill was like a "big tub of manure," the more you stirred it, the more it stank and got on you and everyone nearby. He advised that time and distance from the matter would make things better. Unfortunately, with Jonesy there was no time.

The condescension and discrimination she experienced in the first three weeks after her son's death broke her and the relationship with Sam. It seemed that just the sight of Sam was a painful reminder of a part of her life that she had to forget or go completely insane.

From the death of baby James until she filed for divorce and took a one-way flight back to Brazil, she maybe spoke 50 words to Sam.

Her last words to him were, "I'm gone. Tell all the American Air Force assholes around here that they can kiss my Brazilian *banjo*."

Chapter 17

Birmingham, Alabama
U.S. Attorney's Office
Friday, June 6, 2003
10:00 a.m.

As Sam stood outside the U.S. Attorney's main conference room waiting for the Criminal Division meeting to start, he reflected over his Alabama legal career. He wondered where he was bound.

After his stint in the USAF, Sam had returned to Alabama, and got a job in Birmingham with a big insurance defense firm where disenchantment set in rapidly. The firm required all lawyers to bill at least 2200 hours per year or there would be little chance of a Christmas bonus. The unwritten rule at the firm was bill 2400 hours per year or you should look for other employment.

The work was boring and repetitive. The senior partners got rich, and those like Sam down the food chain got the scraps, while being in the middle of a billing system that was morally and ethically unsound in his view.

Sam knew that with an 8 hour a day, normal forty hour work week, Monday through Friday, which is the usual 8 to 5 job in most of America, one works about 2080 hours, if there is no vacation. Most lawyers have to spend more than one hour in order to honestly bill one hour of time. Billing huge numbers of hours becomes a rotten rat race in which the rats tend to catch you after a while.

When Sam found out that the senior partners borrowed at the end of the year against the firm's account receivables in order to pay bonuses, he decided that hard work and eventual senior partnership were not in the cards for him, so he looked to deal himself out of the game.

Through a friend, Sam got an opportunity to apply for a criminal position with the local Jefferson County district attorney's office. In less than a year Sam had tried two high profile murder cases and gotten convictions in both. Sam found out quickly that it's really true what they say: as a prosecutor you get an enormous rush from wielding the hammer of justice. It's a legal high and it is addictive. After two years, Sam was offered a job as an Assistant U.S. Attorney in the Northern District of Alabama. He jumped at the chance, and began walking the path of a career federal prosecutor.

Sam was from what he sometimes called the "Hanging Judge Parker school of criminal deterrence." In the late 1800's, the Oklahoma Territory was the most lawless place in the United States. To better establish law and order, a federal judge named Parker was sent to Ft. Smith, Arkansas to try and rule over the federal territory.

The first thing that the judge did was to build a gallows that would accommodate several people at one time. He began sentencing a lot of criminals to hang for their crimes. Judge Parker is even reputed to have hung a man for stealing a pocket watch. After some years, law and order was more or less established. He became famously known as the "Hanging Judge."

A reporter from back East supposedly was doing an interview once and asked Judge Parker if he thought that the severity of the punishments he handed down brought law and order to the territory. Judge Parker replied that it was not the severity of the punishments that brought law and order; it was the certainty of the punishments.

In Sam's mind, this principle applied to all criminal cases in society, whether one was applying state law, federal law, or even international law.

Sam also believed in what his local favorite senior federal judge, Judge John H. Hilton, who had been put on the bench in the early 1970's, had to say about being a judge: "The first duty of a judge is to judge." Litigants come to court with issues that need to be resolved promptly, right or wrong. Delays in decision making hurt public confidence in the justice system as much as anything one could name.

Every prosecutor, and every serious trial lawyer for that matter, has a particular way of approaching juries and trying cases, and Sam had his. Lots of lawyers claimed to be great trial attorneys, but as his Uncle John would say, "Everybody holding a pole ain't fishin'." Solid and consistent performances in the courtroom required methodology and a little insight into human communications in Sam's view of things.

First, he believed that you always had to have a clear theme or theory of the case you were trying. If the case was about the theft of government property, theft was the theme. Thus, voir dire questions, opening statement, direct and cross examination of witnesses, jury charges, and closing argument were planned with this theme as the touchstone. If a question, argument, or piece of evidence, no matter how juicy, did not support the case's theme, then Sam would not use it.

Second, he believed that juries and judges did not care to hear the long versions of anything. Radio, T.V., and the Internet had changed everyone's attention spans. The old days of giving arguments that lasted for days were gone. Studies had shown that most people remember the first thing said to them and the last thing said. The stuff in the middle goes mushy in their memories. This is the theory of primacy and recency.

In practice it means that for voir dire, opening statement, direct and cross examination, presentation of evidence, and closing argument, you try to take your best point consistent with your theme, and you make it first in each presentation. You then take your second best point and put it last. It allows one to start on a high note and end on a high note. Sam believed that this approach also made you fully analyze your case and the evidence.

Third, Sam believed that at every turn, one should use charts, models, graphs, photos, and other real or demonstrative evidence. Jurors take in the majority of decision making information by sight and senses and not from the spoken words of the lawyers or witnesses.

Unfortunately, most attorneys are information control addicts who want to present each piece of evidence in a highly controlled format, usually in a boring manner. Lawyers want to present things in bland neat little lines and checked boxes like someone's Internal Revenue 1040 income tax return, while the average juror wants to see the USA Today newspaper with color photos and catchy headlines.

Sam also tried to keep any charts or exhibits simple; "like a telegram to a moron" in the words of Uncle John.

Cases that Sam had handled using these three techniques were generally successful. He still thought that he had used these with some impact on the jury in the Troy Pickering RICO case, but Judge Crowell had taken the jury out of the picture with his Rule 29 judgment of acquittal ruling.

Sam was still chapped and stunned. Karen Kemper and her colleagues at the FBI had marshaled good and admissible evidence of Pickering's fraud, greed, and corruption. The case was sure to be a topic of discussion at the Criminal Division meeting.

Sam sat at the foot of the long conference table. Linda, as the U.S. Attorney, would be sitting at the opposite end. He wanted to be as far away as possible because she could be nasty and most unpleasant when the mood struck her.

When all 32 of the Criminal Division attorneys were seated, the First Assistant, Bill Hughes came in and sat in the chair at the right corner nearest to where Linda would sit. She rushed in a minute later, said the meeting was called to order, sat down, and turned to the First Assistant on her right.

She smiled and stared directly at Bill never turning to Sam and said in an icy tone, "Lawyer Stone, your performance in the Pickering trial was an embarrassment to this office."

Linda continued to smile and look directly at Bill, who was clearly uncomfortable and about to jump out of his chair.

Never looking at Sam, and still with her eyes on Bill, she continued her negative comments. "Your incompetence as a criminal trial attorney is the only excuse I can think of for this disaster. The press is having a field day, and Pickering is threatening civil suits. I have never seen such a public relations disaster for this office."

This was a real show. Sam was being chewed out by a boss who was almost grinning at the First Assistant while never looking in Sam's direction. Everyone else in the room was riveted. Sam thought to himself that if Uncle John had been present he would have described the Assistant U.S. Attorneys in the room as being so tense and so quiet at Linda's first remarks that all you could hear were their assholes slamming shut.

Sam guessed that Linda saw her permanent appointment as U.S. Attorney sliding down the drain and decided to take out her frustrations on him. Sam did not want to add to the show, so he kept quiet. You should never miss a chance to keep your mouth shut in a meeting of this sort. Maybe she was baiting him into some kind of insubordination with plenty of witnesses so she could fire Sam. She was that cunning and capable.

Linda, still smiling at poor Bill and never looking at Sam, said acidly, "You will cease any further efforts in the Pickering criminal matter, including the investigation of his cronies. The FBI has been so notified. I will assign another attorney today to replace you in that regard. You will brief the First Assistant on any pending criminal matters, which he will also reassign."

She paused for effect and continued, still gazing straight at Bill, "You are to be sent to the Civil Division, where your first assignment will be to represent FBI agent Karen Kemper, who has been charged in a criminal complaint with a Class A misdemeanor in the Circuit Court of Winston County for obstructing a sheriff's official criminal investigation. She also is facing a tort suit for assault in the Winston County Circuit Court along with a section 1983 civil rights suit for pushing and threatening the sheriff up there. Johnny Brown faxed over a copies of the charges and the civil complaint 45 minutes ago. Please leave this meeting now, and contact Jane Skipper, the Civil Chief. She will be supervising your new duties."

Holy smoke. Sam realized suddenly that he was being forced into areas of the law that he knew little about. Linda was setting a devious trap for his ruin. A screw-up in representing an agent of the FBI would be grounds for doing anything she wanted to do with Sam's legal career with complete cover for her.

Sam got up and left the room. As he closed the door, Sam looked back and saw poor Bill still under the stare, and now menacing grin, of the U.S. Attorney. Sam felt sorry for him.

Chapter 18

Huntsville, Alabama
Old Duck Hunter's Club
Friday, June 6, 2003
10:00 a.m.

Two men met in an old concrete block hunting club near the Tennessee River. They were at a make shift bar at one end. The place reeked of cigar smoke and cooking grease which was in and on the walls. The smell of alcohol came from the large garbage bins of beer cans and whiskey bottles that had not been emptied in several months. The only decoration in the entire place, was a faded red, white, and blue hand painted banner on the wall behind the bar the said, "Fuck Communism."

"I want a million dollars for the night spot near Redstone Arsenal," said Jeff Duval. "One half million in cash, and my corporation holds the mortgage for one half. The mortgage will be the only paperwork between us. You'll pay 25 per cent of the gross profits to me in cash on a monthly basis. With the Army and NASA personnel, high class government contractors, the rich college kids, and wealth of the redneck land owners, the traffic in drugs, booze, girls, gambling and the rest, should be able to generate over one point five million a year."

"What happens if I can't make the monthly payment?"

"You get to find out whether there is life after death. I personally don't think there is any mystery. I subscribe to the dead dog theory. When you die, you're just like a dead dog along the highway, and that's all there is. You'll find a way to make the payments or you'll be like that same dog on that same earth-bound highway."

They heard a vehicle pull up outside. In a moment through the door came Troy Pickering.

Duval turned to his new night spot partner and said, "You better go. I got other business to attend to."

The man left, and Duval asked Pickering, "What in the hell are you doing here? You know we don't like to meet in front of others. That's one of the rules that have kept us in business all these years."

"Yeah, and the other rule has been that killing is done by the person who needs it done, and no one else. Our plans to scare and distract that female FBI agent and that god- damned federal prosecutor have not worked as well as you planned. It took the Judge to come through in the pinch. My life's been wrecked by the feds for a year now, and I want to cash in and get out."

Duval looked at Pickering and said, "Slow down. You're going to panic and blow our whole set-up. I say that the plan has worked. We paid folks to see that certain teenagers introduced agent Kemper's two kids to drugs, and I know that prosecutor Stone has his hands full on the home front. I went over to Winston County to make sure the daughter was dumped properly, and I had a copperhead delivered to Stone's apartment. The plan has been to keep both of them off base, and it has been working."

Pickering asked, "But what are we going to do now? The feds will still be looking at me, or maybe the state will take up where the feds left off."

"Don't worry. The feds won't turn over your prosecution to the state because we can control those politics. The feds can't try you again because it would be double jeopardy. So we just sit tight and keep a close watch on Stone and the agent. I've heard through the political grapevine that Stone is no longer a criminal prosecutor. It pays to purchase plenty of that 'old Alabama know-who' with political contributions. It's all paying off."

"What do you mean?" asked Pickering.

Duval replied, "Stone is being blamed for the loss of your case. I'm also getting some Washington friends, along with some of the local media types, to pressure the U.S. Attorney's Office about any future investigations. As for the FBI agent, she is about to retire, and I have a plan to keep her more than distracted while she finishes out her career."

"How so?" asked Pickering.

"I got the Winston County district attorney to prosecute agent Kemper for obstructing the investigation of her own daughter's drugged road trip. After all it was never in interstate commerce, so the feds had no official business in the matter. I also hired Johnny "Robert E. Lee" Brown to represent my cousin the sheriff in a civil suit against Kemper for assault. She pushed him aside while leaving that abandoned gas station with her kid. She should be out of action and under our close observation for some time to come."

Pickering said, "Look, what am I going to do in the meantime? Most of my cash has dried up, and I agreed to pay my ringed-tailed whiz-bang lawyer in the criminal case on a contingency fee basis. He's looking to me for $750,000 plus expenses. Any legitimate business income is doubtful because everyone to watching what I do. I've also got some bank loans coming due and some other debts."

"I didn't think you could get a lawyer to take a contingency fee in a criminal case because it's illegal. How did you swing that deal?"

"The greed of some lawyers knows no bounds, and I found one. Not as good as our original attorney from years ago, but good enough to take on my case with a promise not to be paid unless he got me off."

Duval scratched his head and said, "Well, you could always screw the lawyer and the bankers by declaring bankruptcy."

"I've thought of that," replied Pickering. "But, I'd have to file schedules and declarations under penalties of perjury, and it would be easy for the ever watchful feds to nail me on something. I've learned that you always have to keep skunks and federal agents at distance."

Duval went out to his Corvette and retrieved a briefcase from the trunk and came back inside.

He held out the briefcase for Pickering and said, "Yeah, I guess you're right. By the way, next year will be 35 years that we have all been in business. Just hold out until then, and we'll all take a little trip overseas and cash out. In the meantime, I'll loan you $100,000 in cash and put it on your tab. Here, take this case. If you need more, just let me know."

Pickering headed out the door saying over his shoulder, "You know, that tattooed banjo on my left knee hurts from time to time. I'm thinking about having it removed like you know who did 10 or so years ago."

"Suit yourself;" said Duval. "I'm keeping mine. By the way I need another cell phone from the company. I lost the other one somehow."

Pickering said, "O.K. I'll take care of it."

Chapter 19

New Orleans, Louisiana
The French Quarter
Curious Cajun Bar
Friday, June 6, 2003
10:00 a.m.

The most expensive real estate in New Orleans is in the French Quarter, and it had been the most expensive for some time. Over the years it had been a great investment for mobsters, criminals, and others who could manage the politics and muscle it took to keep their investments safe.

Unlike the other 49 states, Louisiana had developed laws from the Civil Law traditions of France as opposed to the Common Law traditions of England and the British Empire. It also developed its own brands of criminals and corruption.

Politics were different in Louisiana. Some rural parts were more akin to a banana republic under a Confederate flag. In New Orleans, corruption at every level of government and business from the lowest police trainees or hotdog street vendors to the highest level politicians and business leaders infected political and economic life.

New Orleans was also dangerously violent in places with a serious murder rate.

Law and order was sometimes a scarce commodity.

A young man in jeans and cowboy boots strolled into the dim lit bar in the French Quarter and with an Alabama drawl spoke to the man behind the cash register, "Jeff said to tell you 'blue banjo' and deliver this package."

The Fed Ex envelope had duct tape in a cross design front and back. Crystal meth was inside contained in double zip locked plastic bags. It had been cooked in a trailer park near Guntersville, Alabama, on the Tennessee River. The trailer no longer existed because the cooker carelessly left an acetone can with the lid unsealed. The fumes from the acetone ignited when someone lit a cigar and threw the match into the sink and it missed. The reaction with other materials, including a full portable propane tank, generated a fireball that could be seen for miles up the river.

"Tell Jeff to lay low for a while. The Feds seem interested in this place all of a sudden. They were asking questions about the ownership of this block in the Quarter at some businesses down on Bourbon."

The young man replied, "O.K. I'll tell him. By the way I just did a job back home in Winston County. I am loaded and looking for some action. Got any suggestions? Jeff said you'd know the hot spots around town."

"Go hit Harrah's Casino for a few hours, and come back here. I know some talented young women who would gladly help you pass the rest of the night for a fee. I'll set it all up for you."

"Thanks. I'll be back around midnight."

He never made it. After losing more than he won at Harrah's, he was getting into his Chevy pick-up, when three Spanish speaking teenagers jumped him, cut his throat with linoleum knives, and robbed him of his wallet and remaining cash. They shoved his body into the driver's seat and fled.

There are some honest and upstanding citizens in New Orleans.

When the body of a young man was discovered by a passing retired cop and his wife from Indiana, the police were called.

The retired cop told the young detective to bag the cell phone that was on the floorboard of the pick-up. The young detective asked why, and the retired cop told him that they should be able to trace the movements of the phone for the past few days for any periods of time that the cell phone was turned on. It might help with the investigation.

Since there was no billfold or identification evidence on or around the body, and since a quick check of the license plate showed that the vehicle had been stolen in Decatur, Alabama, the young detective made a request to the cell phone carrier for assistance.

Within a week, the ownership of the phone was traced to a company in Alabama, whose general manager was named Troy Pickering. Luckily, the cell phone had been on for the past two days, and geographical movements by locations within one square block of accuracy were determined. The cell phone had been switched on at 12:14 p.m. noon two days ago just outside Addison, Alabama, along Highway 278, in Winston County.

The information was passed along to the sheriff of Winston County and to the FBI because of the interstate connection. The sheriff was of little help, but the FBI seemed interested and promised to get back to the detective. The FBI asked that the phone records be faxed as soon as possible. They also asked that any fingerprints on the phone be lifted and preserved.

Within two weeks, latent index and ring finger prints identified a twenty-seven year old high school drop out and petty criminal from Cullman, Alabama named James Stokes. He was missing from his trailer, and a positive I.D. was confirmed by an uncle from morgue photos and a long scar on the left shoulder.

A clear latent thumb print was from a different person. In the opinion of the FBI it belonged to an ex-U.S. Army type named Jefferson Duval.

All of this information was forwarded to the U.S. Attorney in Birmingham.

Chapter 20

Birmingham, Alabama
U.S. Attorney's Office
Friday, June 6, 2003
10:15 a.m.

Most lawyers and businessmen from foreign countries look upon the civil trial system in the United States with fear and loathing. Someone can file a lawsuit against a defendant in tort or contract, conduct discovery of internal business records, and force witnesses and corporate executives to give testimony under oath about the details of the dispute. This is all done usually under the auspices of a local court system, which is subject to political vagaries. For this reason, foreign businesses have traditionally signed arbitration agreements to avoid local courts.

The theory of how civil trials work in the United States generally came out of the adoption of the Federal Rules of Civil Procedure in 1938, and subsequent amendments. Later, most states in the United States adopted similar rules of civil procedure. Facts are to be "discovered" by the parties on their own without the intervention of the court prior to trial. The court always stands ready to decide any legal issues. The scope of discovery is broader that the rules for admissibility of evidence, and privileges, including attorney-client, are construed narrowly in order to provide the maximum disclosure of information.

In federal district courts, which are the basic federal trial courts in the United States, local rules supplement the Federal Rules of Civil Procedure. In addition, most federal district judges have their own policies and practices. This means that a lawyer in federal district court must know the Federal Rules of Civil Procedure, the local rules of the particular district, and the individual judge's policies and procedures.

It is against this backdrop that the United States, like other litigants, must conduct its civil cases. The range and types of civil cases involving the federal government is enormous. Each civil Assistant U.S. Attorney (AUSA) must constantly keep up with the courts, the various agencies and federal employee clients, along with some very specialized claims, procedures, and defenses due to federal causes of action and defenses related to sovereign immunity. Generally speaking, unless Congress has passed a specific statute authorizing suit against the United States, then no lawsuits are allowed.

Sam pondered many of these issues and wondered how long it would take him to get up to practice speed as he entered the Civil Division offices and went into his new supervisor's office.

Jane Skipper, the Chief of the Civil Division, said, "Sam, welcome to Civil. Please have a seat. I understand that you will be representing FBI agent Karen Kemper in a civil case and in a criminal case. Do you have any idea of what's going to be involved?"

"I haven't handled a civil case since the early 1980's when I was doing insurance defense work for a big firm here in Birmingham, so I'm a bit rusty on practice and procedure. I don't know the substantive areas very well either. Other than those concerns, I'm ready to start if you are."

She gave him a sympathetic look and said, "I understand. I've asked two of our most experienced civil AUSAs, Joan Benefield and Jerry Klein, to give you a crash course on procedures and on representing federal employees who have been sued.

Sam said, "Thanks. I really appreciate that."

Jane continued. "I also called the 'NAC' in Columbia, South Carolina, and it just so happens that they have an open slot for an AUSA in their Civil Trial Advocacy course starting Monday. You will get a week of civil exercises that are taped and critiqued. Then, in the second week, you will have to try a mock civil case before one of the federal judges that they bring in from around the country."

The U.S. Department of Justice's Office of Legal Education had established its major training facility on the campus of the University of South Carolina in 1998. It was called the "NAC", which stands for the National Advocacy Center. In 2003, it had been renamed for Senator Fritz Hollins who was instrumental in bringing this federal facility to South Carolina. Political pork has many cuts but the same smell, as Sam's Uncle John would say. The new official name was the Hollins National Advocacy Center, or as some less than respectful AUSAs now called it, the "HAC."

It was a state of the art training center dedicated to the training of federal, state, and local prosecutors and litigators in advocacy skills and management of legal operations. It cost $26 million and had 10 training courtrooms, lecture halls, conference rooms, a dining hall, and guest rooms. More than 14,000 persons were trained there annually. The Center also had a separate building housing its own T.V. station for training and conference broadcasts.

Since the 1980's, all incoming AUSAs, criminal and civil, had to go through a basic trial training course, no matter the level of prior trial experience. Sam had completed the Criminal Trial Advocacy course when he first joined the U.S. Attorney's Office as a criminal prosecutor. Generally, if an AUSA switched from criminal to civil, one was expected to take the Civil Trial Advocacy course. The reverse was true for those civil AUSAs joining the criminal division.

In the days before the NAC was built in South Carolina, all of the basic course training for AUSAs was done at the Main Justice building in downtown Washington, DC. At first, many wanted to see the courses return to DC, but the political forces had kept most of the Department training at the NAC. With the terrorist attacks of 9/11, most of the permanent NAC employees were glad to be out of DC and in South Carolina.

The facilities and courses were first rate. All of the trial practice courtrooms were wired for the latest in technology, and the best experts and lecturers were recruited or hired to teach the courses. The Criminal and Civil Trial Advocacy courses had no equal, even in the private sector.

Sam said, "Thanks. I need all of the help and training I can get in a hurry. Shouldn't I meet with Karen Kemper immediately?"

"FBI agent Kemper has made an official request that she be represented by the U.S. Department of Justice, and her supervisor has certified that she at all times was acting within the scope of her employment. The higher ups at DOJ in Washington, DC have given preliminary oral permission for our office to represent her, which should be confirmed later in writing by them. Before you meet with agent Kemper, I want you to learn a little about our representation functions."

"I see," said Sam.

"I took the liberty of calling her and telling agent Kemper that her request had been approved and that you would be representing her. I also told her that you needed some fast training, and that you would contact her in two weeks or thereabouts. She was taking leave to look after her daughter. I also cautioned her not to speak to anyone about the incident without contacting you or me first. She said she understood."

Jane picked up her phone and over the intercom function asked AUSAs Benefield and Klein to join them. They came in, and after brief hellos, Jane turned to Jerry and asked that he outline some of the issues facing Sam in the state criminal case against FBI agent Kemper.

Jerry said, "First of all, you need to remove the state court criminal case from the Circuit Court of Winston County to the U.S. District Court for the Northern District of Alabama."

Sam said, "Wait a minute. I thought I would have to defend the agent in state court."

Jerry replied, "You can if you and your client want to, but I would not advise it. Do you want some state criminal court system ruling on your federal immunity defenses? I think not. The Civil War established federal supremacy, and you don't want the let the state officials think that they can alter the conduct of federal functions by using and abusing federal employees with state criminal prosecutions."

"Can the state or county prosecutors block the removal to federal court?" Sam asked.

"Not really," he said. "But let me give you some background and also detail the exact procedure. I think that you will then see the tricks and traps."

Sam said, "O.K. Let 'er rip."

Jerry began, "A little history may be helpful. There has always been tension between the state and federal governments over power and jurisdiction. The first federal officer removal statute had to be passed by Congress in 1815 as a part of the customs laws. The War of 1812 was very unpopular in the New England States. To prevent lawsuits and prosecutions in state courts against federal customs officials trying to enforce the embargo on trade with England, Congress passed a special law. It allowed any such state court matters involving federal officials acting under the color of the customs statute to be removed from the hostile state court system to federal court. The statute expired at the end of the war."

Sam interrupted. "How do you know all of this?"

Jerry said, "I looked it up. Several cases track the history well."

Jerry cleared his throat and continued. "In 1833, South Carolina threatened nullification, and in response

Congress passed the 'Force Bill' which provided for the removals of lawsuits and prosecutions involving activities under federal customs laws. As you might expect, new removal statutes were also enacted by Congress during the Civil War in the 1860's. These later became codified and applied in the main to state court suits and prosecutions arising out of revenue law enforcement by federal officials."

Jerry looked around to see if he had lost anyone, and kept going. "In 1948, Congress extended the statutes to cover all federal officers acting 'under color of' office or 'on account of' any authority under any act of Congress. This means that any civil action or criminal prosecution commenced in a state court against a federal officer or agency can be removed to federal court for appropriate disposition by federal authorities."

"Does this mean that by removing a case from state to federal court, the case gets automatically dismissed?" Sam asked.

"No it doesn't," replied Jerry. "That takes an assertion of the federal immunity defense.

"How does that work?" asked Sam.

Jerry replied, "A little history may again help to explain. The most famous case about this issue occurred in Tennessee in the late 1870's, and the case made it to the U.S. Supreme Court in 1880. A federal revenue collector, or 'revenuer', named Davis was seizing an illegal whiskey still when he was shot at by a number of armed men. He returned fire and killed one of his assailants. The grand jury for Circuit Court of Grundy County, Tennessee, returned a murder indictment, and the state prosecutor indicted Davis accordingly."

"You mean that even a state murder case can get removed?" asked Sam.

"You bet," Jerry replied. "The constitutionality of the federal removal authority was challenged in the case, and the court said, 'A more important question can hardly be imagined.' The court let the removal stand."

Sam asked, "Are there any exceptions?"

Jerry replied, "Later, in 1989, the U.S. Supreme Court made it clear in some California criminal prosecutions of U.S. Postal workers for traffic violations that occurred while driving mail trucks that any such removals must be predicated upon a federal defense. The postal workers had failed to raise a colorable claim of official immunity or other federal defense and therefore, the removals to federal court were held to be improper."

"That makes sense," commented Jane.

Jerry continued. "Even if a removal is proper, the federal district court has to decide on motion, or at an evidentiary hearing, whether the evidence supports the federal immunity defense. If you have time, have a look at the decision of the U.S. Court of Appeals for the Ninth Circuit arising out of criminal charges against a special agent of the FBI who fired on the Weaver family during the federal raid on Ruby Ridge, in Idaho. It explores the outer bounds of the Supremacy Clause's federal immunity for the killing of Mrs. Weaver. The appeals court held that material facts were in dispute that had to be resolved by the district court as to whether the federal agent acted in a reasonable manner."

"This is tricky business then," Sam said.

"It can be," said Jerry. "One has to pay close attention to the federal immunity defense and to the procedure."

"How so?" Sam inquired.

Jerry cleared his throat again. "First, you have to put together a petition or notice of removal to be filed in the U.S. District Court. It must recite where the charges are pending, the name of the agent, that the agent was acting under color of office at the time, and that the agent intends to rely on the Supremacy Clause's federal immunity defense. You should attach as exhibits a copy of the state court indictment, a copy of the agent's request for legal representation by the U.S. Department of Justice, and the federal agency's managerial concurrence stating that the agent was acting within the scope of the agent's official duties at all relevant times."

"Do I need to have a hearing in state court about all this?" Sam asked.

"No," said Jerry. "You simply file a notice of the filing of the federal removal with the clerk of the state court from which the removal is made. It's a short form and you attach to it a conformed or stamped copy of the petition or notice that you have filed in federal court."

"Does this automatically stop all state court action?"

"No, it does not, replied Jerry. "The federal judge to which the case is assigned is required to examine the petition or notice of removal and decide whether or not the removal should be summarily dismissed and remanded to state court."

"Does that ever happen?" asked Sam.

"If all of the proper elements are set out in the removal papers, this should not happen. If it does, you can try to mandamus the judge in the U.S. Court of Appeals for the Eleventh Circuit. That would be rare. Assuming there is no immediate remand to state court, the federal judge must set an evidentiary hearing to 'make such disposition of the prosecution as justice shall require', according to the federal statute."

Sam asked, "What does that mean?"

"In practice, we usually file a motion to dismiss, with affidavits and a brief, on the issue of Supremacy Clause federal immunity. We usually try to have the entire case dismissed at this hearing. The procedure calls for the federal judge to have the hearing and determine if the agent's acts were conducted under the color of office. If it is so determined, the federal court issues an order to the state court and to the state court judge to suspend all proceedings. If you can do it, you try to have the federal court rule at the same hearing that the federal immunity defense is sound and that the Supremacy Clause requires that the prosecution's case be dismissed."

"Sounds like some serious work is ahead of me," Sam said.

Jerry commented, "Yeah. The worst case scenario is that the federal judge denies your motion to dismiss, and you have to defend the agent against the state's prosecutors on the merits before a jury in federal court. But, that does beat trying to defend a federal agent in state court."

"I see your point," Sam said. "Have you got a go-by pleading? I think we need to file something as soon as practicable. I would appreciate it if you would review my pleadings prior to any filings by me."

"Be glad to," Jerry said. "First though, let's you, me, Joan and Jane catch some lunch out at Nicki's West. After that, Joan can guide you through the basics of a civil removal."

Sam readily agreed. Nicki's West was the most popular lunchtime restaurant in Birmingham among lawyers, judges, agents, and just about every other person he could think of. It was located near the farmer's market, and the vegetables and main dishes were cooked fresh each day. For a "meat and three" meal it could not be beaten.

At lunch, they encountered Judge Crowell and his entourage of law clerks and office staff. Sam's group kept a distance and made sure they were seated out of earshot.

Joan commented. "I hope we don't draw Judge Crowell. He seems to have a thing about our office these days."

Given the recent Rule 29 experience, Sam tended to agree.

Chapter 21

Birmingham, Alabama
U.S. Attorney's Office
Friday, June 6, 2003
1:00 p.m.

After lunch, they returned to the office and Jane Skipper turned to Joan and said, "O.K. Tell us about the civil case issues as you see them in the civil assault action filed against agent Kemper by Johnny Brown in Winston County Circuit Court."

Joan began, "First, a little legal background and history is in order. This U.S. Attorney's Office has had an interesting role to play in the development of the law concerning private civil suits against federal employees acting in the scope of the federal employment."

Jane interrupted. "Sam, we've had some important cases go to the Supreme Court of the United States that arose in the Northern District of Alabama on these issues."

Sam nodded an understanding.

Joan continued. "Generally, federal agents or employees have been sued in state court for state common law torts or in state or federal court for what we call 'constitutional violations.' We need to consider both, because agent Kemper is being sued under both theories according to the civil complaint filed by attorney Brown on behalf of the sheriff of Winston County."

Sam interrupted, "Is the removal procedure the same for criminal and civil cases?"

"Similar, but not the same," Joan replied. "In a civil case, we file a notice of removal in federal court with a notice of filing in the state court. The case is legally removed at this point. The state court has no authority to proceed from the time the notice is filed. There is no review by the federal district court for possible summary remand, and there is no evidentiary hearing that is automatically scheduled for examination of the question of whether the agent or employee was acting under color of office at the time of the events alleged in the civil complaint."

Sam asked, "Is remand possible at all after removal to federal court?"

"The opposition can file a motion to remand, but those are rarely granted if the notice of removal papers and supporting documents are in order. But we're getting ahead of ourselves here. Let's talk about state common law tort suits first."

Sam said, "O.K. Shoot."

Joan went on. "From 1959 to 1988, federal employees sued in state court for common law torts could get their cases removed to federal court and dismissed on an absolute official immunity basis so long as their conduct was in the outer perimeter of the scopes and lines of their duties at the times of the alleged state common law torts."

"What changed?" asked Sam.

"In the mid-1980's, a man named Erwin was seriously exposed to toxic soda ash while working as a civilian warehouseman at the Anniston Army Depot in Anniston, Alabama, which of course is within the jurisdiction and responsibility of this U.S. Attorney's Office. Erwin sued his federal supervisors, one of which was named Westfall, in state court for negligently exposing him to the soda ash."

Sam asked, "What did the office do?"

"This office removed the case to federal court and got the case dismissed by way of a motion for summary judgment on the traditional absolute federal immunity grounds. The case was appealed, and it wound up in the U.S. Supreme Court. In a unanimous decision in 1988, the court held that in order for an absolute immunity defense to prevail, federal employees must not only show that they were acting within the scope of their employment, but also that their conduct was discretionary in nature. The discretionary aspect was a new and serious wrinkle added by the court."

"What happened?" asked Sam.

"The case shook the foundations of the U.S. Department of Justice because it meant that suits against federal employees would henceforth become fact intensive with little chance of dismissal by way of summary judgment. This is because Rule 56 of the Federal Rules of Civil Procedure requires that there be no genuine issues of material fact in dispute before a summary judgment can be lawfully granted. DOJ would not have enough attorneys to handle the floodgates that had just been opened, and there was widespread panic in the Civil Divisions across the country until a legislative fix was obtained from Congress."

Sam reflected, "Seems that I've heard of the fast passage of the new law. Wasn't it even called the 'Westfall Act'?"

Joan said, "That right. It was rushed though Congress in 1988. It was officially called the 'Federal Employees Liability Reform and Tort Compensation Act'. The trial lawyers and plaintiff's bars across the country never got much of a chance to use the Westfall case. Congress legislatively overruled Westfall to delete the discretionary act requirement that had been judicially imposed by the U.S. Supreme Court."

"So how does it operate?" Sam asked.

"An employee gets sued, asks for our representation, and has his or her supervisor certify that the employee was acting within the scope of the employee's duties. Then the Attorney General's designee, the local U.S. Attorney, certifies the scope in writing, and we remove the case from state court if necessary and file a motion to substitute the United States of America as the defendant in place of the federal employee. The case then must proceed, if at all, under the Federal Tort Claims Act, in federal court. The important part is that the federal employee is cut loose and the United States as a sovereign becomes the defendant."

"Does this mean that the common law assault case against agent Kemper will get dropped because of the substitution of the United States in her place and stead?" asked Sam.

Joan looked around at the others and said, "Probably." The others nodded.

Sam suspiciously asked, "So are there any problems that I can expect?"

"Yes, there are two," said Joan. "There is a special procedure for challenging the U.S. Attorney's scope certification in federal court, and there is the issue of the constitutional rights violation claim in the sheriff's civil complaint. I think you can beat any scope challenge and motion by the sheriff to remand to state court. The law requires the challenger to come forward with specific evidence that contradicts the U.S. Attorney's scope certification. I cannot imagine what that would be in agent Kemper's case. The issue of constitutional rights violation is different, and it requires a little more background."

"Is that what's called a *Bivens* claim?" Sam asked.

"That's correct. As you may recall, in 1971, the U.S. Supreme Court held for the first time that the U.S. Constitution allows for an implied private cause of action for damages against an individual federal official. The case was called *Bivens v. Six Unknown Federal Narcotics Agents* and arose from a warrant-less, no-knock narcotics raid on the Bivens home."

"Why wasn't this a claim or suit directly against the United States?" asked Sam.

"There was no specific remedy against the sovereign under the Federal Tort Claims Act enacted by Congress at the time, because all claims for assault, battery, false imprisonment, abuse of process, and the like, were specifically excluded from coverage under the Act. The United States had not waived sovereign immunity to these specific types of claims. The Supreme Court, in *Bivens*, 'implied' a special cause of action from the Constitution against the federal agents personally. The remedy created was similar to the section 1983 remedy Congress had passed that allowed for civil suits against state officials personally for constitutional rights violations."

"I've heard of these suits, but I have never paid close attention to them," said Sam. "Was a legislative fix tried?"

"Yes," replied Joan. "Congress responded in 1974 with amendments to the Federal Tort Claims Act to provide a remedy against the United States for the torts of federal law enforcement officers executing warrants and making arrests, including the allowance of federal tort claims for assault, battery, and false imprisonment. Many thought this would prevent *Bivens* claims against federal employees for the most part."

"Did it work?" asked Sam.

"No. According to the U.S. Supreme Court in a subsequent decision, it held, among other things, that punitive damages against an individual were not displaced by the amendments. Thus, *Bivens* claims survived the amendment arguments."

"So what happens?" asked Sam.

"Plaintiffs are the masters of their claims, and they typically sue the United States under the Federal Tort Claims Act and, in the alternative, in the same lawsuit sue the individual employee with a *Bivens* claim. You should note, however, that if there is a judgment against the United States, any *Bivens* claim arising out of the same facts against the employee is barred by a special federal statute."

Sam's mind was thinking hard at this point, and he asked, "So what would you recommend that I do with the civil suit against agent Kemper?"

Joan looked at her notes and said, "You have 30 days to remove the civil suit to federal district court from the date the agent was served with the complaint. Do so as soon as you can after you get back from your two weeks of civil training at the NAC."

Sam asked, "What do I do after that?"

"Once the case is removed, you file a motion to substitute the United States on the common law assault claim and another motion to extend time in which to answer on behalf of the agent and the United States for 60 days. That's the normal response time for the United States in most civil suits. If there is a motion to remand, fight it and do the same with any scope of employment challenge. On or before the 60 days are up, file a motion to dismiss or in the alternative for summary judgment."

"On what grounds?" Sam inquired.

"On two basic grounds. First, the United States can be sued under the Federal Tort Claims Act only if an administrative claim has been filed after the United States has been substituted. So the ground is a failure to exhaust administrative remedies as to the common law assault claim because no claim will have been filed with the FBI. As to the *Bivens* claim, the primary defense is that of qualified immunity."

"What's that?" asked Sam.

Joan said, "In 1983, the U.S. Supreme Court, decided the *Bush v. Lucas* case, which arose out of an employment situation at NASA in Huntsville, Alabama. The decision clarified that the court would not supplement any regulatory scheme with new nonstatutory damages remedies in *Bivens* situations. The case marked a cutting back on the expansion of *Bivens* remedies. So, just because you have a judicial remedy under the Federal Tort Claims Act, you are not facing a claim that a new or different remedy needs to be implied. Rather, the main issue in the case will be the agent's defense of qualified immunity, which you should raise by motion at the first opportunity. As long as the agent can show that she was acting within the scope of her duties, you should win and have the case dismissed."

"What if the court denies my motion for summary judgment on the *Bivens* claim?"

"Unlike most civil cases in which you would have to wait until after a trial on the merits in order to appeal, a denial of a motion for summary judgment on qualified immunity gives rise to an immediate appeal. In *Bivens* cases, the Supreme Court recognized the need to allow for immediate appeals of denials of these motions that affect federal officials and the performance of their duties."

"What happens if the court decides to sit on the motion and not rule for a while?" asked Sam.

"If that does occur, and if a court sits around does not promptly rule, this can be treated as tantamount to a denial. An appeal can be immediately taken. Most importantly, it is clear from the case law that a plaintiff is not entitled to discovery in most situations where qualified immunity is raised as a defense."

"It looks like I've got my work cut out for me on two major fronts," Sam said.

Everyone nodded.

Turning to Jane, Sam asked, "Why do you think I've been assigned to this matter?"

She cautiously said, "Because you know the agent better than anyone in the office, and the agent asked that you be assigned to help her. You don't realize the dynamics of federal employee representations and how important it is to the function of the federal government, but you will soon. I think you are the right choice. We are here to assist in any way. Call on us. Egos aren't as big in civil as they can be in criminal."

Sam looked at Jane and said, "I guess it's really true what they say about the differences in criminal and civil from an AUSA's standpoint. On the criminal side we are fast riding cowboys because of the quick paced litigation pressures. On the civil side you have slow going cooks due to the simmering pressures that each case brings to bear because of discovery and the different procedural rules."

"Yes," Jane said. "Also, criminal prosecutors get to pick and choose their cases, and we in civil don't usually. Except for some few affirmative matters, on the civil front, you have to defend what comes in the door as litigation against the United States, its agencies, and employees."

Sam said, "I'm getting that figured out pretty quick. Which do you think is the most difficult, civil or criminal?"

Jane thought for a moment and said, "In civil cases the burdens of proof are less because we typically face the preponderance of the evidence test, as opposed to the criminal beyond a reasonable doubt standard. The lesser proof burdens in civil cases apply to all claims or defenses. Civil cases are, therefore, more difficult to manage because the burdens frequently shift from one party to another during the proceedings or at trial."

Sam said, "Look, no federal case, criminal or civil, is easy. As my Uncle John says, if our jobs were easy, the ignorant, trashy folks out there would have them."

Jane laughed and then turned serious. "Always remember the greatest feature of being an AUSA. When the chips are down, and the going gets tough, and the litigation gets heated up, and your opponent is being a jerk, and some unreasonable federal judge is on your ass, and all about you are legal chaos and confusion, simply ask yourself what's in the best interest of your client, the United States of America, and proceed accordingly with a clear path and clean legal conscience."

"Amen," said Sam.

The others nodded in affirmance.

Chapter 22

Birmingham, Alabama
Sam Stone's Pickup Truck
Friday, June 6, 2003
5:20 p.m.

Sam was listening to Flatt & Scruggs on his Ford F-150's single CD player when his cell phone rang.

It was his Uncle John Stone, a retired U.S. Navy man who lived alone in Cedar Bluff, Alabama. He was 86 years old and had been enlisted as a radioman stationed on an old WWI destroyer somewhere near Surabaya, Indonesia when the Japanese bombed Pearl Harbor in December 1941. He survived being sunk by an enemy submarine in the Battle of the Coral Sea, survived another 30 years of active duty until full Navy retirement, and then he had become a deputy sheriff in Cedar Bluff until his wife of 44 years, Miss Julia, died of emphysema some 16 years back.

There was not much in the way of human conduct that Uncle John had not run across, and he always had some insightful, but usually indelicate, or salty, descriptions of life's encounters.

Uncle John made a beeline directly to the issue of Sam's most pressing concern, marriage. "Direct as a martin to the gourd," as he would say.

Uncle John asked, "How's that bossy wife of yours? Have you divorced her yet?"

Uncle John and Linda had never gotten along. Uncle John loved red bone hounds. His prized red bone, Nickajack, had tried to hump Linda on their first visit after they had been married for 6 months. She cursed a blue streak and tried to kick Nickajack. Linda pronounced in Uncle John's presence that she hated all dogs, and that this humping conduct was only one of the reasons why.

Linda later refused to visit Uncle John's house again. Uncle John kept a civil tongue for the most part about Linda during the early part of the marriage. Recently, however, he had confided in Sam that he thought she was too dammed mean spirited for man or beast.

When Sam had told him that he was in the process of divorce, Uncle John said, "To keep in a marriage or get out, you have to look yourself in the mirror each and every morning and ask yourself the key question: is the fucking I'm getting worth the fucking I'm getting?"

Boy howdy, did Sam know the answer to that question. It really was not worth it anymore.

"Look," said Uncle John, "I need some medical help. I've got a couple of widow women from the Cumberland Presbyterian Church chasing after me, and I may want to get caught. I want some of that 'vitamin V', but everyone says I got to have a prescription. Have you tried the stuff and does it work? If you have about 10 extra pills send them my way."

"Whoa, Uncle John, just ask Doc Rivers over in Centre for the Viagra prescription."

"I can't do that. One of the widows is his first cousin, and the other one is the druggist's younger sister. I can't create a scandal around here."

Sam said, "Let me think about it, and I'll get back to you on that score."

Uncle John asked "I guess you are still working on big cases and projects for the federal government?"

Sam admitted that he was, and Uncle John said, "You had better remember that there are at least seven phases to any big government case or project."

Sam knew he had to ask, so he did. "Oh yeah, what are they?"

"First you have enthusiasm, followed by disillusionment, then depression. After those three comes panic, and then it's a search for the guilty. Punishment of the innocent follows with awards for the non-participants being always last."

Sam started laughing. "I think I'm starting to fit into the pattern."

Uncle John asked, "What are you doing Sunday afternoon? Me and the neighbors are planning a cookout and you are invited."

"What are you having?" Sam inquired.

"I've had a craving flung on me for sodomized chicken on the grill and leather britches," replied Uncle John.

"What?" Sam asked.

Uncle John laughed and said, "You take a whole chicken and pop open a can of beer and shove it up its cavity and the can helps to stand the bird up on the grill. The beer boils and steams the bird as it cooks. Tastes great and is less filling than frying. We also drink a beer or two in the process."

"What's the other dish?"

Uncle John said, "Leather britches. It's an old frontier or Indian dish made from dried green beans, preferably white half-runners. I don't care for Kentucky wonders. In the old days people couldn't can things to preserve food, so they took a needle and thread and strung green beans in a dry attic. After they dried you could use them when you wanted by soaking the beans in water for a day. After that you cook them with some pork fat back. They have a very unique taste that me and the neighbors like."

Sam said, "Uncle John, I'd love to come, but I've got a duty assignment in Columbia, South Carolina for two solid weeks. I'll try to come for a visit when I get back."

"Well, come see me soon. I'm getting old you know, and that's not good."

Sam said, "There's got to be some good in getting old isn't there?"

Uncle John answered slowly, "The only good thing about getting really old is that you outlive your enemies. See you soon I hope." He hung up.

Uncle John was making Sam feel guilty for not visiting him and was doing a good job of it. Sam would have to take Uncle John a gift of some kind on his next visit. Last time, Sam took him some pork chops from some pigs that had been fattened on apples. That drew raves from Uncle John. Maybe another pork package would do the trick.

Sam headed on to his apartment. Steven was supposed to meet him for his second session of banjo lessons. Sure enough, when Sam pulled up, Steven was already there with banjo in hand.

Chapter 23

Birmingham, Alabama
Sam Stone's Apartment on Southside
Friday, June 6, 2003
5:30 p.m.

Sam greeted Steven with, "How's your mom and sister?"

He replied, "They've headed to L.A. for a few days of R & R. Mom said to tell you to call if you really needed to talk with her, but otherwise she would see you in about two weeks."

In Alabama, "L.A." did not mean Los Angeles. It meant Lower Alabama, which usually meant the beach at Gulf Shores, otherwise known as the "Redneck Riviera."

They went inside and got right to it. Steven had his banjo properly tuned, and showed Sam what he had learned from before.

Sam said, "The next technique or style of play is what I call the *folk stroke*. We can add another simple chord at the same time. Some call this right hand playing method the basic strum, others call it folk style, and there are probably other names for it. I like it because it is so versatile and allows one to get out a good banjo sound with some melody notes. It's a great back-up sound for most folk songs. Remember, you can't play lead all the time; it's boring for your audience, and it makes fellow musicians mad."

"Where did you get the name for this technique?" Steven asked.

"A bluegrass purist accused me of 'folk stroking' my banjo one time, so I kept the name. He also accused me of 'folking' around, to which I had to plead guilty."

Steven laughed.

Sam continued. "With you left hand, just like in playing the D7th chord, take your index finger and hold down the second string just above the first fret. At the same time take your middle finger and hold down the fourth string at the second fret. Finally, with your ring finger, hold down the first string at the second fret. The third string is open and not fretted. Brush down across the strings and listen to the C chord. On paper, remember, '1' stands for index finger, '2' stands for middle finger, and now '3' stands for ring finger."

Sam wrote:

C Major Chord
(4th string middle finger (2) at 2nd fret;
2nd string index finger (1) at 1st fret;
1st string ring finger (3) at 2nd fret)

5th	4th	3rd	2nd	1st
G	D	G	B	D
	I	I	I	I
	I	I	(1)	I

```
|   |   |   |  1st fret
|   |   |   |
(2)  |   |  (3)
|   |   |   | 2nd fret
|   |   |   |
|   |   |   |
|   |   |   | 3rd fret
|   |   |   |
|   |   |   |
|   |   |   | 4th fret
|   |   |   |
|  |   |   |   |
|  |   |   |   | 5th fret
```

Sam continued the lesson. "Now we need finger picks. They will make the notes brighter as you play. First, we have a plastic thumb pick. I always score the inside flat bottom with a knife two or three times. This keeps the pick from slipping off one's thumb. If the pick is too tight or too loose on the thumb, you hold the curved edge of the pick next to a light bulb for about 30 seconds to heat the plastic and then you can mold the fit to your particular thumb size."

Sam produced a plastic thumb pick from a bag in his banjo case, scored it with his pocket knife, and saw that Steven had a proper fit.

Sam said, "You will also need a metal finger pick for the index finger. Again adjust the fit to your finger this time crimping inward or outward the metal flanges that clamp the pick around your finger. The flat side should face down and the tip should stick out far enough to prevent your fingernail from getting caught in the banjo strings.

Again Sam gave Steven the metal pick and adjusted it on his finger.

Sam continued. "I always carry extra sets of plastic thumb and metal finger picks in my banjo case. They are easy to misplace, or worse, drop and get stepped on."

Sam grabbed his banjo and began a demonstration. "The folk stroke has three parts that make up one beat. First, cup the middle, ring, and small fingers of the right hand and with the fingernails brush down across some or all of the strings.

Sam demonstrated.

"I'll mark this down as '*Brush↓*'," said Sam. "Second, pick down on the fifth sting with the thumb in the plastic pick."

Sam again demonstrated.

"This will be marked '*T*'," Sam continued. "Third, with the hand on the way back up the index finger with the metal pick, picks up on the 1st, 2nd, 3rd or 4th strings."

Sam demonstrated with four strokes, picking each of the four strings in turn.

"These are sometimes called the melody stings, as opposed to the 5th string, which is never fretted, and is simply the drone string. It is your choice as to which of the melody strings that you pick with your index finger on the way back up. This is marked '*I*'."

Sam then demonstrated the complete hand and finger movements again slowly, and he had Steven do the same.

Sam said, "Now repeat the three parts over and over. Do this very slowly at first and then gradually build up speed. One can actually pick out simple melodies with the index finger while keeping a fast paced rhythm going.

This produces 'galloping' rhythms; good back up for folk and other songs. After the playing becomes automatic, it is easy to sing along at the same time while using the folk stroke. That's the biggest reason for its popularity."

Sam showed Steven the technique by playing "Darlin' Corey" slowly at first, and then he played the song at full speed.

Sam instructed, "As an exercise, I recommend that you play the open G chord using the stroke so that each of the four melody strings are picked up on once by the index finger. Now do the same thing with the C chord, and again with the D7th chord."

He showed Steven the exercise and had Steven attempt it.

Steven started to catch on and said, "I like this."

Sam said, "A good song to practice with is 'Boil Them Cabbage Down', but use the open G chord, and the simple chords, C and D7th."

Sam wrote:

G (open-no fingers on any frets)
Brush↓ T I
Brush↓ T I
Brush↓ T I
Brush↓ T I
"Boil them cab-bage"
C (4th string middle finger (2) at 2nd fret;
    2nd string index finger (1) at 1st fret;
     1st string ring finger (3) at 2nd fret)
Brush↓ T I
Brush↓ T I
Brush↓ T I

Brush↓ T I
"Down boys"
G (open-no fingers on any frets)
Brush↓ T I
Brush↓ T I
Brush↓ T I
Brush↓ T I
"Turn them hoe-cakes"
D7th (3rd string index finger (1) at 2nd fret;
            2nd string middle finger (2) at 1st fret)
Brush↓ T I
Brush↓ T I
Brush↓ T I
Brush↓ T I
"Round"
G (open-no fingers on any frets)
Brush↓ T I
Brush↓ T I
Brush↓ T I
Brush↓ T I
"The only song that"
C (4th string middle finger (2) at 2nd fret;
       2nd string index finger (1) at 1st fret;
       1st string ring finger (3) at 2nd fret)
Brush↓ T I
Brush↓ T I
Brush↓ T I
Brush↓ T I
"I can sing is"
G (open-no fingers on any frets)
Brush↓ T I
Brush↓ T I

"Boil them"

D7th   (3rd string index finger (1) at 2nd fret;
                2nd string middle finger (2) at 1st fret)

Brush↓ T I

Brush↓ T I

"Cab-bage"

G (open-no fingers on any frets)

Brush↓ T I

"Down"

When he finished writing, Sam said, "That's it for today. Next time we'll start you on finger picking."

Steven said, "Sounds great. I think I'm beginning to get the hang of things."

Sam then inquired of Steven, "By the way, do you know much about any controversy that Professor Redmond is having with your college's administration?"

Steven thought a moment and asked, "Do you know who Søren Kierkegaard was?"

"I think he was a Danish philosopher in the 1800's, but that's about all," Sam replied.

Steven said, "Professor Redmond has tried to promote Kierkegaard's notion that religion is truly a matter of existential thinking, and many in the college administration see this as some form of heresy. They don't care that Kierkegaard was a staunch Christian; rather his idea of severing faith from reason is beyond their comprehensions because none of them have ever seriously studied philosophy. It's almost like they are afraid of any ideas that might call their fundamentalist Biblical beliefs into question, even if the ideas would help promote more widespread Christian beliefs in the long run."

"Where do you and the other interested students come down on the matter?" I asked.

"It's hard to generalize. Each student has a set of thoughts and beliefs that are unique to each student. Some are agnostics or doubters in God's existence. Some are atheists or non-believers, and some are what Professor Redmond calls Christian atheists, because they go to church and participate in Christian activities, but in their own hearts and minds they do not believe in God. We also have plenty of students who are existentialists of the Jean Paul Sartre sort, who believe God is dead and that there is no rational basis for God's existence. They ascribe to Sartre's ideas that the outlook for man is generally pessimistic. They like to quote from his famous 1943 essay called *Being and Nothingness.*"

Sam thought to himself, this kid has serious scholar potential. He could probably teach me things. Sam asked, "Where are you in all of this?"

"If you mean the controversy between Professor Redmond and the administration, I'm clearly on his side. If you mean the existential debate, I haven't made up my mind. I am drawn to the existentialism of some Americans, like Henry Miller, who seemed to take an optimistic or enthusiastic view of life and existence. But I have also enjoyed studying Kierkegaard's approach."

"I'm sure you'll do well and write famous books some day," said Sam.

Steven gazed out the window and said thoughtfully, "The world's most famous philosopher never wrote anything that we know of. He was the Greek, Socrates. I guess I'm happy if I can continually examine life each day, just as he recommended."

Sam stood and said, "Next time then. I've enjoyed our discussion. How about another quick lesson tomorrow afternoon? I'm going to be gone for two weeks starting Sunday, and we might as well give you plenty to practice."

Steven said, "Great. I'll come over about three or three-thirty."

Folk Stroke

Chapter 24

Birmingham, Alabama
Sam Stone's Apartment on Southside
Saturday, June 7, 2003
3:30 p.m.

Sam adjusted Steven's shoulder strap on his banjo and began. "Somewhat akin to bluegrass is a two finger picking style called *double thumbing*. It requires the plastic thumb pick and the metal finger pick for the index finger like we used in the folk stroke."

Steven asked, "Is this bluegrass?"

Sam replied, "Not exactly, but probably the most famous double thumber was David "Stringbean" Akeman, who was Bill Monroe's first banjo player with the Bluegrass Boys back in the 1940's. He also played clawhhammer style, but more about that later. Burglars broke into his Tennessee cabin and murdered Stringbean and his wife in 1973 because he did not trust banks and he was always rumored to keep large sums of cash on or around him. As my Uncle John would say, 'It doesn't pay to provide easy pickin's."

"Wow. That's awful," said Steven.

"In a strange twist, twenty thousand dollars in rotted cash was found hidden over the fireplace in the 1990's by subsequent cabin dwellers, according to news reports."

Steven commented, "So the burglars bungled. Let's get on with banjoing."

Sam nodded and said, "Right. The double thumbing technique makes the first string into another drone string because it gets played every other note. The thumb alternates between the 5th string and strings 1 through 4."

Sam picked each string to demonstrate.

"There are four parts to double thumbing: first, the thumb (written as "$T\rightarrow$") picks down on the 1st, 2nd, 3rd or 4th strings (it is your choice as to which string); second, the index finger ("$\leftarrow I$") picks up on the 1st string; third, the thumb ("$T\rightarrow$") picks down on the 5th string; and fourth, the index finger ("$\leftarrow I$") picks up on the 1st string. Now repeat this process over and over."

Sam demonstrated.

"Written down, it looks like this."

Sam started drawing:

5th	4th	3rd	2nd	1st
G	**D**	**G**	**B**	**D**
|	|	$T\rightarrow$	|	|
|	|	|	|	$\leftarrow I$
$T\rightarrow$	|	|	|	|
|	|	|	|	$\leftarrow I$
|	|	$T\rightarrow$	|	|
|	|	|	|	$\leftarrow I$

```
T→ |     |     |       |
|    |     |     |     ←I
|    |   T→    |       |
|    |     |     |     ←I
T→ |    |     |       |
|    |     |     |     ←I
|    |   T→    |       |
|    |     |     |     ←I
T→ |    |     |       |
|    |     |     |     ←I
```

Sam continued. "It produces a driving, fast paced picking style. Advanced double thumbing picks out intricate melody lines by alternating the thumb on the 1st, 2nd, 3rd or 4th strings with the index finger, skipping the 5th string, or using the 5th string sparingly."

Sam demonstrated a quick double thumbing run.

Steven asked, "Where did this style of play come from?"

Sam replied, "Probably this and some other finger picking styles of play developed in the 1850's and 1860's and was patterned on then existing guitar finger picking methods. Three finger bluegrass did not arrive until the 1930's."

Sam paused to let all this sink in.

"Again, as an exercise, I think that you should play the open G chord using double thumbing so that each of the 4 melody strings are picked down on once by the thumb."

Sam wrote:

5th	4th	3rd	2nd	1st
G	**D**	**G**	**B**	**D**
|	*T*	|	|	|
|	|	|	|	*I*
T	|	|	|	|
|	|	|	|	*I*
|	|	*T*	|	|
|	|	|	|	*I*
T	|	|	|	|
|	|	|	|	*I*
|	|	|	*T*	|
|	|	|	|	*I*
T	|	|	|	|
|	|	|	|	*I*
|	|	|	|	*T*
|	|	|	|	*I*
T	|	|	|	|
|	|	|	|	*I*

Sam demonstrated. "Now repeat the same thing with the C chord, and then with the D7th chord."

Steven picked up the technique rather well. Sam had to remind him to go slow and pick the notes with an even tempo.

Sam said, "I know you might get sick of the song, but practice double thumbing 'Boil Them Cabbage Down,' using the open G chord, and the simple chords, C and D7th."

Sam continued to write:

G (open-no fingers on any frets)

T ITI T ITI

"Boil them cab-bage"

C (4[th string] middle finger (2) at 2nd fret;

    2[nd string] index finger (1) at 1st fret;

    1[st string] ring finger (3) at 2nd fret)

T ITI T ITI

"Down boys"

G (open-no fingers on any frets)

T ITI T ITI

"Turn them hoe-cakes"

D7th (3[rd string] index finger (1) at 2nd fret;

    2[nd string] middle finger (2) at 1st fret)

T ITI T ITI

"Round"

G (open-no fingers on any frets)

T ITI T ITI

"The only song that"

C (4[th string] middle finger (2) at 2nd fret;

    2[nd string] index finger (1) at 1st fret;

    1[st string] ring finger (3) at 2nd fret)

T ITI T ITI

"I can sing is"

G (open-no fingers on any frets)

T ITI

"Boil them"

D7th (3[rd string] index finger (1) at 2nd fret;

    2[nd string] middle finger (2) at 1st fret)

T ITI

"Cab-bage"

G (open-no fingers on any frets)

T ITI T ITI

"Down"

Sam said, "Let's take a short break and get something to drink. I'm thirsty. How about you?"

"I'll take a Coke or whatever," said Steven.

Sam went into the kitchen and returned with two ice cold, canned Cokes. He handed one to Steven and asked, "Were you in Professor Redmond's class when he brought up the lawsuit that the Southern Poverty Law Center in Montgomery filed against the Chief Justice of the Alabama Supreme Court over the 10 Commandment Monument? You know, 'The Rock'?"

Steven laughed and said, "Oh yeah. That was a great class. The Professor kicked it off by saying how both sides of the litigation had put the 'fun' back in fundamentalism."

"What did he mean by that?" asked Sam.

"Simply that the focus on the 10 Commandments and the issue of the separation of church and state had caused just about everyone to examine these questions seriously for themselves and engage others in philosophical debates. This, in his view, was a healthy exercise in the long run. He gave out copies of the Eleventh Circuit's opinion that went against Judge Moore, and we discussed portions of it."

"Did the class really go for a federal court opinion? They are usually pretty dry and boring."

"Well, the opinion pointed out that there are differences in the King James Christian translation of the 10 Commandments as opposed to the Hebrew one. The best example is that of the traditional Christian, 'Thou shalt not kill'. In Hebrew, it is 'Thou shalt not murder.'"

"That's a big difference," said Sam.

"The class thought so too. Further, according to the King James Version, this prohibition against killing is found in the Sixth Commandment. For the Catholic and Lutherans, it's the Fifth Commandment."

"I never knew that either," said Sam. "What else did you find out about the decision?"

"One student argued that the Southern Poverty Law Center got a bad result because Judge Moore decided to defy the court's order in the name of God. This set a precedent in the minds of some of Moore's followers that the rule of law could be ignored or disrespected in the name of religion. That was not a political concept or idea that the Center would want to encourage."

Sam said, "I'd heard that some folks were saying that they no longer had to pay child support pursuant to court orders because God told them otherwise. What other 'fun' was mentioned?"

"Yeah, we certainly discussed the impact of the events on law and order. As one of the students commented, there is always a species of *Redneckus Americanus Alabamus* lurking around the shallow end of the gene pool in this state trying to beat the law," said Steven.

Sam laughed.

"Did you hear about the ceremonial destruction of the Eleventh Circuit's opinion?" asked Steven.

"No. I don't believe so. What are you talking about?"

"According to the Professor, the Sunday after the decision came down, a fundamentalist pastor of some church up on Sand Mountain held his congregation over after the morning service for a special ceremony. He had already preached his entire sermon on the vile and ungodly nature of the appellate court's opinion. He took his copy of the decision and asked everyone to follow him outside the church into the sunlight. With everyone in a circle around him, the pastor proclaimed, 'Let this opinion be consumed by the flames of Hell, but let it be lit by the fire of Heaven.' Whereupon he whipped out from underneath his coat a large magnifying glass and set the decision on fire. The preacher also threw into the flames a copy of the U.S. Supreme Court's decision on abortion in *Roe v. Wade*, just for good measure. The congregation went wild."

"I guess Professor Redmond was right," said Sam. "The litigants did put the fun back into fundamentalism. Let's get back to the banjo."

They picked up their instruments.

Sam said, "The next lesson involves simple chord progression. I want you to focus on the basic G, E minor, C, and D7th chords. The E minor chord is new. It has that lonesome country sound."

Sam played it. "I'll write it down."

Sam wrote:

E Minor or Em

5th	4th	3rd	2nd	1st
G	**D**	**G**	**B**	**D**

ǀ	ǀ	ǀ	ǀ
ǀ	ǀ	ǀ	ǀ
ǀ___	ǀ___	ǀ___	ǀ 1st fret
ǀ	ǀ	ǀ	ǀ
(2)	ǀ	ǀ	(3)
ǀ___	ǀ___	ǀ___	ǀ 2nd fret
ǀ	ǀ	ǀ	ǀ
ǀ	ǀ	ǀ	ǀ
ǀ___	ǀ___	ǀ___	ǀ 3rd fret

```
  |    |    |    |
  |    |    |    |
  |____|____|____| 4th fret
  |    |    |    |
  |    |    |    |
  |____|____|____| 5th fret
```

Sam had Steven play the chord, and then said, "For a good left hand exercise, I suggest playing 4 beats for each chord in the following progression: G to Em to C to D7th. This sounds like some familiar songs you have heard, and it produces a good exercise for the left hand. Please keep in mind that the right hand will develop quicker than the left hand. After strumming, do the same using the other right hand techniques that you have learned. The good thing about a banjo is that there are four strings to fret with your four available fingers of the left hand. By contrast, the guitar has six strings that you have to fret with four fingers."

Steven said, "I know what you mean. I've tried to play the guitar and have a harder time with the chords."

Sam nodded and instructed, "Give the sequence a try."

Steven went through the chord progression on his banjo and said, "You are right. This sounds like the music to several folk songs that I have heard."

Sam said, "You now have enough chords to start playing lots of songs. When you are able to play at least three or four tunes, start trying to find persons with other instruments to play with you. Your enjoyment will be enhanced, and the beginner's bad habit of stopping each time you make a mistake and starting over will be broken. Also your rhythm and timing will be greatly improved."

"I believe that I'm getting the hang of the basics," said Steven. "Is that all for today?"

"Yeah. Practice the things I've showed you, and I want to see your progress when I get back in town in two weeks," Sam said, as he started putting his banjo back into its hard-shell case.

Steven asked, "Where did you learn the banjo?"

Sam paused and said, "I asked for a banjo for Christmas when I was 16 years old, and I got one. I tinkered with it for six months because I could not find anyone who really knew how to play it that could teach me. I took my banjo to summer camp in Mentone on Lookout Mountain that summer, and a female counselor told me that her uncle was a good banjo picker and that he taught lessons. He lived not far away over in Rising Fawn, Georgia. She called him, and he invited me to come over get some lessons."

"How did you get away from camp?" asked Steven.

"The female counselor and I were close. She was 18 and had an old VW bug. So we simply left camp one evening after supper and drove down the mountain and over to Georgia. Her uncle was a Georgia Fish and Game official, and he had learned to play from a bluegrass and folk artist by the name of Walter Forbes."

Steven asked, "I never heard of him; who was that?"

"Forbes cut some records for RCA in the early 1960's. I've got some of his recordings around here somewhere. I'll let you listen sometime. Anyhow, the uncle gave me four lessons over a 10-day period, and then told me that I was on my own. He said that I obviously was serious about playing and to keep it up. He told me to seek out other pickers when I got back home, and to listen to music and watch others play. He also told me to get copies of Pete and Peggy Seegers' books and to develop my own style and be proud of it."

"Seems like you've told me the same thing from the beginning," said Steven.

"Words of wisdom Steven," Sam replied.

"Any other wise words that you learned?" asked Steven.

"The uncle also made another good point about playing the banjo. You should be honest about your limitations and never suffer from delusions of adequacy."

They both laughed.

Steven asked, "What are your best shots at words of wisdom that you have learned to live by? The Professor always asks the students to continually think about that question."

Sam thought for a moment. He reached into his banjo case and pulled out an old 3 by 5 note card that was well worn. He looked at it briefly and said, "I wrote the following down when I was in my early 20's. I learned some of these things from an old time banjo player I met one time from Alexander City. Others I added or modified. I think about them from time to time."

Sam copied on a separate pieced of paper for Stephen:

Life Propositions:

1. Change is inevitable –learn to enjoy it

2. Face your fears-if nothing else, it adds excitement to your life

3. Exercise as much reason as possible between 1 and 2- it produces the best results and helps out when judging decisions you have made in hindsight

4. Conflict is a part of us and life-manage it any way you can

5. Belief in God can help you through the really bad times

Steven asked, "Have these really worked for you?"

Sam replied, "Well, I'm not speaking from the burning bush. These are just some thoughts about personal survival. I should add that playing the banjo is also a help in times of stress."

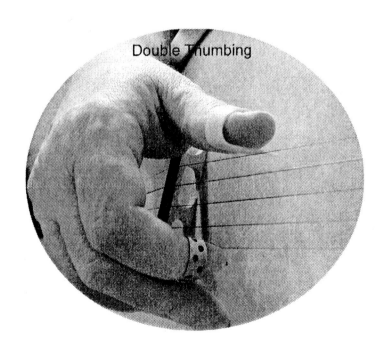

Chapter 25

Columbia, South Carolina
National Advocacy Center
University of South Carolina Campus
Sunday, June 8, 2003
6:30 p.m.

The Civil Chief, Jane Skipper, had called the Director of the Constitutional Torts section of the U.S. Department of Justice and arranged for Sam to meet with an expert on representing federal employees in situations like that of Karen Kemper. The expert had flown down from Washington to Columbia, South Carolina to teach at the Civil Trial Advocacy Course and to coach Sam specially. Their first meeting was to take place at the National Advocacy Center on the University of South Carolina campus in downtown Columbia, South Carolina.

Sam walked into the bar and lounge on the third floor and spotted a group of about 12 Assistant U.S. Attorneys drinking and joking around out on the porch overlooking the rear grounds of the facility.

Sam went up to the group and said, "Hi. My name is Sam Stone and I'm looking for Jason Sherrod from 'contorts' at Main Justice."

"I'm Jason," a voice answered. "Let me introduce you to the Civil Trial Ad course instructors for the first week of training. I've told them a little about your situation, and they have agreed to help out. This group has a combined total of about 350 years of civil experience, and there is practically nothing that they have not encountered in the world of civil practice on behalf of the United States."

"Gee thanks," Sam said and each member of the group introduced themselves.

They were from all over the United States. This particular group of instructors had met over 20 years ago, and they tried to teach the first week of the civil trial advocacy course once a year as a group. They started out as a teaching unit when the training was done in Washington, D.C., and they had continued their annual teaching reunion when all DOJ training moved to Columbia, South Carolina.

Jason asked Sam, "How about giving us a fast run down of the criminal complaint and the section 1983 civil suit there in Alabama. Grab a beer or a soda first if you like."

Sam said, "I'll get something later." He gave them a quick and dirty rundown of what had happened, including his transfer from criminal to civil.

Someone in the back commented, "That's pretty wild. Not even Ripley would believe that these are legitimate state court actions."

Jason said, "Yes, but Sam has to deal with the two cases properly, regardless of the merits. I think he first needs to focus on his role in representing agent Kemper."

There was a nodding of heads all around.

"Let's begin," said Sam.

Jason said, "The first thing you must realize about representing a federal employee is that legal representation is limited."

"What do you mean, 'limited'?" asked Sam.

"Have a look at the acknowledgement of the conditions of representations that your FBI agent client must sign. It says clearly that while the Department of Justice furnishes an attorney, the client acknowledges that the representation can only be for what conduct reasonably appears to have been within the scope of official federal employment."

Sam asked, "The FBI I represent is about to retire. Would I still represent her after that?"

"Yes," said Jason. "We represent retired federal officials all the time. It's not a problem."

"Do I represent the client or the United States?" inquired Sam.

"Good question. Some of both is the short answer," replied Jason.

"Are there privileged attorney client communications with an agent that is being represented?

"Yes, but if there is any conflict between the agent's interests and those of the United States that you discover, then you must withdraw and advise the client to seek private counsel," said Jason. "In some cases the United States will pay for it. By the way, an agent is entitled to retain private counsel at any time. The agent has the option to keep you on at the same time."

Sam asked, "Why would a federal employee want to do that?"

"You as government counsel cannot do certain things that might be of strategic benefit to the client, like file a counterclaim for a bad faith lawsuit. A federal employee would need private counsel for that. It's Department policy to defend employees but not to advance claims for them. Also, as you might expect, you cannot advise, encourage, or make any claims against the United States on behalf of the represented employee."

"What about judgments and appeals?" asked Sam.

"We represent the employee on appeal, even sometimes to the U.S. Supreme Court. As to judgments, an adverse money judgment can be entered against the individual employee, and he or she may be personally responsible for payment."

"Wait, what about indemnification by the United States?" Sam interjected.

"There is no right to indemnification or reimbursement generally. However, if there is a final judgment against the individual and the United States jointly, the United State would pay the judgment, and the individual would then be off the hook for compensatory damages and the like. This would not be true for any punitive damages. By federal law the United States cannot be held liable for punitives, and therefore, the client is responsible."

"Can that happen?" asked Sam.

"Sure," said Jason. "In the case that you have with the FBI agent, you will substitute the United States on the common law assault claim under the Federal Tort Claims

Act. The case may eventually go to trial on the *Bivens* claims of intentional violations of constitutional rights to the person. Likely, the judge will have both matters sent to the jury, even though the Federal Tort Claims Act matter is advisory only because there is no right to a jury trial in FTCA cases."

"So where is the likely bottom line for my FBI agent client?" asked Sam.

Jason looked around the group of instructors, and said, "I discussed the case with the teaching group and the general consensus is that you should be able to win everything on motions, assuming a decent federal judge, with the possible exception of the FTCA tort and the *Bivens* claims in the civil suit. Improper motive of the agent and intent are going to be your battle grounds."

"Do you mean this turns on the subjective intent of the agent?" asked Sam.

Jason said, "No, the agent is entitled to qualified immunity if a reasonable official, acting in the same circumstance faced by the agent, and possessed of the same knowledge, could have believed the conduct to be lawful. That's the legal test, but I must admit that some judges confuse it with elements of subjectivity. Those cases are appealed."

"Does that mean that in the worse case scenario, where my client's motion to dismiss or for summary judgment is denied, I can expect at least one trip to the U.S. Court of Appeals for the Eleventh Circuit before there is any trial?"

Jason said, "You catch on fast."

One of the instructor group leaders for the civil course chimed in, "Welcome to civil trial work for the United States. It's the most fun you can have as a professional adult with your socks on. And you are really in luck because one of the moot court cases for exercises and trial for the next two weeks is a *Bivens* type assault case. We will make sure you get the defense side when you do your mock trial before a federal judge in week two."

Another instructor spoke up and said, "At least you are not facing a *pro se* plaintiff which is what we get a lot of these days in *Bivens* cases. Many of those situations are too stupid to talk about. It's no fun engaging in a war of wits with someone who is unarmed."

"Just give any of us a call if you get too bogged down or overwhelmed. You are a part of the largest law firm in the world, and we always try to help each other in civil. There are very few egos here. Learn all you can and try to enjoy yourself while you are here in Columbia. We'll all try to stop and give you pointers from time to time. Please ask us questions. Somebody in this group has probably faced just about anything you can come up with."

Sam said, "Thanks. I plan to work hard."

Jason said, "Don't work too hard. Burying yourself in work is a cheap trick to avoid real thinking."

Sam said, "Well, I do plan for some relaxation. On Fridays, when I've been here in the past, I head over to Bill's Music Shop & Pickin' Parlor across the river for some bluegrass music. A lot of the local groups turn up and play in different rooms. It's great."

Jason said, "Well, if you like bluegrass, why don't you join us down at Delaney's Irish pub on Tuesday for our brand of music. We play and sing some ourselves. You might get a kick out of it."

Sam said, "Thanks. Can I bring my banjo?"

"Absolutely," said Jason.

Everyone else also enthusiastically approved.

By the end of the first week of training, Sam had acquired a new level of confidence in his civil case abilities from the teaching group. Maybe civil work would not be so bad in the U.S. Attorney's Office.

Chapter 26

Perdido Key, Florida
Flora Bama Bar
Monday, June 16, 2003
1:30 p.m.

Before a hurricane named Ivan in 2004, the most famous bar and restaurant in the Alabama-Florida panhandle area of the Gulf Coast was the Flora Bama Lounge Package Store & Oyster Bar & Grill. Its loyal customer base hopes for a rebuilding. It straddled the state line between Alabama and Florida on Perdido Key's beachfront. The Flora Bama sponsored the Polar Bear dip on New Years and the Mullet Toss on the last full weekend in April. There were other assorted live entertainments on or around the premises throughout the year. It was the social focal point of life on the Redneck Riviera.

It was also the meeting place for Jeff Duval and his business associates from time to time. They did not make themselves into public spectacles like some of the young drug traffickers who had more money than sense. These 'drugees' on occasion got drunk in bars along the coast and showed off by wadding up one hundred dollar bills and having a bar fight with them, leaving the wadded bills on the floor for the spectators.

There was too much money at stake for Duval and his cronies to be attracting too much attention with such antics. Their low key policy had been the mainstay to survival over the years. It had worked well, with the only major glitch being Pickering's recent indictment by the feds.

There were five in Duval's group all together that still met once a year in Gulf Shores. These five originally ran into one another at the helicopter school at Ft. Rucker, and everyone was from Alabama. Now, each one lived close to a U.S. Army installation. Duval lived in Huntsville near Redstone Arsenal; Troy Pickering lived near the Anniston Army Depot and near what was Ft. McClelland; Tom Wassel lived in Phenix City, near Ft. Benning, Georgia; Ben Blake lived in Savannah, Georgia, near Ft. Stewart; and Robert Nolan lived in Atlanta, near Ft. McPherson. Each had a blue banjo tattooed on his left knee.

Between them they owned numerous beachfront properties on Gulf Shores, even though their ownership was hidden by Netherlands Antilles Corporations, which were in turn held by Panamanian offshore corporations. These latter corporations were held in the names of nominees, so that true ownership could not be traced. Finally, these entities were held by a special trust created in the Cayman Islands.

The trust had been created in 1972 and was financed by a bearer share corporation in Panama that traded only offshore so that nothing could be taxed. The bearer share corporation's true ownership could not be traced either, and the banking transactions stayed hidden behind Panama's strict bank secrecy laws which allowed for Swiss style numbered accounts and the like. The Caymans had similar secrecy laws, but had common law type courts and traditions which had been inherited from England.

Over the years the main corpus of money was kept in the bearer share Panamanian corporation. It had grown from $12 million in 1972 to $130 million in 2004. Originally, there had been $15.6 million, but $3.6 million had gone into the Cayman trust to buy properties, including beach front properties on Gulf Shores when it was selling for cheap.

The trust also owned restaurants and bars in the New Orleans French Quarter, a small vineyard in California's Napa Valley, condos in Vail, Colorado, and a townhouse near Central Park in New York City. It was hard to value the real estate investments at this point, but it was beyond any of the group's wildest expectations.

The trust was set to terminate at the end of 35 years, which was coming up soon. The main Panama corporation with its huge amount of cash would also be divided up at that same time in all likelihood.

Each lived very well, but not so lavishly to call too much attention to themselves. They had to stay below the federal authorities' radar screens. The state law enforcement officials could be bribed or otherwise paid off or "handled." All engaged in criminal activities, but these were usually geared to stay out of federal interests or federal jurisdictions.

Most owned or operated businesses near military bases in the form of bars, restaurants, and nightclubs. Cash business was a must. How else could certain large deposits be explained from time to time? Some, like Pickering, also got into state contracts, with its easy corruption and political payoffs. Again, a lot of cash changed hands.

The U.S. income tax laws taxed individual citizens and residents on their worldwide incomes, no matter what the source.

Duval and his associates never declared any income from their vast foreign holdings. All filed federal and state income tax returns, but none checked the box on the federal return that required a disclosure of signatory or other authority over foreign accounts and the like. All cheated like mad on their individual and business returns.

As Robert Noland liked to boast, "My Form 1040 is my first offer."

It was Noland that first approached the others back in 1967 about financial opportunities in Vietnam. His cousin had been a master sergeant who ran an enlisted men's club for the U.S. Army near Saigon. He had shocked the family after two consecutive tours in Vietnam by renouncing his citizenship and moving to Switzerland. He had made so much money on the black market that he could not come back to the states.

The others asked how he did it, and Noland said, "It had something to do with MPC's. If my cousin could make a ton of money, we should be able to do even better. He was dumb as a stump, and we are all geniuses by comparison."

They all said what the hell. All of them were bound for Vietnam whether they liked it or not, so they might as well make it worth while.

"MPC" stood for Military Payment Certificate. They were issued by the U.S. military, and the certificates looked like paper money, but with differing colors and designs. MPC's were used in places like Vietnam in an attempt to control the black market and to stabilize the local economy by preventing the trafficking in U.S. dollars.

Officially, the use and possession of dollars by service personnel was outlawed, and only MPC's could be used by the in-country troops to make purchases at the base exchanges and clubs on post. One could be court martialed for using dollars in Vietnam.

MPC's could be exchanged for the local currency, the piaster, in order to make purchases on the local economy; however, local currency could not be converted back into MPC's officially.

A black market arose in this situation despite official regulations. Many service personnel sold their rations of alcohol and tobacco on the local market in exchange for MPC's which many civilian locals seemed to readily possess due to fraud and theft.

To prevent this local trade in MPC's the U.S. authorities would from time to time, without notice, announce a conversion day or "C-day". Only persons with authority to lawfully posses MPC's could convert their old MPC's to the newly printed versions of the MPC's. The old ones became worthless, and no one on the local economy wanted to be left holding the bag, so to speak.

Into to this mix in the late 1960's came the Hindu moncychangers. They had been in Southeast Asia for years, but became prominent in places like Saigon as the war in Vietnam escalated. They exchanged piasters, MPC's or just about anything else. They somehow managed never to get caught with worthless MPC's on conversion day.

Their main business operated around the demand for dollars by North Vietnam and by other Communist countries that needed dollars for the purchase of war materials and international trade. By 1968 the demand for dollars was so great that a Hindu money changer in Saigon would give a serviceman MPC's or piasters in exchange for dollars at the rate of 5 to 1.

They would even take checks if drawn on U.S. dollar accounts back in the states. Of course this latter approach was too risky for most service personnel, because one was likely to get caught and sent to jail due to the cancelled check evidence that wound up in the U.S. banking system.

When Duval and his cronies first arrived in Saigon in 1968, they found out about the 5 to 1 deal offered by the Hindu traders, and considered writing checks, but Tom Wassel had a better idea. He was a helicopter mechanic who had been the Army longer than the others. Prior to Ft. Rucker, he had been stationed in at Ft. Kobbe in the Panama Canal Zone. He told the group that there was no exchange rate between the U.S. dollar and the Panamanian Balboa, and that you could have a numbered bank account in Panama with all the benefits of bank and corporate secrecy laws.

Duval and the others immediately decided to open an account in Panama and start writing checks to the Hindu moneychangers out of it. They sent Duval on his next leave to a lawyer in Panama City, Panama. He set up an offshore corporation in the name of the lawyer as nominee so that none of their names appeared.

Duval took 100 bearer shares that signified ownership of the corporation and opened a numbered checking account with $10,000. He placed the shares in the bank's special safety deposit box. Unique instructions were left at the bank.

Bearer shares, warned the Panamanian lawyer, were just that. Whoever possessed the shares owned and controlled the corporation. Transfer was easy and no names generally showed up in transactions. The downside was that they could be lost or stolen. By hook or crook, whoever who was the "bearer" was the owner.

After Duval returned to Vietnam from Panama, the group elected to have blue banjos tattooed on their left knees for special identification and for other reasons. Each also had a piece of paper with a drawing and code given to them by Duval.

Plans were laid to go off like clockwork. They would write a check in Saigon on the Panamanian bank account and get 5 to 1 back in MPC's and piasters. They would take the proceeds and buy high grade diamonds and emeralds from the base exchanges and on the local economy. The group also would buy special gold necklace jewelry made of 24 carat links. They planned to stay away from drugs and other items that were strictly illegal to possess.

The group also planned to have someone travel back to the states with a permanent change of station move with the goods every 6 months. Sometimes they could rotate more often. Each of them also planned to volunteer for extensions of duty so that each could spend at least two years in Vietnam "conducting business."

The jewelry would be sold stateside and the moneys taken to Panama and deposited into the bank account.

The U.S. military would provide free transport because servicemen could always catch "hops" on military flights each day to practically anywhere in the world where there was a military air base. The military bases in the Panama Canal Zone were easy enough to get to for them.

In late 1968, Duval wrote the first check to the Hindu moneychangers for $5,000. In return he and his group received $25,000 in MPC's and piasters, which they promptly converted into the highest grade diamonds and emeralds they could buy. Within 6 months they had transported the goods stateside, sold them, and deposited the moneys in the numbered account in Panama, which grew tax free. Panama did not tax offshore investments, and Duval and his cronies were not about to tell the I.R.S.

The next check was for $25,000 and the Hindu moneychangers gave them $125,000 in MPC's and piasters. Again there was a 6 month turn around. From 1968 to 1971, only five checks were written, but they allowed Duval and his crowd to deposit $15,625,000 in their secret account in Panama. The last load of diamonds, emeralds and gold took a huge moving effort by all in the group, but it was well worth it.

In 1972, Duval sent Pickering to the Caymans with $3,625,000 to set up the trust that was to purchase the beach front properties at Gulf Shores and other targeted real estate with income potential around the United States. Haight & Woodhouse, Chartered Accountants, in Georgetown, Grand Caymans, accommodated Pickering's every need.

Each of the group's original members was made a beneficiary of the trust, and Pickering was made the trustee. He in turn empowered the accountants to keep their names secret, and to conduct all the other real estate investments through foreign corporations created and controlled by the trust. They provided similar services for lots of Americans who wanted to conceal their finances and ownerships.

At the accountant's suggestion, Pickering also executed a special Last Will and Testament, which along with some other important papers, were kept in a special safety deposit box in Georgetown at a bank also recommended by the accountants. They advised him not to carry or posses any documents in the U.S. that showed any indications of foreign financial interests or ownerships. They also advised him not to make too many trips back and forth to the Caymans because his passport would show evidence that could raise suspicions by the U.S. taxing authorities. The accountants agreed to meet with him outside the U.S. from time to time, but in other countries.

All of the current group, except Pickering, was assembled at a back corner table at the Flora Bama. He came in 30 minutes late looking hung over and disheveled.

"Man you look like Joe Shit the ragbag," said Duval, who offered him a box of Cuban cigars that looked like small torpedoes. "Have one of these Montecristo Number Two's that I had brought in from Cuba. Each was rolled on the inside of a Cuban virgin's thigh. I guarantee you will feel better."

Pickering said, "No thanks. I need a big drink. This legal wrangle with the U.S. Attorney's Office in Birmingham has had me dragging ass, scattered to hell and gone, and tripping over mouse turds."

Duval replied, "Look, you've got to stay focused and keep all your shit in one sock. Didn't you learn in helicopter school that you can't ride in all directions at one time even if you are in a multidirectional machine?"

"Yeah, but I'm still worried that the feds aren't going to give up so easy."

Duval said, "Look, we got the charges dismissed against you, and we've got the FBI agent and Assistant U.S. Attorney off base and pinned down. You might say that we have them 'in training'."

Pickering paused and said, "I'm not sure that your 'training' as you call it is going to work. Training those two is like baptizing a bear, it generally won't take."

Chapter 27

Birmingham, Alabama
Sam Stone's Apartment on Southside
Friday, June 20, 2003
5:30 p.m.

Sam had Steven demonstrate what he had learned thus far on the banjo, and said, "O.K. You're doing great. We will now introduce you first to *frailing* and then to bluegrass."

Steven grinned and replied, "I'm ready."

Sam began. "Frailing a 5-string banjo is a unique art form. In some circles, this playing style is called frammin, flammin, whamming, rapppin, beatin, knockin, or clawhammer. It first appeared in the 1840's when the 5-string first was popularized by Joe Sweeney and his traveling minstrel show. In more recent times, the 1900's, performers on the Grand Old Opry, such as Uncle Dave Macon, Dave "Stringbean" Akeman, and Grandpa Jones, kept frailing alive and well."

"I think I've seen Grandpa Jones on some old re-runs of Hee Haw," said Steven.

Sam continued. "Many folk artists consider this a pure form of 5-string banjo playing and refuse to play any other styles. It is also a method that has been traditionally well liked in Appalachia. It produces a fast and driving rhythm with some melody notes. Many players use no picks, not even a thumb pick. It is fun to simply grab your banjo and start playing without having to look for any finger picks. Personally, I like to use a thumb pick when I frail. I think it makes for a better ringing banjo sound."

Sam demonstrated the style by playing 'Darlin' Corey.'

Sam said, "To frail a banjo, one first has to decide whether to use the right hand index or middle finger to pick the melody notes. The melody notes are played with the back of the nail of one of these fingers by picking down on the 1st, 2nd, 3rd or 4th strings."

Sam demonstrated.

"I prefer to use the middle finger because I can keep a finger pick on my index finger and switch into and out of the double thumbing style of play. I like to cup my middle, ring, and little fingers of my right hand, while keeping my index finger pointed straight."

Again, Sam demonstrated for Steven.

The phone rang, Sam saw the caller I.D., and answered, "Hello, Professor."

Professor Redmond asked, "Is Steven there? I'd like to speak to him."

Sam turned and handed the phone to Steven. "It's for you."

Steven said, "Hi Professor, what's up?"

"My sources tell me that the Gates Scholarships will be announced in the next month or so. Thought you would want to know. I'm keeping my fingers crossed."

Steven said, "That's great. I hope it's good news too."

They both hung up.

Sam asked, "What's going on?"

Steven replied, "The Cambridge Gates Scholarships are to be announced soon, and the Professor is getting excited."

Sam said, "Look, if you get that scholarship, I'll take you on a free trip to Nashville to see the Grand Ole Opry and maybe even arrange a tour of the Gibson banjo works."

"That would be super. I'll take you up on that offer," said Steven.

Sam said, "Now back to frailing. To frail, allow your right hand and forearm to move in a counterclockwise, circular set of motions down towards the strings."

Sam demonstrated the right hand movement. "First, pick down on one of the melody strings with the back of the middle finger's nail."

"I write this down as "$M\downarrow$"."

Sam wrote and then continued.

"Second, pick down across some or all of the strings with back of middle finger's nail ("$M\downarrow$") or the back of the nails of the cupped three fingers.

Sam showed Steven.

"During this second phase, one's thumb is rested on the 5th string."

Sam again demonstrated.

"On the hand's movement back up, the thumb picks the 5th string ("-T").

Sam wrote this down, and then said, "In other words, you have to make a slight delay in picking the 5th string with the thumb. Some players silently say to themselves, "bump-diddy" to get into the correct rhythm of play."

Sam said as he wrote, "I write frailing as '$M{\downarrow}M{\downarrow}$-$T$'."

Sam played a few bars and said, "For some people, frailing is an easy method to learn. I have known others, however, that could play every other style of banjo but this one, and found it impossible. My advice is to keep trying."

Steven asked, "How did you learn?"

Sam replied, "I learned the method on my own by asking around about it, looking at Pete Seeger's book on the subject, and by listening to it being played on records. After about 3 weeks, I started to get the hang of it. Learning can be simply a matter of persistence. Frailing was for me."

Sam then made Steven go through the right hand motions very slowly, especially the part about resting the right thumb on the 5th string and plunking it on the way back up.

Sam then said, "As an exercise, you should play the open G chord using frailing so that each of the 4 melody strings are picked down on once by the back of the middle finger's nail, or back of the index finger's nail if that is the melody finger you choose to play with."

Again, Sam demonstrated, playing each of the four strings in turn.

"You should repeat the same exercise using the 4 melody strings with the C chord, and then with the D7th chord."

Sam showed the complete exercise to Steven using each of the chords, and said, "Now practice 'Boil Them Cabbage Down', using the open G chord, and the simple chords, C and D7th."

Sam played the song and then wrote:

G (open-no fingers on any frets)
M↓M↓-T
M↓M↓-T
M↓M↓-T
M↓M↓-T
"Boil them cab-bage"
C (Middle finger on 4th string at 2nd fret
    Index finger on 2nd string at 1st fret
    Ring finger on 1st string at 2nd fret)
M↓M↓-T
M↓M↓-T
M↓M↓-T
M↓M↓-T
"Down boys"
G (open-no fingers on any frets)
M↓M↓-T
M↓M↓-T
M↓M↓-T
M↓M↓-T
"Turn them hoe-cakes"
D7th (3rd string index finger (1) at 2nd fret;
    2nd string middle finger (2) at 1st fret)
M↓M↓-T

M↓M↓-T

M↓M↓-T

M↓M↓-T

"Round"

G (open-no fingers on any frets)

M↓M↓-T

M↓M↓-T

M↓M↓-T

M↓M↓-T

"The only song that"

C (4^{th string} middle finger (2) at 2nd fret;
    2^{nd string} index finger (1) at 1st fret;
    1^{st string} ring finger (3) at 2nd fret)

M↓M↓-T

M↓M↓-T

M↓M↓-T

M↓M↓-T

"I can sing is"

G (open-no fingers on any frets)

M↓M↓-T

M↓M↓-T

"Boil them"

D7th (3^{rd string} index finger (1) at 2nd fret;
    2^{nd string} middle finger (2) at 1st fret)

M↓M↓-T

M↓M↓-T

"Cab-bage"

G (open-no fingers on any frets)

M↓M↓-T

M↓M↓-T

M↓M↓-T

M↓M↓-T

"Down"

Sam had Steven go through the exercise correcting any mistakes that he saw. Steven was really making good progress.

When they finished, Steven asked, "When are we going to start on bluegrass?"

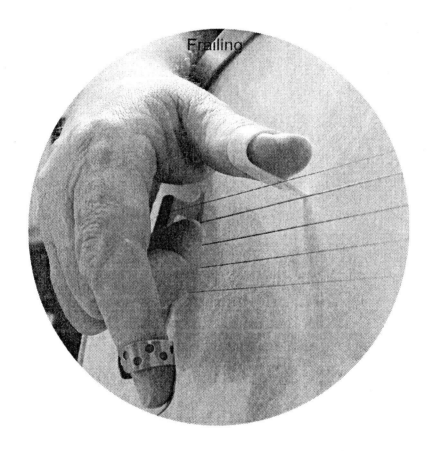

Frailing

Chapter 28

Birmingham, Alabama
Sam Stone's Apartment on Southside
Friday, June 20, 2003
5:45 p.m.

Sam said, "Right now. For your first lesson in three-finger picking or *bluegrass*, you must learn about *rolls*. This requires a plastic thumb pick, along with metal picks for the index and middle fingers."

Steven asked, "Do all bluegrass pickers use similar picks?"

Sam said, "Maybe not all, but all the ones I have ever seen do."

Sam produced another metal finger pick and added it to Steven's thumb pick and index finger pick that had been used in folk stroking and double thumbing.

Sam continued. "A bluegrass roll is generally eight notes played in a certain sequence. In music terms, these are typically 1/16th notes. Rolls are usually played back to back. Because there are three fingers playing eight notes in sequence over and over one gets a syncopated sound called bluegrass."

Sam held the banjo up horizontal so Steven could see, and said, "The right hand should be anchored in place with the tips of the ring and little fingers touching the banjo head just above the bridge area. This allows the thumb, index and middle fingers to pick."

Sam then had Steven anchor his right hand in a similar fashion.

Sam continued, "There are numerous rolls. The first roll to be learned is called a forward roll. Other rolls to be learned are called backward and reverse rolls, and sometimes other names. I'll write all of them down."

Sam demonstrated the roll on his banjo.

"For your first forward roll, the following is required: first, the index finger, written down as '$\leftarrow I$', picks up on the 1st, 2nd, 3rd or 4th strings. It is your choice as to which string."

Sam demonstrated by picking one of the four strings.

"Second, the middle finger '$\leftarrow M$', picks up on the 1st string."

Again, Sam demonstrated.

"Third, the thumb '$T\rightarrow$', picks down on the 5th string."

Sam used his thumb to demonstrate.

"Fourth, the index finger '$\leftarrow I$', picks up on the 1st, 2nd, 3rd or 4th strings. Again, it is your choice again as to which string.

Sam demonstrated, using his index finger.

"Fifth, the middle finger '$\leftarrow M$', picks up on the 1st string."

Sam used his middle finger.

"Sixth, the thumb '$T\rightarrow$', picks down on the 5th string."

Sam demonstrated.

"Seventh, the index finger '$\leftarrow I$', picks up on the 1st, 2nd, 3rd or 4th strings. Again, it is your choice again as to which string."

Sam demonstrated.

"And eighth, the middle finger '$\leftarrow M$', picks up on the 1st string."

Sam completed the demonstration.

"Now repeat, so that each note is evenly spaced."

Sam then demonstrated the complete 8 note roll technique very slowly and had Steven attempt the same.

Sam wrote:

5th	4th	3rd	2nd	1st
G	**D**	**G**	**B**	**D**
		$\leftarrow I$		
				$\leftarrow M$
$T\rightarrow$				
		$\leftarrow I$		
				$\leftarrow M$
$T\rightarrow$				
		$\leftarrow I$		
				$\leftarrow M$
/	/	$\leftarrow I$		
				$\leftarrow M$
$T\rightarrow$				
		$\leftarrow I$		
				$\leftarrow M$
$T\rightarrow$				

|	|	←*I*	|	|
|	|	|	|	←*M*

Steven's progress was awkward at first, and he said, "I don't know if I can get the hang of this."

Sam said, "Look, you are using muscles in your fingers and thumb that have never been used or developed before. That's why you practice the rolls before you try to play too much in the way of different tunes. It takes a little fine muscle development."

"How long will it take?" asked Steven.

"It depends on the person, and their practice skills and dedication. I suggest that you try to practice for smoothness and even notes as opposed to speed. One must learn to walk before running and the same applies to bluegrass. In a good week to ten days one should be able to crank out at least one tune. You should do the following exercise in open G tuning."

Sam demonstrated and wrote:

5th	4th	3rd	2nd	1st
G	**D**	**G**	**B**	**D**
|	*I*	|	|	|
|	|	|	|	*M*
T	|	|	|	|
|	|	*I*	|	|
|	|	|	|	*M*
T	|	|	|	|
|	|	|	*I*	|
|	|	|	|	*M*
|	|	|	|	*I*
|	|	|	|	*M*

T						
T	|	|	|	|
|	|	|	*I*	|
|	|	|	|	*M*
T	|	|	|	|
|	|	*I*	|	|
|	|	|	|	*M*

Sam continued, "Play the eight notes in the roll twice in open G. Then do the same thing with the C chord, and again with the D7th chord."

Sam demonstrated the entire exercise.

Sam had Steven do the same, and then said, "Now you are ready to play 'Boil Them Cabbage Down', using the open G chord, and the simple chords, C and D7th."

Sam first demonstrated and then wrote:

5th	4th	3rd	2nd	1st
G	**D**	**G**	**B**	**D**

G (open-no fingers on any frets)

|	|	|	*I*	|
|	|	|	|	*M*
T	|	|	|	|
|	|	*I*	|	|
|	|	|	|	*M*
T	|	|	|	|
|	|	|	*I*	|
|	|	|	|	*M*

"Boil them cab-bage"

C (4th string middle finger (2) at 2nd fret;

2nd ^{string} index finger (1) at 1st fret; 1st ^{string} ring finger (3) at 2nd fret)

```
 |    |    |    I    |
 |    |    |    |    M
 T    |    |    |    |
 |    |    I    |    |
 |    |    |    |    M
 T    |    |    |    |
 |    |    |    I    |
 |    |    |    |    M
```
                "Down   boys"

G (open-no fingers on any frets)

```
 |    |    |    I    |
 |    |    |    |    M
 T    |    |    |    |
 |    |    I    |    |
 |    |    |    |    M
 T    |    |    |    |
 |    |    |    I    |
 |    |    |    |    M
```
        "Turn them hoe-cakes"

D7th (3rd ^{string} index finger (1) at 2nd fret; 2nd ^{string} middle finger (2) at 1st fret)

```
 |    |    I    |    |
 |    |    |    |    M
 T    |    |    |    |
 |    |    |    I    |
```

```
 |    |    |    |    M
 T    |    |    |    |
 |    |    I    |    |
 |    |    |    |    M
```
"Round"

G (open-no fingers on any frets)

```
 |    |    |    I    |
 |    |    |    |    M
 T    |    |    |    |
 |    |    I    |    |
 |    |    |    |    M
 T    |    |    |    |
 |    |    |    I    |
 |    |    |    |    M
```
"The only song that"

C (4th string middle finger (2) at 2nd fret; 2nd string index finger (1) at 1st fret; 1st string ring finger (3) at 2nd fret)

```
 |    |    |    I    |
 |    |    |    |    M
 T    |    |    |    |
 |    |    I    |    |
 |    |    |    |    M
 T    |    |    |    |
 |    |    |    I    |
 |    |    |    |    M
```
"I can sing is"

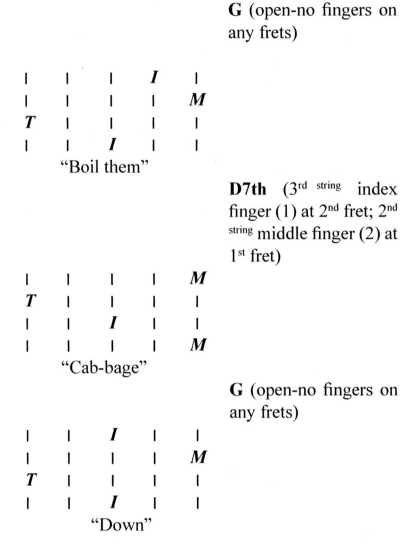

G (open-no fingers on any frets)

"Boil them"

D7th (3rd string index finger (1) at 2nd fret; 2nd string middle finger (2) at 1st fret)

"Cab-bage"

G (open-no fingers on any frets)

"Down"

After playing the song, Sam said, "I should point out that the 8 note sequence of rolls being played back to back has to be altered in the last line ('Boil them Cabbage Down') in order to make the picking fit the song. This happens frequently in bluegrass. While bluegrass is generally described as a series of 8 note rolls being played back to back, the reality is that tunes require modification in order to work. As my Uncle John would say, 'nothing is perfect in life and nothing is perfectly easy.'"

"Is he another Alabama backwoods philosopher?" asked Steven.

"Yes, or something close thereto. He's been around a lot."

Steven asked, "What other keen insight has your Uncle passed on to you? Professor Redmond always asks students for local wisdom and the like that they have learned from families and friends."

Sam thought for about ten seconds and said, "Uncle John thinks that if women could control their feelings of envy and if men could control their emotions surrounding their egos, the world would be a happier and easier place to live in. That's about as deep as he's ever gotten with me."

"That's some concepts worth bringing up in the Professor's class," said Stephen.

Sam then gave Steven another demonstration of the roll exercises and song. "One should practice roll after roll and concentrate on smoothly spaced notes and even sound levels for each note. Next time, additional forward, backward, reverse, and partial rolls will be learned. I will introduce them to you as you progress."

Steven inquired, "Last time we had a lesson, you said that you played the banjo to avoid stress. Have you got any other suggestions about dealing with stress?"

Sam reflected and then said, "As you get older, things that cause stress can change, but in periods of stress for me I have learned to write things down, read a good story, break problem tasks into smaller units, use the word 'no' more often, practice breathing slowly, avoid negative people, and pet a friendly animal."

Steven asked, "Anything else?"

Sam reflected and said, "I don't want to seem preachy, but drugs and alcohol are temporary fixes that won't work to alleviate stress in the long run. Unfortunately, that's a lesson that most people have to learn for themselves, and some never learn. Try not to be a slow learner on this score."

"I would have thought that you, as a musician, would be a little more open minded about drugs and alcohol," said Steven.

"Well, just remember the old saying that is one of my Uncle John's favorites," said Sam. "If you are too open-minded, your brains will fall out."

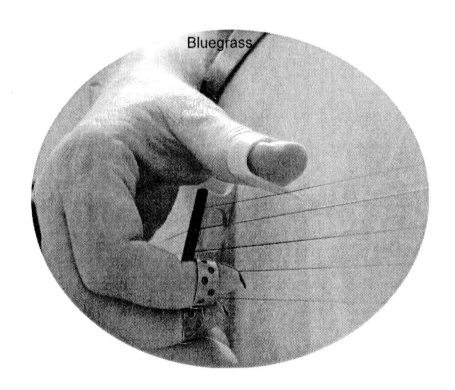
Bluegrass

Chapter 29

Point Clear, Alabama
Grand Hotel
Saturday, June 21, 2003
8:30 p.m.

The old Spanish maps called it Punta Clara, and the English settlers kept the name in a translated version, Point Clear. A hotel of some sort had been there since the mid-1800's, and the structure had been used as a hospital during the Civil War. With fires and other disasters, none of the original buildings remained. The current Grand Hotel had a series of old and new additions. It remained a popular resort although management of the huge resort and grounds with 550 acres had become a difficult task.

One could still get high tea at 4:00 p.m., but the good old days of the 1930's and 1940's of catering strictly to the social elite, such as when Franklin Roosevelt and his entourage would come for a visit on their way to the Little White House in Warm Springs, Georgia, were gone.

Judge Crowell sat in a wicker chair in the Bird Cage Lounge sipping his third rum punch which he had had the barmaid make according to his strict instructions. He learned the formula from an old bartender in Barbados on one of his many trips to the Caribbean. It was so good that he had actually paid $20.00 for the recipe because the old bartender did not want to give it up for free. You needed a good medium dark rum, Mount Gay or Black Seal, preferably not a Bacardi product.

One then followed a rhyming formula:

> One of sour,
> Two of sweet,
> Three of strong,
> Four of weak

The "one of sour" was one part freshly squeezed lime juice. Key limes were the best. "Two of sweet" was two parts simple syrup or sugar water or just sugar in a pinch. The "three of strong" was three parts rum, and the "four of weak" was ice. One could add cinnamon, nutmeg, orange slices, fresh pineapple chunks, sprigs of mint, a top floater of real port, or anything else one liked after the basic rhyming formula was followed.

Judge Crowell often remarked that he was no longer an apprenticed alcoholic; rather he had finally earned his masters papers.

Duval came up behind the Judge and asked, "Are you having a Jubilee by yourself tonight?"

In late summer, an amazing natural phenomenon sometimes occurs after midnight but before dawn on Mobile Bay's Eastern Shore. The locals call it a "Jubilee." It starts with an overcast day, with winds from the east over a calm bay surface. Somehow the waters become oxygen deprived, and all of the bottom feeders, including flounders, crabs, lobsters, shrimps, eels, and you name it, rush together towards the Eastern Shore.

The populations of Daphne, Fairhope, and Point Clear ring bells, blow horns and whistles, and hurry to the shallow waters with nets, buckets, tubs, and anything that can scoop up the wealth of sea life. The feasting and partying on fresh seafood that almost jumps out of the bay and into cooking pots and pans is truly a Jubilee. Large quantities of alcoholic beverages are also consumed.

"No Jubilee," said the Judge. "It's not late enough in the summer. I'm just trying to take some pressures off."

"Our good buddy Troy Pickering says to tell you thanks for cutting him loose. That's the only time any of us have come close to legal disaster over the years. Hopefully, the feds will stand down, and leave Pickering to the state and locals so that we can control things."

The Judge said, "Look. I told the group years ago to stay out sight from the feds. That's the best legal advice ya'll ever got, and it has worked. The other advice was not to spend, but invest wisely with slow distributions connected with cash businesses. You've done that well. Now the bigger problem is how to finally wind up things without giving up citizenships or becoming fugitives. Any big mistakes and it may come to that, whether you like it or not."

Duval looked away and said, "I don't think the feds are going to do much more. Besides, I have a good scheme going to keep their main players occupied, while keeping tabs on things."

The Judge asked, "How much apiece do you think the final shares will work out to be?"

Duval grinned and replied, "I'm figuring on about $50 million each."

"That should keep me in rum punches for quite a while. Now you better leave. No use taking a risk on being seen with me."

Duval said, "That's fine. I was just going. I've been invited by a couple of hot young women to meet up the road at Judge Roy Beans's bar in Daphne for drinks, and I don't want to be late.

"Don't let those women trap you," said the Judge.

"Well, it's like the story of our populist Governor Big Jim Folsom. He was quite a party goer. Once, while in the middle of an election campaign, he was on the road and was invited by his political opponents to a motel for a 'social evening.' Big Jim's political advisors said, 'Big Jim, don't go. We hear that they are going to have loose women and lots of whiskey. It's a set-up and a trap.' Big Jim's response was, 'Well, I'm going to the party anyhow. If you bait a trap with whiskey and pussy, you're going to catch ol' Big Jim every time.'"

The Judge laughed. "I've heard that one before about our former gov, but I always enjoy its retelling.

Duval said, "I've always taken your other advice and never married. You always said, 'if it flies, floats or fucks, rent it.' That's been good advice. I'll keep you posted any other developments."

The Judge reflected that the most lucrative clients he had ever had were Alabamian by-products of the Vietnam conflict. They had come to him years ago with some minor criminal matters, and he had developed their trust to the point that they finally cut him in. He showed them how to spread money around to politicians and the like, while keeping a low profile. His advice had really paid off for them and the Judge.

Karen Kemper and her daughter wandered into the bar looking for the dining room. They had driven over from the beach to have an early supper by the bay. Karen spotted Judge Crowell taking to someone she did not recognize and turned quickly and left the bar area before the Judge spotted her. She did not want to have a conversation with a judicial jerk, which would no doubt spoil her evening with her daughter. She wondered who the stranger was that had made the Judge laugh. He did not look familiar.

Chapter 30

Birmingham, Alabama
U.S. Attorney's Office
Friday, June 27, 2003
4:00 p.m.

Sam was glad it was Friday because it had been a busy week.

On Monday, he had filed a notice of removal in federal district court of the criminal case against FBI agent Kemper and gave notice to the Circuit Court of Winston County of that fact. Sam also filed a notice of removal of the civil suit and gave a similar notice to the Clerk of Court in Winston County.

As bad luck would have it, the first case was assigned to Judge Crowell, and because the civil case was related to the criminal one, he also got that case assignment. The U.S. District Court assigned cases utilizing a random system so that one could not shop for the various judges, and, in turn, the judges could not pick and choose case assignments.

In the civil case, Sam filed a motion to substitute the United States as the defendant on the common law assault claim, and he moved for a 60 day extension from June 6 in which to answer the complaint or otherwise file motions with respect to the sheriff's case. In most cases in which the United States is sued, it has 60 days in which to answer, as opposed to private litigants, who have only 20 days.

The United States gets the extra time because it has to consult with its agencies that, in turn, have to investigate the matter and provide a litigation report to the U.S. Attorney. The extension motion was granted on Wednesday, and that meant that Sam would file a motion for summary judgment on or about August 5. That would put off action on the civil front while he worked to get the criminal charges taken care of.

On Tuesday, Judge Crowell entered an order in the criminal case denying any summary remand of the proceedings back to the Circuit Court of Winston County. That was a big relief. Once that order landed on Sam's desk, he started working on a motion for a hearing and a motion to dismiss.

Sam had Joan Benefield and Jerry Klein in the office review his motions. As a further precaution, he faxed a draft of the motion to dismiss to Jason Sherrod for additional suggestions. He also coordinated everything with the FBI's Office of Legal Counsel.

By Wednesday, Sam filed a motion for a hearing, and by Thursday, he had filed a motion to dismiss the criminal case based upon the Supremacy Clause's federal immunity defense. He attached a declaration of agent Kemper under penalties of perjury to his motion which in bare bones fashion outlined the phone call, her report to her supervisor, her trip to Winston County, and her encounter with the sheriff.

In federal court proceedings a special federal statute permits one to filed declarations under penalties of perjury in lieu of using affidavits which would require notarization. Sam also attached a declaration from her FBI supervisor corroborating Kemper's outline of events.

On Friday, the U.S. District Court set a hearing and the motion to dismiss for Monday, July 14, 2003.

In the meantime, Sam got notice that his final divorce hearing was scheduled for 2:00 p.m. on Monday, June 30. If he survived the divorce, he planned to cash in all of his frequent flyer miles and take a 5 day trip to California's Napa Valley and soak his miseries in food and wine. He was really feeling the need to get away.

Jane Skipper came by his office on Friday afternoon. She looked a little perturbed. "I know you are busy," she said. "But I have been directed by the U.S. Attorney to give you a special assignment."

"What kind of assignment?" asked Sam. "Some suicide mission?"

Jane tried not to laugh. "No. Nothing that dramatic, but it is a little odd. You are familiar with the fact that we have jurisdiction over several military installations in the Northern District."

Sam said, "Sure, I've prosecuted plenty of crimes on military bases under the Assimilative Crimes Act, which gives our office criminal jurisdiction over most crimes on military reservations."

"Well, apparently, the U.S. Attorney is tired of prosecuting civilian shop lifters and employee thefts at the base exchanges because she considers it a waste of valuable office resources. The base exchange managers on the other hand want to maintain some level of deterrence."

"So what does that have to do with me as a civil attorney?" asked Sam.

"In 1993, the Alabama Legislature passed a special civil statute to deter employee theft and shoplifting which allows civil penalty recoveries against offenders. The civil action permits a recoupment of the full retail value of any merchandise, expenses and attorney's fees."

Sam could see it coming and cleared his throat.

Jane continued. "The U.S. Attorney has directed me to inform you that you are to be in charge of this new civil penalty recovery program. You are to meet with the Base Exchange managers as soon as possible. They are being directed to contact you with each and every shoplifting and employee theft case that comes their way."

Jane shook her head and looked down at the floor. She was not happy having to give him this task.

"Let me get this straight. The U.S. Attorney wants me to file civil penalty actions against all employee thieves and shoplifters at the base exchanges in the Northern District?"

"That's about the size of it," said Jane. "I'll try to find you some paralegal or secretarial help. I had plans to use you in other civil matters, but those plans were expressly rejected by the boss. It's a dog assignment, and I'm sorry."

"That's O.K.," said Sam. "I'll figure out something."

What he would figure out, he did not have a clue. Linda was certainly being creative in making his life miserable. Hopefully, what went around would come around.

Chapter 31

Birmingham, Alabama
U.S. District Court
Monday, July 14, 2003
2:00 p.m.

Nancy Hankins, Judge Crowell's law clerk, came into the courtroom and said, "The judge would like to see just counsel in chambers."

Sam turned to Karen Kemper and said, "I don't like this. I'm about to make the judge mad. I intend to make him put everything on the record, even any in chambers proceedings."

Sam asked Wallace Pinkerton, the official court reporter, to follow them into the judge's office.

The prosecutor for Winston County, George Farwell, led everyone into chambers.

He greeted Judge Crowell with, "Howdy Judge. Good to see you again. It's been a while."

The Judge saw the court reporter, and asked, "Is Wallace necessary? I just thought we would have a friendly chat about the case. Who asked for the reporter?"

Sam volunteered, "I did judge. This case is very important to the FBI and the U.S. Department of Justice. Everything needs to be on the record."

"Well if that's the way you want it, then that's the way it'll be. Wallace, take this down." The Judge waited while the reporting equipment got set up.

Sam opened his file to take notes.

The Judge continued when the reporter was ready. "This is the case of the State of Alabama versus Karen Kemper, Criminal No. 04-C-603-S. The government attorney has removed this criminal case from the Circuit Court of Winston County on questionable grounds. The removal flies in the face of federalism and respect that the federal and state governments should have for their respective legal jurisdictions. I've read the motion to dismiss and the declarations of the FBI people, and I have read the opposition filed by the prosecution."

He paused for effect and then continued on in a more stern voice. "The activities in Winston County were not in anywise in interstate commerce, and therefore, there was no federal FBI jurisdiction over the matters being properly investigated by the local sheriff. The agent was there for personal reasons related to her daughter's drug addiction, and she should not have obstructed the sheriff's investigation. Unless the federal government can give me good reason, I am intending to deny the motion to dismiss, but allowing the prosecution to go forward with its criminal prosecution in this court under my control as trial judge."

Judge Crowell turned and glared at Sam.

Sam thought to himself. Why is this being done in chambers and not in open court? Thanks be that Jane Skipper had told him to be sure to have the court reporter present at all times no matter what.

He needed to make a clear record, so Sam said, "Judge, with all due respect, the U.S. Attorney's Office believes that a complete and formal hearing is needed so that a proper record of evidence and testimony can be established."

"Well, you should have put everything in evidence by way of declarations or affidavits. I don't think a hearing is necessary. You can't change the facts. George, what do you think?"

George Farwell smiled and said, "I'm with you Judge. I don't think a hearing is necessary."

Judge Crowell said, "Mr. Stone, you are asking for trial by battle or ordeal and it's not necessary."

Sam responded, "All I'm asking for is an evidentiary hearing. I thought those old common law forms of action were abolished."

Sam did not want to argue the case until all of the evidence was clearly in the record.

Judge Crowell, in a condescending tone, said, "I don't think so. The laws and statutes passed in England before the emigration of our Alabama ancestors are a part of our common law. Some states have common law acquisition statutes as early as 1787. Alabama was created in 1819, but had territorial courts prior to that time which were operating on acquired common law principles which were later subsumed by the courts of the state. Trial by battle and ordeal were not abolished by Parliament in

England until 1819. Thus, the argument can be made that they are still a part of Alabama's common law."

Sam could not believe that a federal judge was saying this on the record.

Sam commented, "I thought that the common laws of England which were inconsistent with the Constitution, laws and institutions of the thirteen original colonies and Alabama were left behind. That's one of the reasons there was a revolution in 1776."

The Judge turned red. "I like my analysis better. If we have a hearing, what witnesses will you call?"

Sam replied, "I have subpoenaed the sheriff. I plan to call agent Kemper's supervisor, and I plan to call agent Kemper. There could be another witness or two depending on how things go."

The Judge asked, "Do you really plan to put your client on the stand when she is facing criminal charges? She has the right not to incriminate herself you know."

It suddenly appeared clear to Sam that the Judge did not want her to testify.

Sam said, "I have discussed this situation with my client, and we both think it best that she testify. We have the burden of proof on the federal immunity defense, and she holds much of the evidence."

The Judge winced. "How are you going to deal with the lack of interstate involvement?" he asked.

"Once you have heard all of the facts and circumstances, the defendant contends that this should not be a problem."

"O.K.," said the Judge, "I'll grant you a hearing. But make it short and sweet. If you simply repeat the evidence in the declarations or affidavits with nothing new, I'll consider holding you in contempt for wasting the court's time. Let's start the hearing in 5 minutes."

Sam went directly back into the courtroom and spoke with Karen. "Listen, I'm putting you on the stand first up. I'm going to ask that you tell your story but I cannot ask leading questions. Judge Crowell is one of those judges that has a fetish about leading examinations. Be sure to cover more than is in your declaration with specifics. The Judge is hung up on a lack of interstate commerce involvement to give the FBI jurisdiction. I think he's wrong and off base but we need to figure on some evidence to fill that gap if we can."

Karen asked, "Do you think the Winston County prosecutor or the Judge will ask me questions about interstate involvement?"

Sam said, "You can bet on it. Why?"

She said, "What I have to say about the subject will be much more effective if they, and not you, ask the questions. I just got some new info."

Just then Judge Crowell came in.

The courtroom deputy announced, "All rise and come to order. The United States District Court for the Northern District of Alabama is now in session. The Honorable Judge Nathan Bedford Crowell presiding. God save this honorable court."

The Judge said, "Be seated. Mr. Stone, call your first witness."

Sam did not have a chance to find out what new information Karen had, and he was concerned, but he trusted her instincts.

On the way to the stand she saw Sam's concerned look and whispered, "Trust me."

Karen was sworn in and Sam conducted a 30-minute examination, which brought out the phone call she received, her daughter's leaving of the Cahaba Heights Rehab clinic, the phone call to her supervisor, her arrival in Addison, and her encounter with the sheriff.

When Sam took a long pause to look at his notes, Judge Crowell impatiently interjected, "I have not heard a word about interstate commerce and the FBI's jurisdiction. Now please Mr. Stone, fish or cut bait."

Sam looked at Karen, and asked, "Can you answer the Judge's concerns Ms. Kemper?"

She looked directly at the judge and said, "The phone call I first received warned me to stay away from cases like Troy Pickering's and then told me that my daughter was in an abandoned Gulf station on Highway 278 just east of Addison."

"We know all of that," said the Judge impatiently.

Karen continued with her testimony. "This morning my office received a final report that a satellite cell phone belonging to one of Troy Pickering's businesses was found near the body of James Stokes of Cullman, who was murdered in his truck in New Orleans two weeks ago. The phone had been turned on the entire day of Thursday, June 5, the date in question. An examination of the phone records has shown that at about noon the phone's location was within 100 yards, plus or minus, of the Gulf station in Addison, Alabama. I have the reports in my file here today."

"That's not conclusive of anything," said the Judge.

"The satellite cell phone shows an interstate commerce connection," said Karen.

The judge paused to think and said, "What else?"

Karen responded, "We also found Stokes' fingerprints in the filling station on a discarded cigarette pack and on a Bud Light bottle. We plan to subpoena Troy Pickering to this hearing, along with another man whose print turned up on the satellite cell phone."

"And who would that be?" asked Judge Crowell with an air of arrogance.

Karen said, "A clear right thumb print on the phone, according to U.S. Army records, belongs to a man named Jefferson Duval."

Sam asked, "Jefferson Duval? Was he ever stationed in the Panama Canal Zone and did he have a banjo tattooed on his knee?"

Judge Crowell suddenly went into a coughing fit and declared a recess.

In about 15 minutes, the Judge's law clerk, Nancy Hankins, came into the courtroom. She said that the Judge was not feeling well. He had asked her to inform all the parties that he had reconsidered the defendant's motion to dismiss the criminal charges on the basis of her federal immunity defense, and that he intended to grant the motion. An order to that effect would be forthcoming.

Karen hugged Sam and said, "Thanks. I don't know what happened, but I would bet that there is a connection between Judge Crowell, Pickering, and Duval. The old military photo of Duval we pulled looked a little like a stranger that I saw the Judge with in the bar of the Point Clear Hotel recently. I'm going to dig around some."

Sam scratched his head and wondered what he was missing. The Judge certainly changed his attitude in a hurry. Oh well, he was not going to look this gift horse in the mouth. Getting the criminal charges dismissed was a huge win.

It made his final divorce from Linda 2 weeks ago a little less painful for Sam. Linda had managed to saddle him with most of the debts of the marriage, but he had kept her out of any of his retirement funds. She was still bitter. Sam wanted just to get on with life.

Judge Crowell had a meeting with Duval and Pickering later that day at a truck stop on I-20 between Birmingham and Anniston. He told them that he had saved their asses from being subpoenaed by the feds by dismissing the criminal case against agent Kemper. Duval said that was a disappointment, but that there was still the civil case. He suggested that the Judge not dismiss it so readily. Judge Crowell reluctantly said he would see what he could do.

Chapter 32

Birmingham, Alabama
Sam Stone's Apartment on Southside
Tuesday, July 22, 2003
5:30 p.m.

Sam said, "For today's lessons we will start out with some left hand musical tricks of the trade that give variety to the songs you play. First, the harmonic chimes, then vamping the strings with full chords, followed by sliding, hammering on, and finally, pulling off."

Sam laid his index finger lightly across the strings at the 12th fret and plucked his banjo with the thumb and two picking fingers of his right hand. A soft chiming sound was produced.

Steven asked, "What's that called again?"

Sam replied, "Chimes or harmonic chimes. Try it."

Steven did, and got good resulting chimes on the first try.

Sam nodded, "Good going. You can get chimes at the 5th, 7th, 12th and 19th frets and on past the 19th fret on the strings over the banjo head if you want."

Sam wrote this information down for Steven.

"Next, let's look at vamping the strings. This technique is useful for playing back-up with other musicians when you allow others to take the melody leads. You must use a full chord pattern, so let me digress about those first. There are three ways to play a full chord on the 5-string banjo. You know the first one already, it's the bar chord we did in the beginning."

Steven played open G and then a C chord using his index finger across all of the four strings at the 5th fret. "You mean like this?" he asked.

"That's it," said Sam. "Now use all 4 of your left hand fingers like this. I call it the F chord position because it is the first full chord on the neck that is after the nut in which all four fingers must be used."

Sam demonstrated and then had Steven try it. Sam said, "I'll write it down also."

He wrote:

F Major Chord
(3rd string index finger (1) at 2nd fret; 2nd string middle finger (2) at 1st fret; 4th string ring finger (3) at 3rd fret; 1st string little finger (4) at 3rd fret)

```
5th   4th   3rd   2nd   1st
G     D     G     B     D
_____
 |     |     |     |
 |     |    (1)    |
 |_____|_____|_____|  1st fret
```

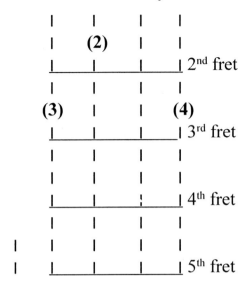

"Now try what I call the D major chord position." Sam showed Steven and again had him try it. "Again, you must use all four fingers of the left hand. I'll write it."

Sam wrote:

D Major Chord
(3rd string index finger (1) at 2nd fret; 2nd string middle finger (2) at 3rd fret; 4th string ring finger (3) at 4th fret; 1st string little finger (4) at 4th fret)

5th	4th	3rd	2nd	1st
G	**D**	**G**	**B**	**D**

```
 |       |     (2)     |
 |_____|_____|_____|  3rd fret
 |       |      |       |
(3)      |      |      (4)
 |_____|_____|_____|  4th fret
 |       |      |       |
 |   |   |      |       |
 |   |___|_____|_____|  5th fret
```

"Now, you should have figured out that there are three ways to play each major chord between the nut and the 12th fret. After that, the chords repeat until you run out of frets."

"So what's this got to do with vamping?" asked Steven.

"Well, hold the strings about half way down to the frets in any major chord position, and pick or brush the strings with the right hand. It gives out a vamping or damping sound like pressing on the petals of a piano. Like I said, it's great for back-up when playing with other musicians."

Sam then demonstrated a simple slide on the first string which started at the 2nd fret and ended at the 5th fret, followed by hammering on and pulling off at the third string second fret.

After each demonstration, Sam had Steven perform the same techniques.

Holmes suddenly came into the room and went to the door looking anxious.

Sam said, "Let's take a short break. Looks like my dog has heard the call of nature."

Steven said, "Mind if I come along? I'd like to stretch my legs."

As soon as Sam opened the door, Holmes dashed off to his favorite tree.

Chapter 33

Birmingham, Alabama
Sam Stone's Apartment on Southside
Tuesday, July 22, 2003
6:00 p.m.

Sam and Steven started following Holmes down the street, and Sam asked, "What have you been studying lately, anything interesting?"

Steven replied, "I've been looking at the works some of the most influential philosophers and mathematicians. Sir Isaac Newton in 1687 published his famous *Philosophiae Naturalis Principia Mathematica*, setting out the fundamental laws of motion and gravitational theory. He also discovered the secrets of light and color and invented calculus. Newton is usually regarded as the most influential scientist in history. As brilliant as he was, however, he was obsessed with alchemy, theology and Biblical chronology."

"So what are you saying about him?" asked Sam.

"No one has science figured out, and sometimes it's hard to tell the kooks from real contributors. There are a lot of people that believe a new big break is about to occur, but some theories and researchers are hard to follow."

Sam inquired, "Do you mean another discovery equivalent to Einstein's theory of relativity?"

"Yes. That's exactly what I'm talking about. It may have already occurred, and we don't know about it."

"What do you mean?" asked Sam.

Steven replied, "Except for a very few people, little was understood about Einstein's theory of special relativity, which he published in 1905, and later his general theory, until Sir Arthur Eddington lectured and published fundamental explanations in the mid-1920's. Einstein commented that Eddington's work was the finest explanation of his theories in any language, but if the average person were to pick up Eddington's publication, they would not understand much. It's mostly a book of complex geometrical and mathematical writings. It took a young Bertrand Russell, in 1925, writing an 'ABC' book about the subject to provide a non-mathematical explanation that the world could understand. Some things are hard to explain, even in plain English, and they take a while to sink in."

Sam said, "I guess you are right. After all, people are still fighting about teaching Darwin's theory of evolution in some parts of this country."

Steven laughed and said, "That's why I want to study at Cambridge. I figure that news of any great scientific, philosophic, and mathematical discoveries will likely surface there, and I would like to be close around when it happens."

"Sounds like a reasonable plan," said Sam.

Steven continued. "Some have recently theorized that the speed of light may vary, which would call into question a basic part of Einstein's general theory of relativity. Fundamental research is being done with particle accelerators and time microscopes. NASA in Huntsville has created a device that is being launched into space to test Einstein's general theory. That kind of research and the debate that goes on about cosmology are exciting to me."

Sam looked around and whistled for Holmes to turn around and head back to the apartment. Holmes obeyed as was his usual and ran back all the way.

Sam turned to Steven and asked, "What do you think about all the scientific conspiracy theories associated with the likes of Leonardo da Vinci and others that have surfaced in popular novels in print of late?"

"Not much," said Steven. "You could take the same approach and create the belief that the ancient Egyptian's use of square and compasses held the secrets of Einstein's theories because circles, triangles, and geometry are used to explain and illustrate his special and general theories by most writers and lecturers."

They entered Sam's apartment and picked up their respective banjos.

"Back to banjoing, and simpler things," said Sam. "For this lesson I want you to start trying additional bluegrass rolls. I'll write them down. Try not to play tunes until you can do these smoothly. If you want to do some songs, or try to perform, use some of the other styles that I have taught. I really believe that you will be a better bluegrass player if you don't try to play too many songs until you have mastered smooth roll techniques. Trust me on this."

Steven said, "O.K., but I want to play some songs as soon as I can."

Sam said, "I understand that, but let's go through this my way for now. The first roll I showed you was a forward roll that looked like this.

Sam wrote:

5th	4th	3rd	2nd	1st
G	D	G	B	D
|	|	*I*	|	|
|	|	|	|	*M*
T	|	|	|	|
|	|	*I*	|	|
|	|	|	|	*M*
T	|	|	|	|
|	|	*I*	|	|
|	|	|	|	*M*
/	/	*I*	|	|
|	|	|	|	*M*
T	|	|	|	|
|	|	*I*	|	|
|	|	|	|	*M*
T	|	|	|	|
|	|	*I*	|	|
|	|	|	|	*M*

Sam had Steven give it a try while he looked on and made corrections. Sam make Steven repeat the roll several times.

Sam then said, "Now the next roll is another forward roll."

He demonstrated it slowly and had Steven perform the technique.

Sam said, "It looks like this."

He wrote:

5th	4th	3rd	2nd	1st
G	**D**	**G**	**B**	**D**
|	|	*T*	|	|
|	|	|	*I*	|
|	|	|	|	*M*
T	|	|	|	|
|	|	|	*I*	|
|	|	|	|	*M*
|	|	*T*	|	|
|	|	|	*I*	|
|	|	*T*	|	|
|	|	|	*I*	|
|	|	|	|	*M*
T	|	|	|	|
|	|	|	*I*	|
|	|	|	|	*M*
|	|	*T*	|	|
|	|	|	*I*	|

"The next roll is what I call a modified forward roll," said Sam.

He again demonstrated it to Steven and had him perform the exercise several times.

Sam said, "Again, I'll write it for you."

Sam wrote:

5th	4th	3rd	2nd	1st
G	**D**	**G**	**B**	**D**
		T		
			I	
				M
T				
				M
			I	
		T		
				M
		T		
			I	
				M
T				
				M
			I	
		T		
				M

Sam showed Steven the next roll, which he called a "backward roll."

He played the roll and then had Steven do the same, with several repetitions.

Sam wrote:

5th	4th	3rd	2nd	1st
G	**D**	**G**	**B**	**D**
				M
			I	
T				
				M

			I	
T				
				M
			I	
				M
			I	
T				
				M
			I	
T				
				M
			I	

Finally, Sam showed Steven what he called a "mixed roll." Sam played the roll and then had Steven do the same.

He wrote:

5th	4th	3rd	2nd	1st
G	**D**	**G**	**B**	**D**
				M
			I	
				M
T				
				M
			I	
				M
T				
				M
			I	
				M
T				

```
 |      |      |      |     M
 |      |      |      I     |
 |      |      |      |     M
 T      |      |      |     |
```

Sam said, "That's a good bit of learning for today. I think we'll leave it there until next time. Some banjo pickers say that you should try to use the thumb as much as possible to pick out the melody lines. It makes for a stronger sounding melody. I tend to agree. Think about it as you practice all of these rolls. You can also practice the rolls without your banjo. Simply try to do them on your desktop, thigh or belly at odd moments during the day."

Steven asked, "When do I get into some songs?"

"Once you have mastered the rolls, I will teach you individual songs, but not until then, except for 'Boil Them Cabbages Down.' Remember, it's the training of the right hand finger muscles and smooth coordination that is the most important to develop first if you want to play good bluegrass."

"I know," said Steven.

"If you show good progress, I'll begin teaching you 'Cripple Creek' and a few other songs next time. How's that?" asked Sam.

"Sounds great. Thanks. When's our next set of lessons?"

Sam replied, "Well. I'm planning a much needed vacation to California's Napa Valley starting the end of this week. Then, I return and I have to go to the base at Redstone Arsenal outside Huntsville for a few days. So, just to be safe, let's say in the middle of the first week in August. You have plenty to work on."

"Yeah, and maybe by then I'll have heard about the Gates Scholarship and Cambridge."

Chapter 34

Napa Valley, California
Restaurant
Friday, July 25, 2003
4:30 p.m.

Sam cashed in his frequent flyer miles as planned and flew
into San Francisco on Wednesday. He spent the night at
a small hotel near Fisherman's Warf. The next morning
early, Sam rented a car and drove up through the Sonoma
Valley into the heart of the California wine region. His
plan was to tour Sonoma's sights and then head east to the
Napa Valley, which ran a north and south parallel. This
was just the kind of out-of-Alabama experience he needed
to try and gain some perspective and put some order back
into his life.

Sam toured the Glen Ellen vineyards in the late
morning, and in the afternoon, took a trip to the Jack
London State Historic Park. He had never been a particular
Jack London fan, but he had read *The Sea Wolf* (1904) in

college, and Sam had seen movies made of *The Call of the Wild* (1903).

At the visitor center and park, however, Sam became fascinated with London's life. London was born out of wedlock in San Francisco in 1876, and raised by an ex-slave because his mother remained ill. A man named John London married Jack's mother in 1876, and the family later moved to Oakland where Jack grew up hard and tough as a laborer in the mills and canneries. The Oakland Free Library and others encouraged him to read, while he worked various jobs and sometimes raided oyster beds in the Bay.

At the age of 16 he managed to purchase a sailing sloop, the *Razzel Dazzle,* and he began a life of serious drinking and hanging out in waterfront bars. He also became known for his street orations, and he ran unsuccessfully for mayor several times on the socialist ticket. Jack London was called the "Boy Socialist of Oakland."

London's socialist views were formed at an early age, probably as a result of the hard work experiences in his youth. Later, his restless and sometimes reckless spirit caused him to join a sealing expedition to Siberia, to set out for the gold rush to the Klondike in Alaska in 1897, and to become a war correspondent during the Russo-Japanese War in 1904.

Sam was struck by the fact that London was America's first popular and financially successful working class writer. He was also struck by the fact that he had married twice.

First, in 1900, he married his math tutor, Bess Maddern, who he apparently did not love, but with whom he had two daughters. In 1905, London married Charmian

Kittredge, his secretary, whom he did love. London referred to her as his "Mate Woman." They had only one child, a female that lived only a day and a half.

This later fact made Sam think briefly about Jonesy. He wondered what had become of her.

In 1905, London decided to purchase what he named the Beauty Ranch. He had a 15,000 square foot mansion called the Wolf House built on a mountainside. Just before it was finished in 1913, it accidentally burned to the ground. London was broken hearted, and he never rebuilt. He died at the ranch at the young age of 40 from uremic poisoning in 1916.

Sam walked the trail of a little over a mile to the Wolf House ruins and stopped by the London's grave on a small hill not far away. Sam resolved to put the past behind him, and seek some adventures of his own, but not at the reckless pace of a Jack London.

He drove from the Sonoma Valley over Mount Veeder into the Napa Valley and checked into a bed and breakfast on the outskirts of Napa. The next day, Friday, he got up at 8:00, ate a big breakfast and toured the wineries of Robert Mondavi, Opus One, and Silver Oak.

Sam wound up in the early afternoon at the Robert Louis Stevenson Silverado Museum in the small town of St. Helena, 12 miles to the north of Napa. He was amazed that the famous author, in 1880, had honeymooned in a small cabin on the slopes of Mount St. Helena.

He asked the museum attendant advice on a place to eat supper, and she recommended a small family owned restaurant that catered to the locals 3 miles to the south that was on his way back to Napa.

The restaurant wasn't crowded. The waitress, after taking his order of a filet of beef with polenta and porcini mushrooms, a grilled artichoke, a fresh salad, and a glass of local red wine, commented, "You must be from the South. I detect a certain accent."

Sam said, "Yes. I'm from Alabama. I bet you don't get too many visitors in your restaurant from there."

To his surprise, she said, "As a matter of fact we do. There is a group of Alabama men that have some interest in the Southern Accent Winery, which is down the road a mile or so and off the highway about another mile."

"How do you know they are from Alabama?" asked Sam.

"They have always joked about the lack of barbecued pork on our menu, 'like we have back home in Alabam'," she said in a dramatically faked southern voice. "They could be from some place else, but with their slow drawling speech, I'd say they were from Alabama or close to it."

Sam asked, "Did they give you any names? Alabama is a small place. I might know them."

The waitress rubbed her chin thinking and said, "Maybe… one was named Stovall. No, that's not right. His name was Duval. That's it."

Sam thought to himself. It can't be the same Duval, or could it? He decided to tell Karen about this strange coincidence of names and see what she thought. He pulled out his cell phone and called her but he got no response. He left a brief message that he would talk to her next week. Out of habit, he checked the phone messages on his office recorder back in Birmingham. The only message of real interest was from Uncle John.

Sam decided to call him. He dialed his number, and Uncle John answered on the third ring.

Sam said, "Uncle John. This is your nephew Sam. Did you try to call me at the office?"

"Where are you?" asked Uncle John.

"I'm out in Napa Valley, California, and just sitting down to supper."

"I had supper hours ago and it sure was good. Bet what I had was better that what they're serving you in California."

"Beef, polenta, and artichoke are what I'm about to have," said Sam.

"Groundhog, homegrown beefsteak tomato slices, and grits are what I had."

"You're kidding me," said Sam. "How did you cook the groundhog? In the grits?"

Uncle John laughed and said, "No. The groundhog was grilled. It was really old-fashioned pork sausage made locally. You know, ground hog. Ground-up pork, get it?"

Sam started laughing too.

Uncle John said, "Now the large stone ground grits from a mill in Tennessee took a half hour to cook, but they were better than any polenta dish you'll ever find in California."

"You're probably right. Uncle John did you need something?" asked Sam.

"I just completed the Stone family history and wanted you to have a copy of it. I ought to warn you that some of the old photos of your ancestors tend to prove Darwin's theory. When are you coming for a visit? I hope you've unloaded that witch of a wife by now and are not tied down."

"I am divorced finally. And as soon as I get back I have to go up to the Army base at Redstone Arsenal to begin filing civil penalty cases against shoplifters. After that, I'll call and come by on my way back to Birmingham."

Uncle John said, "Civil penalties against shoplifters? That seems a waste of your time and talents. You better look into the legality of that."

"What do you mean?" asked Sam.

Uncle John replied, "I had a friend in the sheriff's department down in Calhoun County some years ago near Ft. McClelland, and he said there was some jurisdictional glitch about enforcing Alabama's civil laws on base. Seems like I recall that in the Navy we had similar problems at the Charleston Navy Shipyards in South Carolina when I was stationed there."

Sam said, "Thanks, Uncle John. I'll check on that. Here comes my supper. I'll see you soon after I get back in a week or so. Have a good night."

"Hey, don't forget the vitamin V. It's supposed to make your sticker peck out, even at my age."

Sam said, "Goodnight, Uncle John." He clicked off the phone.

Sam had to hand it to Uncle John. He still had an active mind and zest for life. Sam hoped he himself would be that spry if he managed to live that long.

For desert the waitress talked Sam into having Bananas Jack, a dish named after the current cook, who claimed to have invented it. Bananas were peeled and placed in a shallow baking dish, and each was sprinkled with cinnamon sugar. Over the top was poured a mixture of equal parts honey and Madeira (or tawny port). This was baked for about 20 minutes until piping hot. The bananas and liquid mixture was finally placed in a serving bowl with a heaping tablespoon of sour cream. The dishes, especially the desert, were exceptional, and Sam started to relax for the first time in a long while.

On the drive back to the bed and breakfast in Napa, Sam wondered if Jonesy would have liked to have been called his "Mate Woman." He laughed to himself. No doubt she would have had strong opinions about the subject with some choice, and no doubt, descriptive language.

Chapter 35

Birmingham, Alabama
Sam Stone's Apartment on Southside
Wednesday, August 6, 2003
5:30 p.m.

Steven asked, "Don't you think I should buy a better banjo? This one is old and beat up. I keep having to adjust the bridge and the tailpiece. I'd like a fancy one."

"Look. The neck is true and the fret board is in good shape and not warped. The pegs don't slip too much yet, so that you have to constantly retune. It's not fancy, but it looks O.K. and plays well for your needs. Someday when you have more money than sense, you can be picked up in a Lear jet and flown to Nashville, where for a mere thirty to forty thousand dollars, you can have a custom built banjo presented to you in a special ceremony."

"Do fancy banjos really cost that much?"

"You bet. The prices have gone through the roof at the high end. Right now though, you can buy a really fine instrument for two to three thousand dollars. Low-end beginner banjos can be had for as little as $100. A little judgment is called for."

"Mine just doesn't sound right; certainly not like yours," said Steven.

"Give me your banjo for a minute." Sam picked "Cripple Creek" first in a bluegrass style, and then stopped and switched to "Darlin' Cory" in a folk stroke style. Sam handed the banjo back to Steven.

"See, it's the music and the player that counts, not the instrument or how fancy the inlays are. Now let's try some of those bluegrass rolls that I showed you last time. We're not looking for speed, but for smooth and evenly spaced notes; speed can be developed later."

Steven properly demonstrated all of the bluegrass rolls that Sam had shown him before taking his trip to California.

When Steven finished, Sam said, "That's really good. Now we'll start on some tunes. I want you to watch me closely as I play, and then we'll go back through each song so that you can find the fingerings up and down the fret board. We'll start with an exercise that I made up some 15 years ago from parts of songs that are good for warming up. It has several different songs and tunes built in. I pass it on to you for what it's worth."

Sam continued, "As I've said before, warming up is really important in banjo playing. I try never to pick up the instrument unless I have at least 30 minutes minimum to play. An hour is better. I think that practice for only say 5 minutes hurts your skills. After 10 or 15 minutes of this exercise, I'm warmed up and ready to play other styles and songs."

Sam tuned his banjo and adjusted his finger picks. "I use the folk stroke for the word parts, and then I pick bluegrass style for the banjo tunes after each chorus in which the tune is named."

Sam sang and picked the tunes for Steven.

When he finished, Sam said, "It looks like this."

Sam wrote:

Banks of the Tennessee

Verse 1:
(G)   (C)   (G)
We farmed corn fields my brother and me
                                        (D7th)
Down on the banks of the Tennessee
(G)   (C)   (G)
Plowed new ground with an old gray plug
                                (D7th) (G)
And sold corn whiskey by the gallon jug.

Chorus:
    (G)   (C)   (G)
    Run down shack and an old ban-jo
                                (D7th)
        "Going Up Cripple Creek" is all I know, if it
    (G)   (C)
    Hadn't of been for my drinking so
        (G)   (D7th)   (G)
        I'd have been a thinking clear long time a-go.

[Do banjo break of "Cripple Creek"]

Verse 2:

I lost the farm and my mon-ey

    Down on the banks of the Tennessee

I never took any good advice

    Lost all I had to cards and dice

Chorus:

    Run down shack and an old banjo

        "Old Joe Clark" is all I know, if it

    Hadn't a been for my gambling so

        I'd have been a rich man a long time ago

[Do banjo break of "Old Joe Clark"]

Verse 3:

The prettiest girl I ever did see

    Lived down on the banks of the Tennessee

Her eyes were blue and her hair was red

    And her lips were sweeter than gingerbread

Chorus:

Run down shack and an old banjo

"Home Sweet Home" is all I know

If it hadn't a been for my rambling so

I'd have been married a long time ago

[Do banjo break of "Home Sweet Home"]

Verse 4:

[Repeat Verse 1 and others as desired]

Sam had Steven follow him through each fret change for each bluegrass song until Steven had the patterns roughly correct. In no time, Steven was picking the tunes, but with a few mistakes.

Sam commented, "When you make a mistake in picking a tune, try to keep going rather than stopping and starting over. Some beginning pickers make the mistake of always starting over and they never seem to be able to play a complete tune. It also makes its difficult to play with others if one is always stopping and starting over."

"What should I do if I can't remember the chord progressions or how a tune is played?" asked Steven.

"You can borrow some of my books with banjo tablature or find similar banjo tablature on the Internet."

Steven said, "Sounds good. Show me 'Grandfather's Clock' in bluegrass style."

Sam did, and in no time Steven was picking it up.

The phone rang, and Sam picked it up. "Hello Karen. Yes, he's right here."

Sam turned to Steven and said, "It's your mom."

Steven took the phone and asked, "Is everything all right? What? That's terrific. I'll go see Professor Redmond right now. Bye. I love you mom."

A grinning Steven turned to Sam and said, "I got the Gates Scholarship to Cambridge. Can you believe it? Professor Redmond wants to see me as soon as I can get over to his office. He's called a news conference for 10:00 a.m. tomorrow morning to make the official local announcement. He wants to see me for about 30 minutes to prepare me for the news event."

"How about I drive you over to the college? I'd like to congratulate the Professor on having trained such an outstanding student."

They got into Sam's Ford F-150 and headed down toward the college. Sam put a Bill Monroe CD into slot and turned up the sound.

Sam said, "I guess I owe you a trip to Nashville and the Grand Ole Opry."

Steven just smiled and nodded.

The light was red at the corner of Richard Arrington, Jr. Boulevard and University Avenue. Coming down the steep hill, Sam saw the red light and hit the brakes. The brakes failed completely, and Sam's pickup truck was T-boned by an Alabama Power Company truck on the passenger's side.

It was later determined that there were punctures in the brake fluid lines of Sam's pickup. Someone had wanted harm to come to him.

The good news was that the UAB hospital emergency room was only a block or so away. Sam was badly bruised and had several cracked ribs, but he was otherwise O.K.

The bad news was that Steven's condition was far worse. He sustained a broken right leg and two severely detached retinas. Steven was blind.

Chapter 36

Birmingham, Alabama
U.S. District Court
Monday, August 25, 2003
2:00 p.m.

Sam blamed himself for Steven's broken leg and blindness despite the clear evidence that someone had tampered with his brakes. First a snake and now the brakes. Who was that damn mean, and who disliked him that much? At least the snake had hurt no one.

Karen was not happy with Sam either. She was strictly business in her relations with him. Karen was facing FBI retirement in two months with a drug dependent daughter and a disabled son. Her world was not working out the way she had planned. She tried hard not to blame Sam for Steven's condition, but too many "what ifs" automatically surfaced every time she thought about the truck accident. Karen considered having Sam sued for negligence but Steven said he did not want that. She was bearing up but it was plain difficult for her to be around Sam.

The Gates Foundation was notified of Steven's medical change of status. Because of the Foundation's strong non-discrimination policies concerning the disabled, Steven was given a year to recuperate, rehabilitate, and make arraignments to accept the scholarship if he wanted to and was able. After one year, the scholarship would be cancelled and given to someone else if Steven did not use it. There was an initial outpouring of help in the Birmingham community for Steven, led by Professor Redmond.

Sam did not get to speak directly with Steven for several weeks after the wreck. In the meantime, he did find out through the Professor that Steven wanted to figure out a way to accept the scholarship within the year that had been given to him. There were many things to consider and a great deal of rehabilitation and learning that would have to be done.

On August 5, Sam filed a motion for summary judgment instead of an answer in Karen's remaining civil case asking for a full dismissal. The original motion to substitute the United States as the defendant on the common law assault claim had not been ruled upon by Judge Crowell. This worried Sam somewhat, so he also addressed those issues again in his brief to the court.

Sam did not know why the Judge was holding onto the motion to substitute. The Plaintiff had not filed a motion to remand. So it looked like the case would stay in federal court.

Sam was aware of the fact that a federal court, at any time, on its own motion could dismiss a case if it thought that there was no subject matter jurisdiction. This was true whether not the parties consented to federal jurisdiction. Even federal appellate courts sometimes dismissed cases on this basis despite the wishes of all the parties to stay in federal court.

Federal courts were said to be courts of limited jurisdiction, as opposed to the typical state trial courts, which were said to be courts of general jurisdiction.

In defense of the *Bivens* claim, Sam raised qualified immunity. His motion for summary judgment claimed that agent Kemper was at all times acting within the scope of her duties as an FBI agent in her encounters with the sheriff in Winston County.

On August 6, the court issued a scheduling order indicating that any opposition by the plaintiff should be filed by August 18, and any reply by the defense was due on or before August 21. A hearing on the motion and all pending issues was set for Monday, August 25, at 2:00 p.m.

At the hearing the courtroom was somewhat crowded. Linda sat in the back with Jane Skipper. The U.S. District Court had given Linda the appointment as U.S. Attorney the week before, and Linda was showing up and showing off as much as possible.

Joan Benefield and Jerry Klein were also present from the Civil Division. The FBI Special Agent in Charge or SAC for Birmingham was in the audience, along with two other agents. Sam sat at the defense table with Karen and an FBI attorney named Roslyn Furmeister, who had flown in from DC headquarters.

The sheriff of Winston County was present with his attorney, Johnny "Robert E. Lee" Brown. A paralegal and a junior associate joined them.

Just prior to the beginning of the hearing, Brown walked over to Sam and said, "I'm still pissed off at you for filing that motion *in liminie* against me personally about my facial expressions in the Hicks trial before Judge Hilton. You are going to lose today, and I am going to enjoy trying this case against your client. No holds barred."

A year and a half ago Sam had indicted Brown's client, Jerome Hicks, for bank fraud, and because Johnny Brown had developed a reputation to shaking his head, making sour facial expressions, and the like to the jury during his opponent's opening statement and presentations throughout trial, Sam had actually filed a motion limiting this conduct with the court, and Judge Hilton had granted it, much to the embarrassment of Brown. This had put a crimp in his typical courtroom theatrics.

Sam looked Brown in the eye and said, "You'll get to try this case against my client only if the Eleventh Circuit says so first."

Brown turned away sharply and went back to his table as the hearing began.

The Judge's usual courtroom deputy was out sick so the duties of announcing the court open fell to the Judge's newest law clerk, Sally Whipple, who was clearly nervous.

As she put down the phone, Judge Crowell came into the courtroom. Sally announced in an unsure, squeaky voice, "All rise and come to order. The United States District Court for the Northern District of Alabama is now in session. The Honorable Judge Nathan Bedford Crowell presiding. God save us all."

The courtroom erupted with laughter.

Judge Crowell shook his head and sternly said, "Everyone be seated and come to order. Ms. Whipple, please get the court announcement correct in the future.

Write it out and plainly read it if you have to. I'll not tolerate another such mispronouncement."

Sally teared up and had to hold her head down for the rest of the proceedings. A wave of sympathy for her swept through the courtroom. Sam thought to himself that Judge Crowell was demonstrating what a complete and total jerk he was.

The Judge announced the case. He asked if the plaintiff was ready and then asked the defense. Both sides announced "ready."

"Since we are here on the defendant's motion, the court will hear from Mr. Stone first. What says the defense?" asked Judge Crowell in an icy tone.

Sam went to the lectern and said, "It looks like the plaintiff does not oppose the defendant's motion to substitute the United States on the common law claims of assault, and therefore, unless there is any opposition, I would ask that it be done and that the plaintiff proceed on that claim in accordance with the administrative requirements of the Federal Tort Claims Act."

At this point, Johnny Brown stood and said, "Plaintiff consents to the substitution of the United States and will voluntarily dismiss that particular claim without prejudice while we file an administrative claim with the FBI. I understand that upon denial or after 6 months plaintiff can file suit and have a bench trial."

Judge Crowell looked disappointed, but said, "Very well. So ordered."

Sam then said, "The remaining major issue is the defendant's qualified immunity to the *Bivens* claim."

The Judge interrupted Sam, "Mr. Stone, do you have any other facts or evidence other than what you have presented in your motion for summary judgment and reply?"

Sam had a bad feeling about what was about to happen. He said, "No, Judge. I don't."

The Judge leaned back in his high backed chair and said, "I have reviewed all of the facts presented and the entire file. Your arguments concerning Ms. Kemper's qualified immunity defense are almost frivolous in the court's view. You, Mr. Stone, are guilty of intentionally misleading the court in your moving papers or else you are guilty of abysmal legal ignorance."

The harsh words stung Sam, but he did not flinch.

The Judge paused and then continued, "Defendant's motion for summary judgment based on qualified immunity is denied. There are genuine issues of material fact in dispute and the defendant is not entitled to judgment as a matter of law within the meaning of Rule 56 of the Federal Rules of Civil Procedure. I already have an order prepared to that effect. Do you have anything else Mr. Stone?"

Sam had plenty, but he held his tongue. Obviously, Judge Crowell was baiting him, and hoping that Sam would say or do something that would allow the court to sanction him.

"No, your honor. The defense has nothing further for now." Sam turned away from the lectern and was about to step away when he realized that the Judge was still glaring at him and that he had not been formally excused. Some judges would sanction a lawyer for failing to ask to be excused. Sam realized that he was about to step into that very trap.

Sam quickly turned and faced the Judge, asking, "May the defense be excused?"

Judge Crowell reluctantly said, "Yes. These proceeding are over for now." He banged his gavel.

Sally Whipple weakly said, "All rise."

The Judge got up and quickly left the bench.

The noise level in the courtroom picked up dramatically.

Linda came over to Sam and said sarcastically, "Another poor performance."

Jane Skipper kept quiet.

Karen asked Sam, "What happens now?"

Sam replied, "I've prepared a Notice of Appeal to the Eleventh Circuit which will be filed late this afternoon or first thing in the morning."

Chapter 37

Birmingham, Alabama
U.S. Attorney's Office
Thursday, September 18, 2003
1:30 p.m.

Linda Lott dropped in on the Civil Division meeting. It was held at least once a month to discuss cases, office policies, and other topics of common interest.

After the support staff had left, and only the attorneys remained, Linda tuned to Sam and asked in front of all the other Assistant U.S. Attorneys, "Can you give me an update on the civil penalty program that was assigned to you some time ago? I have detected little or no progress. Do you have any excuses? Please enlighten all of us lawyer Stone."

The increased tension in the room was noticeable. Everyone seemed to be looking for cover. Even Jane Skipper shifted around uncomfortably in her chair.

Sam looked at Linda and asked, "Have you ever heard of federal enclave jurisdiction?"

Linda replied, "Of course I have. We try crimes committed on military bases all the time under the Assimilative Crimes Act."

"That's not what I am talking about. I mean federal enclave jurisdiction for civil matters on base. Have you come across that issue before?"

"No," said Linda emphatically, as she turned red with anger or embarrassment. "What in the hell are you talking about?"

Sam smiled and replied, "Let's take Redstone Arsenal as our best example. Between 1942 and 1943 the U.S. government acquired approximately 44,000 acres in Madison County, Alabama, next to Huntsville, by purchase and condemnation in order to establish Redstone Arsenal military base."

"So what?" asked Linda.

"Be patient. I'm getting to it." Sam looked at some notes and continued. "On November 2, 1942, and April 9, 1943, the State of Alabama issues two patents which ceded exclusive criminal *and civil* jurisdiction over these lands to the United States."

Sam used special emphasis on the words "and civil."

Everyone in the room watched quietly.

"Under the *McGlinn* doctrine, which was established in 1885 by the U.S. Supreme Court in the case of *Chicago, Rock Island & Pacific Railway Company v. McGlinn*, the civil law of the state existing at the time of land acquisition by the Federal government applies on base until it is superceded by federal law."

Linda was quiet.

Sam continued. "The State of Alabama has had no authority to pass civil legislation that applies on Redstone Arsenal after the dates of cession of exclusive jurisdiction. The civil laws of Alabama in existence in the early 1940's are frozen in time on base. The civil penalty statute that you asked me to enforce was passed by the Alabama legislature in 1993. It has no application on Redstone."

Sam paused for effect. The room was dead quiet.

He continued. "If I took action against someone based on that statute I would get hit with a *Bivens* suit for taking or attempting to take someone's property in violation of known statutory and/or constitutional rights."

"This can't be right," said Linda. "We get sued under the Federal Tort Claims Act and use state law all the time for acts and omissions on base."

"Yes," said Sam. "But the FTCA has a special provision that directs the U.S. to use local state law in FTCA cases. That law does not apply to thefts of property at the base exchanges. I have a legal memorandum on the entire subject that I plan to give to you and the civil chief in the next 5 days. The enforcement of a civil penalty program by me would have been a total disaster."

Linda got up out of her chair and left the conference room without another word.

Jane turned to Sam and asked, "Where did you find out about the *McGlinn* doctrine? I've never heard of it."

"My Uncle John, who is retired from the U.S. Navy and local law enforcement, tipped me off. I called at few JAG offices around the state and I finally located an enclave research file that someone had put together in the 1960's. It covers every base in Alabama. I just got a copy, and I'm using it for my memo."

Jane said, "Make sure we keep a copy for our central files."

Sam did not tell the Civil Chief that he had found out that Linda should have known about the issue, because in 1993, her father's contracting company had been sued by a power company under a 1988 utility service penalty statute for theft of power from a power company's generators on a base. The suit had been dropped due to the *McGlinn* doctrine. Sam had tracked down Uncle John's friend in Anniston who knew about the whole story and then some.

Sam believed that Linda had knowingly set him up for a fall by giving him this assignment. Fortunately, Sam had discovered the jurisdictional flaw before filing suits against any shoplifters.

He intended some payback for Linda. Sam knew that if he stayed patient and kept a close watch on her, he would get a chance to strike back. Her conduct toward him had been unprofessional and unpardonable. Sam needed to wait until the right time and place.

In the meanwhile, he had other worries. He called Karen at home.

"It's Sam. How are you doing?" he asked.

"I've officially retired from the FBI and I'm looking for contract work. I need money for Lauren and Steven. His first eye surgeries went so, so. They've tried to reattach his retinas with microsurgery. Steven can see light in his left eye now, and his right one may take another surgery. The surgeries and healing processes are slow. It's heartbreaking, and the medical expenses are mounting. Local charities have helped, but there is always some new expense."

"I'll try and get some investigator work sent your way," said Sam. "The briefs in your civil appeal to the 11th Circuit will be filed in the next two weeks. Hopefully, we can get a favorable decision in the next few months."

"That's the least of my worries these days," said Karen. "Steven needs a lot of help. He tries to do things but becomes frustrated."

"Should I try to talk to him?" asked Sam.

"No. Not now. Steven has to work out some things for himself. He'll let you know personally if he wants to talk. Professor Redmond stays in as close a contact as anyone. He's helped a good bit."

"Take care then," said Sam. "Bye."

They both hung up.

Sam wondered if Steven still made any effort to play the banjo.

Chapter 38

New York, New York
The Algonquin Hotel
Tuesday, September 30, 2003
8:00 p.m.

Linda Lott liked to stay at the Algonquin Hotel on West 44th Street when she visited New York City. The Algonquin was the most famous literary hotel in the United States. H. L. Menchen considered it one of his favorite places. Dorothy Parker, Robert Sherwood, Edna Ferber, George S. Kaufman, Robert Benchley, and others met regularly in the Rose Room at what became known as the "Algonquin Round Table" in the 1920's. Famous guests at the Algonquin have included Eudora Welty, Gertrude Stein, Helen Hayes, and William Faulkner, who wrote his acceptance speech for the Noble Prize in literature there in 1950.

Linda did not care about its literary history. She liked the hotel because it was near Times Square, the Theater District, and was reasonable in price by New York standards. Her father had indicated that he needed to see a business associate in New York and that her presence would be helpful to him. They flew up from Alabama together, and she had talked him into staying at the Algonquin.

Her father had arranged a meeting in the Blue Bar of the hotel. Linda preferred the Lobby, where sometimes you could catch a glimpse of the rich and famous as they came in or out, but that was too open for her father. He would not tell her exactly what the problem was, rather that it had to do with an old contracting associate.

The meeting was set for 8:00 p.m., and just as they entered the bar, a balding man in his mid-50's raised his hand and motioned them over to his table.

He said, "Hello, Mr. Lott, I'm Tom Wassel. Please, you and your daughter, join me for a drink. I've been expecting you."

Linda and her father sat down.

"Mr. Lott. You are behind on some payments, and you need to catch them up as soon as possible. I don't want to refer your promissory notes for collection, but I will if I have to. So what can you pay?"

Linda's father said, "I'm strapped and I won't have any significant money for three months. That's when I finish the current construction contract at the Anniston Army Depot."

"Look. My group helped you get that contract through our political influence. We want the payments you promised. We don't care where you get the money. That's your problem."

Linda interjected. "What's going on? I don't like the sound of your threats."

Her father said, "It's O.K. With a little help from you, this can be worked out. Right, Mr. Wassel?"

"What in the hell does that mean?"

Wassel said, "Do you want me to explain this to her?"

Linda's father nodded.

"Mr. Lott owes my group a ton of money. We are prepared to defer payment for 6 months, but we would like a favor or so from the U.S. Attorney's Office."

Linda said, "Just a damn minute. You better be careful. I'll have you indicted."

Wassel said, "I don't think so. Not unless you want to see your father and mother spend the rest of their natural lives in jail. So listen up. This is not so bad. We just want you to squeeze your husband's balls a little bit as his boss. That's all we are asking. It's a small favor over a small issue that really should not affect your official position on any pending cases. We just don't want him thinking too much about some of his old encounters. I understand that you don't like the son of a bitch anymore anyhow."

Linda said, "He's no longer my husband. We got divorced at the end of June. What have you got going on that involves him?"

"That's not important. Can you reassign his duties to make his job harder and him busier or not?" asked Wassel.

Linda was puzzled. She had been considering doing something else to Sam anyhow, given the fact that the civil penalty for shoplifters plan had fallen through.

She scratched her right side and said, "I could give him bankruptcy and collections. He'd be in court and on the road just about every day, and he would not have time to think about any of his 'encounters' as you call them."

"Good," said Wassel. "That sounds perfect. Now would you also like our help with some politicians that could get you that Presidential appointment as U.S. Attorney?"

Linda smiled and said, "Tell me more, but not too much. If you know what I mean. Where are you from, Mr. Wassel?"

"Down around Phenix City," he said with a grin. "But I have access to a townhouse near Central Park just about any time I want it. I like to come to New York a good bit."

"So do I," said Linda. "So do I."

Her father stood and let out a sigh of relief. He went over and asked the bartender to bring a round of drinks, all doubles.

Chapter 39

Rio de Janeiro, Brazil
Arpoador Apartment
Monday, October 13, 2003
9:30 a.m.

Jonesy lived in a fourth floor apartment that overlooked the head of Ipanẽma (*dangerous waters* in local Indian language) beach. She actually lived on Arpoador (*harpooner* in Portuguese), which was the beach and set of rocks close to where Copacabaña and Ipanẽma beaches meet in Rio de Janeiro. The area was the center of sophistication and cultural chic.

The greater city of Rio had an estimated 15 million people, and most of them enjoyed the beach life and soccer with a seemingly religious fervor. Jonesy lived in one of the most desirable places in Rio. It was everyone's dream in Brazil to live at the beach. Despite its social and economic problems, Rio was still one of the world's most wonderful and beautiful cities.

The name "Rio de Janeiro" meant "January River" which was the name given to the area by early Portuguese explorers in 1502. They thought the bay they had sailed into in January was the mouth of a wide river. It turned out to be an illusion, but the name stuck.

The city has the famous Sugarloaf Mountain overlooking Botofogo beach and the Rio Yacht Club, the Christ the Redeemer statute on top of Corcovado (*hunchback*) Mountain, the Tijuca Forrest, the Dois Irmãos (*two brothers*) Mountain at the end of Leblon beach, the Rio-Niterói Bridge across Guanabara (*arm of the sea* in local Indian language) Bay, and various other mountains and lakes in a tropical setting.

Less than 40 miles away is the old royal city and mountain resort of Petrópolis with its Summer Palace and Imperial Museum displaying the Dom Pedro II era of Brazilian royalty. About 30 miles further into the mountains is the town of Teresópolis, which was named for Dom Pedro II's wife, the Empress Tereza Cristina.

In Rio itself, the optimism, irreverence, and hedonism of the *cariocas* that flock to the beaches daily are an endless source of entertainment for apartment dwellers that live overlooking the South Atlantic Ocean.

A person born and raised in Rio has traditionally been called a *carioca*. Each takes pride in the natural beauty of Rio, and demonstrates daily a joy for life that is generally unmatched anywhere in the world. This is even true for many of the poor who live in *favelas*, or shanty villages, on the hills around the city.

From outward appearances, Jonesy had everything. She had grown up as a *carioca*, and she had a beautiful place to live in the best part of Rio. She also enjoyed a

professorship in anthropology at the prestigious Federal University of Rio de Janeiro (UFRJ).

Yet, life had recently dealt her some hard blows. She had remarried an international executive with the Bank of Brazil, and they had shared an exciting but childless relationship. Jonesy enjoyed their discussions about international banking, and she especially enjoyed travel with him on his business trips to Hong Kong, Singapore, Dubai, Paris, Zurich, and London. Sadly, he had been killed in an automobile accident a year and a half ago on the highway from Rio to São Paulo.

Now, the worst news had come to Jonesy. She had just been diagnosed with breast cancer. She needed to undergo surgery and chemotherapy. It would take at least three months. It took money to make sure she got the best treatment possible, and it looked as if she would have to mortgage the apartment to see her through all of the medical procedures.

Jonesy was also concerned that she might need to have high dose chemotherapy with autologous stem cell rescue if all of the other treatments did not stop the cancer. She was advised to have this done in the United States if it came to that point of medical necessity.

She was a true *carioca*, but in the face of cancer, it was hard to maintain genuine optimism.

Due to some recent, severe depressive episodes that she had not experienced since leaving Panama, she sought psychiatric help. The sessions forced her to take mental trips back through her life, especially her first marriage to Sam. It was not pleasant for her.

She learned, however, that she needed to face the fears and demons of her past in order to find any peace or happiness in the present.

Chapter 40

Montgomery, Alabama
U.S. District Courthouse
Wednesday, January 14, 2004
2:00 p.m.

Ever since October, Sam had been assigned by Linda to bankruptcy and collections in the Civil Division. He stayed busy and on the road traveling to U.S. Bankruptcy Court hearings two and three days a week in Huntsville, Anniston, Gadsden, and Tuscaloosa.

He did, however, retain Karen Kemper's civil case, which was on appeal to the Eleventh Circuit. Sam was constantly busy. The cases weren't particularly hard; there were just lots and lots of them. One had to react daily and stay on top of things.

Sam did most of his work for the Internal Revenue Service. Tax liens and debts for back income taxes predominated in the vast numbers of Chapter 13 wage earner plans and Chapter 7 liquidations that were filed by individuals each year in the Northern District of Alabama.

Ever so often there would be a Chapter 11 business reorganization case filed, but again, it would generally be the IRS that Sam would represent. He got to know the IRS agents and attorneys very well.

U.S. Bankruptcy Courts were a part of the U.S. District Court system. They wielded enormous power because they had virtually nationwide and sometimes international jurisdiction. Things moved quickly, and there were few long or drawn out cases with the typical discovery fights that one saw with most civil cases in U.S. District Court. Occasionally, there would be an adversary proceeding in U.S. Bankruptcy Court, but not often. These were resolved with bench trials, so that they were generally disposed of rapidly.

The local bankruptcy bar was a close and tight knit group that was a pleasure to work with for the most part. An attorney's word still meant something, which was a necessity, because the cases moved so fast that one did not have time to put everything in writing each day.

Some days Sam felt that he was as far removed from his old criminal prosecution practice as he could get. He rarely saw Linda, and he tried to keep a low profile around the office.

Sam talked to Professor Redmond and learned that Steven had regained limited sight in his right eye, but he could only get weak light and no real vision in his left one. His broken leg was healing, but with all his medical problems, Steven would need personal assistance in order to accept the Gates Scholarship. Things were not looking hopeful.

Steven needed plenty more rehabilitation and training. He would also need special monetary assistance, and his family was not in sound financial condition.

Sam remembered one of his first wife's favorite sayings, *dar um jeito*, or make a way. He intended to do that for Steven if he got the chance.

Sam found out that Steven had tried to continue playing the banjo. In Sam's mind that was a good sign. He hoped that Steven would call him sometime about playing.

All of these thoughts went through Sam's head on his way to Montgomery to argue Karen's appeal before an Eleventh Circuit panel of three judges.

The headquarters for the Eleventh Circuit was in Atlanta, and the circuit had jurisdiction over cases from Alabama, Florida, and Georgia. The old Fifth Circuit had been split in 1981 to create the Eleventh, and a new Fifth Circuit which had jurisdiction over Mississippi, Louisiana, and Texas. It was the Fifth Circuit that had had jurisdiction over the federal courts in the Canal Zone.

The Eleventh Circuit panels of judges hearing appeals sometimes traveled to different federal courthouses around the circuit for the convenience of local attorneys. That was the reason Sam went to Montgomery instead of Atlanta for the appellate argument.

The new federal courthouse and courtrooms in Montgomery were spectacular. The traditionally laid out courtrooms were spacious and well lighted. No expense had been spared on the construction and decoration. In Sam's view, it was what a modern courthouse should look like. He did not care for the modernistic, small, and poorly lighted courtrooms of the Hugo Black Federal Courthouse in Birmingham.

There were two cases that were argued ahead of Sam on the docket so he got a sense of how active the panel was going to be in its questions in his case.

When Karen's case was called, Sam went up to the podium and began, "May it please the court, my name is Sam Stone, Assistant U.S. Attorney, and I represent Karen Kemper, a former FBI agent, the appellant in this case."

Chief Judge Harold Cooksey interrupted Sam, "Counselor, we have read the briefs and we think we understand the factual record. So a recitation of the facts and procedural history can be dispensed with. What is the central legal issue as you see it?"

The other two judges on the panel nodded accord.

Sam had hoped for such active judges. There was nothing worse than an inactive panel that appeared to be fossilized and said or asked nothing during an argument. One could never get a read on the case from inactive appellate judges. Sam always enjoyed appellate work, regardless.

Linda, on the other hand, had always disliked most appellate courts. She frequently said that appellate judges were like the warriors that hid up in the mountains while the battle was going on and came down after it was over with to slay all of the wounded.

Sam responded, "The issue is whether a reasonable official, acting in the circumstances faced FBI agent Karen Kemper, and possessed of the same knowledge she had at the time, could have believed her conduct to be lawful."

"That's correct. Why do you think the district judge obviously missed the central issue?"

Sam felt a wave of relief. These judges really understood the facts and the issues relating to Karen's defense of qualified immunity. Sam had to be careful. He did not want to say the wrong thing and piss off the panel.

"Perhaps he confused the seeming subjective motives of the agent into the situation. Some cases that I have cited in my brief illustrate the point and how the notion of subjective motives is against U.S. Supreme Court and this Court's precedents."

All three panel members nodded their agreement with what Sam had just said. Sam knew that he had the upper hand so he made the tactical decision to stop. "Unless your Honors have any additional questions, I will rest and reserve the balance of my time for any rebuttal if necessary."

Rebuttal was not called for. The panel listened politely to Johnny Brown's theatrics, and when he had finished, they asked Sam if he wished any time to reply.

Sam stood up and said, "The appellant waives rebuttal. All essential points were established in my opening remarks."

"Very well," said Judge Cooksey. The three judges on the panel then looked at one another, huddled briefly, and nodded to one another. Sam could not hear their brief conversation.

Judge Cooksey looked at Sam and said, "We don't usually act immediately after oral argument, but in this case we think it best to issue an immediate decision. The law and the facts are clear. Therefore, please inform your client, former agent Kemper that the Eleventh Circuit intends to uphold her defense of qualified immunity. An opinion and mandate will issue directing the district judge to dismiss the case against her."

Sam thanked the panel. He came away with the distinct feeling that the Eleventh Circuit Judges knew the district judges over which they presided very well. Sam was also glad that they obviously cared deeply about the litigants. He was elated that they had rendered an immediate ruling and that Karen would not have to wait for an opinion to be handed down as happened with most cases. Sam quickly proceeded out of the courtroom and into the hallway to phone Karen with the good news.

Chapter 41

Tuscaloosa, Alabama
U.S. District Courthouse
Monday, January 19, 2004
11:00 a.m.

Sam had ten cases on the bankruptcy court docket and was talking to a bankruptcy trustee who was hired to help the bankruptcy court administer it cases. She pointed out to Sam that in some complex cases the trustee or court could hire special trustees or administrators to take charge of and/or recover assets from lying and cheating debtors, especially if the court could be shown a substantial likelihood of recovery. Courts everywhere were getting more and more active in criminal collection situations.

Sam said that he would keep that in mind. He had not had the situation come up yet. She said that if it did, she had a list of private attorneys, forensic fraud investigators, former IRS and FBI agents, and the like, who would jump at the chance to be hired. Sam filed the thought away.

Sam finished his last case about 11:00 a.m. As he was leaving the courthouse, an attorney from a large Birmingham firm named, Millwood & Walsh, approached Sam.

He said, "Pardon me, Mr. Stone. You don't know me but my name is Bill Stubbs. I'm a partner with the Millwood firm and I represent the 1st Coosa Bank & Trust. Could I have a private word with you? It will only take a minute."

"Sure," said Sam. "Let's walk toward the back where I'm parked."

As they walked, Stubbs inquired, "I believe that you had a criminal case this past June against a man named Troy Pickering, is that right?"

Sam nodded his head and said, "Yes, and Judge Crowell Rule 29'd it out of court, much to my great disappointment."

Stubbs said, "Yeah. That's what I heard. Look, in a nutshell, Troy Pickering owes the Coosa Bank close to a million dollars on some personal notes and on some guarantees. They are all due and the bank is afraid that he might disappear or flee the country or jurisdiction. Do you know if the federal government has any claims against him at this point? Like maybe the IRS?"

"If we did, what would you want us to do? Get the federal court sign a writ of *ne exeat republica*, barring him from leaving the country?"

Sometimes the IRS would get this special writ granted in federal court barring some delinquent taxpayer from "exiting the republic" or leaving the country.

Stubbs laughed. "No. Nothing quite so dramatic, but that would be fun to watch if you did. We had something more basic in mind, like putting him into involuntary bankruptcy and appointing a trustee and hiring auditors and/or investigators to see what they can unearth and recover. There's more than one way to skin a fat cat."

"Could these seekers of Pickering's riches be hired on a contingency fee basis?" asked Sam.

"I think so. Although, they would probably want expenses paid up front. We could work a deal about splitting those kinds of costs."

"Give me your card and phone number. I'll ask around with the IRS. Could be that there is some way to nail Pickering. I'll help if I can." They shook hands.

Sam had a sudden idea for possible employment for Karen Kemper. She would certainly be motivated in the case of Pickering.

He called Karen on his cell phone, but Steven answered. "Hello."

Sam said, "Hi Steven. How are you holding up?"

Steven replied, "I'm taking things day to day. Some are better than others. Professor Redmond says that if Homer, Galileo, Milton and Helen Keller can overcome their sight disabilities then I can too. Not being able to see very well is difficult to get use to. It makes me feel stupid at times."

"Are you playing the banjo any?" asked Sam.

"Yeah, at little, but I detect small differences in sounds with my banjo that are distracting. I think two of the tuning pegs are slipping, the strings need changing, and it's hard for me to adjust the bridge and tailpiece. I guess I won't be the Ray Charles or Ronnie Millsap of banjoists anytime soon."

"Maybe I can find you a better banjo or fix up your old one," said Sam. "You could aspire to play like Doc Watson."

"What I need is better sight first. I still want that Gates Scholarship."

The conversation was getting difficult for Sam. "Make a way" thought Sam to himself. He wanted help make a way for Steven if there was anything that could be done.

Changing the subject Sam asked, "Is your Mom around?"

Steven said, "No. She went to the Wal-Mart."

"Tell her to give me a call. I may have an employment idea for her. Thanks and take care." Sam closed his cell phone. He sighed and almost started to cry. Life for some was not fair.

Sam drove through the University of Alabama's main campus on the way back home to Birmingham. It was only an hour's drive back to the office, and he was in no hurry at the moment. The campus brought back fond memories of undergraduate and law school.

As he passed by the Gorgas House located on the 12 acres of campus officially designated as the Gorgas-Manly District, he started having recollections about the Panama Canal Zone. He stopped and took a brief tour of the stately old house.

Josiah Gorgas, had been born in Pennsylvania in 1818, and he was the Chief of Ordinance for the Confederacy in the 1860's. He later he served as President of the University of Alabama.

More importantly, his son, William Crawford Gorgas, who was born in 1854 in Alabama, became known as the world's leading sanitation expert. In 1904, he took on the task of destroying mosquitoes in the Canal Zone, which led to wiping out of malaria and yellow fever so that the canal could be built. Without him, the canal project would have likely been a failure.

Sam's thoughts about the early days of the canal construction led to thoughts about the time that he spent in the Canal Zone in the 1970's. He sincerely hoped that Jonesy had found some happiness.

Chapter 42

Columbus, Georgia
Jordan City
Smokey Pig Number One
Friday, February 6, 2004
1:00 p.m.

It's often said that there are more barbecue joints per person in the area of Columbus, Georgia and Phenix City, Alabama, than in almost any other area of the world. Most of the establishments always seem to be full of customers and none seem to go bankrupt. In local arguments over who has the best pork barbecue, invariably the names "Smokey Pig Number One", located in Jordan City on the Columbus side of the Chattahoochee River, and "Smokey Pig Number Two", located on the Phenix City side, come to the fore.

As a result of Sam's informal inquiries with the IRS about Troy Pickering, an IRS agent in Columbus, Georgia had called Sam and invited him to drive down for an informal chat.

The IRS agent suggested that they meet and have lunch at the Smokey Pig Number One. She faxed Sam a map of how to get there. It was about a three-hour drive down Highway 280 from Birmingham. Sam told her that he would meet her there at 1:00 p.m. Eastern Time, and that she could recognize him by his white shirt, black blazer, and tie with American flags all over.

As Sam walked in the main entrance of the Smokey Pig, in Jordan City, a middle-aged female with red hair, wearing a gray pantsuit, approached and asked, "Are you Sam Stone from Birmingham?"

Sam said, "Yes, I am. You must be Donna Bailey from the IRS."

She responded, "That's right. Let's get some barbecue, and we can talk."

Agent Bailey ordered a sliced, inside and out meat, barbecue pork sandwich and a large, sweet iced tea. Sam did the same.

They took a table in the main dining area, and after a few bites, Agent Bailey said, "Troy Pickering and a local yokel named Tom Wassel appear to have some investments together in real estate along Victory Drive just outside the main post at Ft. Benning. We've been watching them for years, but we can never seem to put a case together on them or their friends and associates."

"What kind of real estate are we talking about?" asked Sam.

"Strip clubs, beer joints, biker bars, topless bars, fast food joints, and the like. None of the land title records are in their names. Foreign corporations own the places, as best we can tell, from the Netherlands Antilles. There the records of ownership stop short of showing who the persons are behind the owning companies. All the real estate taxes are paid like clockwork each year."

"Why do you believe that Pickering and Wassel have interests in these places?"

"Several of the club mangers over the years have told local undercover drug agents that Pickering and Wassel own and control the places. We've brought tax cases against some of the girls that worked in the bars and clubs and they have told us the same thing."

"Anything specific?" asked Sam.

"One said that Pickering had regular business contacts in the Cayman Islands. The only problem is that we have no real proof. No one in my office wants to take on a real federal investigation because of the time, effort, and money involved. They prefer the easier cases these days. My higher ups say it's strictly a local law enforcement matter. That's why we're having lunch at the Smokey Pig instead of a conference in my office downtown."

"So what do you think can be done?" asked Sam.

"Start looking for foreign connections to Pickering or Wassel. There's got to be some. These guys are dirty, and they are pros at dodging taxes. But like all crooks, I'd bet a dollar against a doughnut hole they have made a big mistake somewhere."

"Can you think of anything else that could be significant about Wassel or his operations with Pickering?"

"No. Not really."

Agent Bailey suddenly laughed.

"What is it?" asked Sam.

"One of the strippers we tagged for back taxes a few years ago said that Wassel had a funny looking blue banjo tattooed on his left knee."

"That is funny," said Sam. "Look. Thanks for the barbecue conference. Believe it or not you have given me some good information. I have some new ideas that I intend to put into play. I'll let you know if they work."

Sam bought a bottle of barbecue sauce on the way out. He had a lot to think about on his trip back to Birmingham.

Chapter 43

Birmingham, Alabama
U.S. Attorney's Office
Thursday, February 12, 2004
3:30 p.m.

The Civil Conference Room was full of files in banker's boxes, and there was hardly enough room for the meeting called by Sam. All present had interests in Troy Pickering's finances. Bill Stubbs represented Coosa Bank, Susan Wartzog represented the Alabama Department of Revenue, Phil Coulter represented North Anniston Contractor Suppliers, and Sam represented the IRS.

"What do you mean that it takes at least three creditors to put someone into involuntary bankruptcy?" asked Sam.

Bill Stubbs replied, "That's what the bankruptcy code says. It also says that the creditors must hold claims against Pickering that are not contingent as to liability or the subject of a bona fide dispute. They must amount to over $10,000. I don't think that is a problem. Let's go around the table and see what we have. The bank has $975,446.03 in judgments on personal notes and guarantees."

Susan Wartzog said, "The State of Alabama has tax judgments in the amount of $257,983.17."

Phil Coulter added, "Pickering's debts with my client are just over $500,000, but only $147,045.50 has been taken in judgments."

"The IRS could only find a $23,794.96 income tax deficiency from three years ago which Pickering has acknowledged but not paid. Time has run on protests or appeals. The IRS is still looking." Sam opened a folder and continued. "I have good reason to believe that Pickering, and probably some of his associates, are holding real estate in the U.S. through offshore means."

"How can you be sure of this?" asked Stubbs.

"Some of what I'm about to say is based on hearsay, but my own investigation shows that Pickering and his running buddies, own substantial real estate assets through Netherlands Antilles corporations. A company, or likely a trust, maintained in the Cayman Islands, in turn holds these."

"What evidence do you have about that?" asked Wartzog.

Sam said, "An unnamed IRS agent has looked at the real estate records connected to one of Pickering's close business associates and found real estate holdings by Netherlands Antilles Corporations. According to the agent, hearsay has it that Pickering has business contacts in the Caymans. As some of you may know, the usual format for doing business there is through a Caymans Trust owning real estate back in the U.S. via Netherlands Antilles companies."

Sam did not tell them that in one of his recent civil cases involving FBI agent, Karen Kemper, a cell phone belonging to Pickering or one of his businesses came up in an evidentiary hearing. The phone had been recovered from a crime scene, but the full story was not put into evidence because Judge Crowell cut the hearing short.

According to Karen, the phone records showed overseas contacts that the group would be interested in. In particular, the records showed a number of suspicious calls over the past two years from Gulf Shores, New York City, New Orleans, Vail, and Napa Valley to some chartered accountants in Georgetown, Grand Caymans, by the name of Haight & Woodhouse. She never got to that part of her testimony about all the phone's interstate and international contacts, but she had been prepared to present it all.

Phil Coulter asked, "So what would be our plan. Bring an action here and in the Caymans and conduct a search?"

"No," said Sam. "If I understand the bankruptcy laws, we file an action in U.S. Bankruptcy Court in the Northern District of Alabama. It will be a petition by all of our respective clients to put Troy Pickering into involuntary bankruptcy under a Chapter 7 in order to liquidate his personal assets to satisfy the debts."

Stubbs added, "Other creditors may also want to join in once we get the petition filed and notices go out."

Coulter asked, "Don't you think Pickering will fight this tooth and toenail?"

"I don't think so," replied Sam. "He would have to answer too many questions about his finances under oath in a federal proceeding. Pickering knows that I would be on him with a criminal referral like a duck on a june bug for any misstep. He won't even file an answer to the petition."

"I'm still a little unclear. How do you think this will work?' asked Wartzog.

"We file the petition, and the bankruptcy judge grants it. The court then appoints an interim trustee who legally stands in the shoes of Pickering to his exclusion. The trustee is able to go into any jurisdiction with a certified copy of the court's order of appointment and make claims on any of Pickering's assets."

"Can the interim trustee go to the Caymans and have the court's authority recognized?" asked Coulter.

Sam replied, "Yes. It's been done before. The Caymans' legal system is based upon the English common law like ours and there has been little problem in the past with their recognition of our bankruptcy laws. They have similar ones that we recognize."

"Do you have anyone in mind for the trustee appointment?" asked Wartzog.

"Yes," said Sam. "Bill has recommended Milton Amason, an attorney with trustee experience. I am also recommending that Amason hire former FBI agent, Karen Kemper, as his assistant for the Caymans investigations. She knows a good bit about Pickering already, especially about his businesses and associates. She also has close contacts with the relevant federal agencies. I think that she can ferret out his assets here and in the Caymans if anyone can."

Stubbs said, "If there are no other discussions, let's get the ball rolling and file the Petition for Involuntary Bankruptcy that I have prepared. You should notice that it does not mention the Caymans or our suspicions about foreign assets. I suggest that we keep that information to ourselves until the interim trustee is able to act. All we need right now is a very plain petition."

Sam helped pass out copies of the document. He hoped this plan would work. Sam had been put in charge of collections for the Civil Division so he had told his Civil Chief about the plan in general but not the details of the unique approach to nab foreign assets held in the Caymans. He did not trust Linda, and the less information available to her through his immediate boss the better.

Chapter 44

Georgetown, Grand Cayman
Cayman Islands
Monday, March 15, 2004
10:00 a.m.

The Petition for Involuntary Bankruptcy against Pickering went off like clockwork. Pickering was served but refused to respond, just as Sam predicted. Milton Amason was appointed as interim trustee, and he hired Karen on Sam's recommendation.

Both were to be advanced expenses by the petitioners, and be paid 15 percent out of any recoveries. Amason and Karen agreed on a 60/40 split. The Bankruptcy Court approved the fee arraignment.

Karen thanked Sam earnestly for this opportunity to get back at Pickering and to potentially solve some of her financial problems. Sam said that he was simply more than glad to help. They quickly drew up a plan of action, which was put into immediate play by Karen.

At her strong suggestion, she and Amason flew into Georgetown, Grand Cayman on a Sunday evening, and were ready for their first encounter with the Haight & Woodhouse accounting firm the next morning.

At 10:00 a.m. they entered the accounting firm's offices, showed their identifications, and presented officially certified copies of appointment and other court documents.

At first the junior accountant said that he would have to refer the matter to a senior partner. The senior partner insisted that he had to consult with legal counsel. Legal counsel said he had to consult with local government officials.

However, after a three-hour wait, the senior partner finally said, "Please step into our conference room. Any and all files and records that we have on Troy Pickering will be made available to you."

With that he left, and within 15 minutes, the junior accountant brought in four large plastic boxes of records. They had hit the mother lode. All of the real estate holdings through a Caymans trust with Netherlands Antilles corporations were there. The records started in 1972 and ran up to the present. Real estate investments from New York to New Orleans to the Napa Valley were all there.

Karen noticed a special file that contained a copy of a Last Will & Testament for Troy Pickering. A local bank, whose address was just across the street, named the Caribbean Bank & Trust of Georgetown was listed as the holder of a safety deposit box. An extra key was taped to the folder.

She showed this to Amason, and they immediately walked across to the bank and presented identifications and appointment documents. After an hour of checking, the bank's manger gave them access to the safety deposit box. It had $200,000 in cash, a Last Will & Testament, and a curious sheet of paper with the following chart and diagram:

B.B. key-3 Inch Length
Peghead-3/8 Inch Square
5th string peg-1/8 Inch Square
(1 ¼ Inch from Rim)
Neck-2 Inches Length
   -1/8 Inch Width
   -1/16 Inch Thickness
Pass & Password-Fraternity Style
Blue Tattoo Left Knee
O-S-U-S-A-N-N-A-H

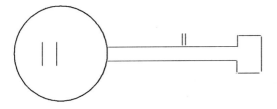

Karen said, "I wonder what this is about. Some key to more treasure?"

Amason replied, "We have enough to keep us busy and fee'd for now. Bring everything, including the chart and diagram. We'll close the safety deposit box. We need to take all of the contents and the other accounting and real estate records back to Birmingham. I predict that it will be several months and possibly a year before all that we have found can be sorted out and disposed of under the court's procedures. I think you and I are on our way eventually to a hansom reward for our efforts."

Karen said, "I just wish I could see the expression on Pickering's face when he finds out that his ill gotten gains are gone."

Amason laughed. "He should beware the Ides of March and the power of the U.S. Bankruptcy Courts."

Chapter 45

Birmingham, Alabama
Sam Stone's Apartment on Southside
Friday, March 19, 2004
5:30 p.m.

Sam brought home a xeroxed copy of the sheet of paper with the chart and diagram and laid it on his kitchen table. It remained a puzzle that no one had figured out as yet. He had just fixed a BLT sandwich and some sweet iced tea when the doorbell rang. Sam put the sandwich down and headed for the front door.

He opened it and stood staring at a pretty woman with green eyes, who said, "*Como vai* (*how's it going*), Sam, it's been a long time."

"Jonesy? Is it really you? Please, uh, come in if you like." Sam was dumbstruck.

She said, "I would like to talk with you for a little while. I need to get some things off my mind."

"Please. Come in and sit a spell as we say in the South. Would you like some iced tea or something to eat?" Sam asked.

She said, "No, but please put this pint of vanilla ice cream in your freezer. I just bought it, and I'm afraid it will melt and make a mess."

Jonesy handed him a small paper sack, and Sam started for the kitchen.

As he exited the living room, Holmes made an appearance and went directly to Jonesy who began to pet and play with him. She was seated on the sofa with Homes at her feet just like he had always belonged there when Sam returned.

"Nice Lab," she said.

"Yeah," Sam said. "He's been a good and loyal companion."

"How have you been?" she asked.

He said, "Good, for the most part. I remarried but recently got divorced. No kids, just my banjo and Holmes there at your feet. I now work as a federal employee with the U.S. Attorney's Office, and the divorce has left me a little strapped financially. I still have a ways to go until I can retire. But my health is fine, and I generally enjoy my work. What more could I ask for?"

"Very little I suspect," she said and looked away.

"Tell me about yourself. You are looking well. Why are you in Birmingham?"

Jonesy paused and said, "I got remarried to a banker in Rio, and I had a job teaching anthropology at the Federal University of Rio de Janeiro. We had an apartment at the head of Ipanẽma beach near Arpoador in Rio, but he was killed two years ago in a car crash. Neither of us wanted children so we did not attempt any. He got fixed so that I could stay off the pill. Unfortunately, I've recently been diagnosed with breast cancer, and I came to Birmingham to the Kirklin Clinic for treatment. It has some of the finest medical facilities in the U.S., and it was easier to schedule treatments there than in New York, Houston, or Miami. I have no health insurance to cover the medical bills, and I have had to borrow and mortgage everything."

Sam said, "Jonesy, I'm so sorry. Is there anything I can do to help?"

"Yes," she said. "My doctors say that there is a psychological component to serious cancer treatments, and that I should make sure that I maintain a positive view of my world for the treatments to be the most effective."

Sam wasn't sure where all of this was going so he kept his mouth shut and let her talk.

She looked directly at him and said, "Sam. I've been seeing a psychiatric counselor, and despite my initial denials, I've come to realize that I have carried a lot of emotional baggage over the years as a result of our marriage and divorce. Please don't get me wrong, I'm not blaming you. I've been blaming myself for a long time. Hardly a day has gone by that I did not think about our time together, the good and the bad."

Jonesy paused and looked away for a moment. She swallowed hard and then continued. "My counselor says I need to confront the situation head-on, and to try to put it behind me. I need to forgive myself first and then ask you for your forgiveness. This is not easy for me, because asking forgiveness is a hard thing in my way of being, but it's why I'm here. As they say in Brazil, *dar um jeito,* or make a way. That's what I want to do."

Sam said, "Jonesy, I'll do or help in any way that I can. You don't need to ask for my forgiveness. There is nothing to forgive. Things happened that we could not control. I certainly don't blame you for anything. I've always been sorry that things did not work out, but fate dealt us some wild cards. I guess we both played them the best we could in the circumstances. What can I do for you?"

She smiled and said, "Talk to me. Let me spend a part of the evening with you. Maybe I can discover a way to get my mental state ready for tomorrow's first round of cancer treatments."

Sam said, "Sure. You are totally welcome here. I see that Holmes likes you, and I am at your disposal. I was about to have a sandwich and some iced tea. Would you like the same or something else?"

She brightened somewhat and said, "I would like that. Can I help you fix any thing?"

Sam said, "No, but come on into the kitchen so that we can talk and catch up. It really is good to see you."

Sam got up from his chair, and Jonesy followed him into the kitchen. She spotted the xeroxed chart and diagram on the table and asked what it was.

Sam told her that the original had come out of a safety deposit box in the Cayman Islands. He also said that it could be the key to additional illegal moneys, but that he could not connect the dots as yet.

Jonesy said, "The bottom part looks like a banjo to me."

Sam said that similar blue "banjo" was tattooed on the left knee of a criminal businessman in Alabama who had placed the chart and diagram in the safety deposit box, therefore, he thought that the "B.B." meant "blue banjo."

Sam also said that the same criminal could be connected to a former U.S. Army type that Sam had encountered in Panama. But he still could not figure what the entire chart and diagram meant.

She stared at the page for about a minute, and said that it made no sense to her either. Jonesy, however, thought to herself, *a oportunidade faz o ladrão,* or the opportunity makes the thief.

She asked, "If you had all the money in the world, what would you do with it?"

Sam laughed and said, "Give it to you for what you need, and take the rest and be like Bill Gates at Microsoft. I'd set up a foundation to do good works."

She misted up and turned away to hide her emotions, asking, "Where is that sandwich and iced tea?"

Sam handed her his and started putting another sandwich together. They made some small talk until both finished.

Jonesy said, "Hey, I have a surprise dessert for us. I was told to fatten up for the treatments and that's why I brought the ice cream. Do you have a couple of wine glasses and a blender?"

Sam got out the glasses and the blender, and she said, "Go into the other room while I make this. I want it to be a surprise. I need my bag out of the living room."

Sam fetched her bag and handed it to her. He then retreated to the couch in the living room wondering what she had in mind. He heard the blender going at high speed for a minute or so, and then into the room came Jonesy, handing him a glass of chilled white liquid with some sort of brown spice sprinkled on the top. She had a similar glass in her hand.

She said, "Take a sip. I think you will like this."

Jonesy came over and clinked his glass and sat beside Sam on the couch.

Sam said, "Here's to better times."

She looked him in the eye and winked, "*Salut.*"

Sam took a sip and said, "Wow. That's great stuff. What's in this concoction?"

She smiled and said, "Its basically vanilla ice cream and a certain liqueur run through the blender with a little cinnamon sugar sprinkled on the top. Can you guess which liqueur?"

Sam tasted the drink again, thought for a minute, and said, "No, I can't. What do you call this?"

Jonesy smiled and said, "In Brazil, I call this *líquido de amor*, or liquid love. I left a note with the formula and the rest of Drambuie and other stuff for you in the kitchen. I won't need them starting tomorrow. By the way, do you have a CD player? I have some *fados* (*folk songs*) that I would like very much for us to hear."

She handed Sam a CD from her bag, and he got up and put it on. Holmes got up and left the room.

As Sam settled back down on the couch, he drained his glass and said, "Jonesy, this drink is wonderful. You could sell this and make a fortune."

She laughed, finished her glass, and said, "Can I use your bathroom for a moment? I need to freshen up."

He said, "Sure, right around that corner on the right. If you hit the bedroom, you've gone too far."

Jonesy took her bag and left him on the couch. She still looked as great as ever to Sam. It was hard to believe that she had cancer. Sam let his mind run about the good times they had had in Panama.

The music was a collection of female vocals singing mostly slow, sad folk songs in Portuguese with only guitar accompaniment. Jonesy was taking her time in the bathroom, but what did it matter. It was great to see her again, even if it was under difficult circumstances for her. After 25 or 30 minutes she came back into the room and sat down beside Sam.

She smelled of the tropics and her hair was let down. She crossed her legs and Sam could she that she still kept a nice tan.

A jolt of sexual energy started up in him which could be seen through his pants. Jonesy saw this too, and with her hand touched the bulge and said, looking into his eyes, "*Nênê*, you still care for me. How wonderful."

Sam was slightly embarrassed.

She kissed him gently and said, "Please make love to me."

Sam took her hand and led her to his bedroom where they renewed a passion that Sam had thought was gone forever.

Sometime later, as they lay in each other's arms, Jonesy said, "*Nênê*, I'm truly sorry."

Realizing how difficult that was for her to say, Sam said, "The past is over and it's O.K. I'm sorry too."

She kissed him and said that she had to go. Sam asked about seeing her again.

Jonesy said, "My treatments last 10 days here, and then I have some recuperation time. I would prefer not to see you again until I am well. I want to keep the memory of this evening close to my heart while I go through what

I have to go through. After I am cured, I wish to have you as a part of my life again if that is possible. Think about it. *Dar um jeito*, make a way. I left you my address and phone number in Rio in the kitchen."

She got up, dressed, and left. She tearfully kissed Sam at the door, and said, "*Nênê*, thank you for helping me. I will always love you. Come and visit me in Rio after I am well. *Ciao*."

Sam shut the door and went to bed. When he awoke the next morning, he went into the kitchen to fix a cup of coffee. There was a note from Jonesy underneath a small bottle of Drambuie. Beside the bottle were two plastic capped drug containers. The note had her address and phone number. It also had the formula.

The note said:

> Put vanilla ice cream in the blender and add as much Drambuie as you like, but not too much. One of the plastic containers has cinnamon sugar which is added at the last with just a sprinkle or two over the top after the liquid is poured into the glass. The other container has Viagra tablets. They are entirely optional. I powdered up one for your drink.
>
> Love,
> Jonesy.

Sam started to laugh. What a woman.

Then he had a thought. Sam might have to furnish some of this Brazilian liquid love potion to his Uncle John.

Chapter 46

Panama City, Panama
Bank of Brazil
Monday, April 12, 2004
10:30 a.m.

A woman in a black pants suit, blond wig, and sunglasses stepped into the Bank of Brazil in Panama City's financial district on Avenida Federico Boyd. The bank was on the first floor of a 32-story modern office building overlooking the Bay of Panama.

The woman asked in English to speak to the manager. She was directed to take a seat by the male receptionist.

In a few moments, a female manager dressed in a dark blue skirt and white blouse came out and asked, "How may I help you? My name is Ms. Fernandez."

The woman smiled and said, "My name is Ms. Smith. I am here for a special safety deposit box. I believe the number is 11."

The manager said, "Yes. That would be a very special box at this bank. I must check the records for certain matters."

She turned and went into a nearby office. The bank originally established boxes 1 through 25 with specialized instructions for opening which were maintained in a safe kept only by the manager. Each owner had provided customized instructions for opening these boxes. After retrieving small leather zipped banker's pouch from the safe with the instructions to the bank concerning box 11, the manager read carefully the letter contained in the pouch and then returned to the woman.

Ms. Fernandez said, "There is a pass and a password. Do you have these?"

The woman responded, "Yes. I have both. Which would you like first?"

"That is for you to present correctly. It's part of the special instructions."

"Very well." The woman rolled up her pants leg and showed the blue banjo tattooed on her left knee. "That is the pass, correct?"

The manager looked carefully at the tattoo and asked, "May I touch the tattoo to make sure that it is a real one? It's a part of the verification procedure."

The woman nodded approval.

The manager pinched the skin around the banjo image and saw that the tattoo was in fact real.

After she finished, she said, "The pass is alright. The password is next."

The woman responded, "The password must be lettered back and forth between us."

"Please begin."

"No, you begin," said the woman.

"No, you must begin," said Ms. Fernandez.

"O," said the woman.

"S," said the manager. They continued back and forth until "O-S-U-S-A-N-N-A-H" was finally spelled out with the woman saying the final "H."

"The password is correct," said Ms. Fernandez. "Do you have the key?"

The woman opened her handbag and produced a key that looked like the blue banjo tattooed on her left knee. She handed it to the manager for inspection.

With the key in hand, Ms. Fernandez unzipped the pouch and produced a similar one. She said, "Even the locks and keys were customized for these bank boxes. Please follow me."

They went through three steel security doors in succession, each of which was locked behind them. They finally entered a special vault with safety deposit boxes of various sizes from floor to ceiling. Ms. Fernandez used both keys to open the door of box 11.

She slid out the long square box, and said, "You may take this to the room just outside the vault for viewing. Please lock the door behind you. Ring the bell on the wall when you have finished, and I will come for the box and place it back in the vault."

The woman thanked her and quickly took the box into the viewing room and locked the door. When the box was opened, she saw that it contained 100 bearer shares of a Panamanian corporation named, "Alabama Investors, Inc."

There were articles of incorporation also which listed the name of an attorney, Jose Padilla, of Padilla &

Hernandez, Abogados (*attorneys*) of Panama City, Panama as nominee. There was nothing else in the box. No other names appeared on any document. She took the shares and articles, closed the box, and rang for Ms. Fernandez.

The woman was led back to the manager's office. Ms. Fernandez asked, "Did you find everything satisfactory?"

"Yes, but I need a small favor. Can you direct me to the law offices of Padilla & Hernandez?"

"Of course," she replied. "They occupy the top three floors of this building. Take the elevator to the 32nd floor for the reception."

The woman took the elevator as directed.

At the reception desk she said, "My name is Ms. Smith. I would like to see attorney Jose Padilla about my corporation called, "Alabama Investors, Inc."

She was directed to wait. The receptionist made a call, and in a few moments, a gray-haired attorney in his 60's came out and said, "My name is Jose Padilla. How may I be of service?"

The woman asked, "May we speak in private?"

Padilla said, "Certainly." He escorted her into a small but lavish conference room and offered her a seat.

She sat down and opened her handbag and pulled out the shares and the articles of incorporation for Alabama Investors, Inc.

Holding the shares, she turned them on the table and showed them to Padilla. She looked into his eyes and said, "I am the owner because I am the bearer of this corporation's shares. I believe you set it up and that you have probably maintained it over the years. I want to hire you to liquidate the corporation and transfer the proceeds to an account that I have set up in Switzerland. Please charge any reasonable fees and expenses and take them out of the proceeds. Can you do that?"

He said, "Certainly."

The woman handed him a piece of paper with the National Bank of Berne's address, telephone number, and numbered bank account and routing instructions.

She said, "Please wire the funds as soon as possible. How long will it take?"

Padilla said, "For my two per cent in fees it takes 30 days. But for five per cent I could probably do it in 10 days. I believe the assets are mostly liquid in offshore accounts."

The woman said, "In that case, I'll give you ten per cent if you will get the transfer done in 3 days and use ever what influence you have with the banks to corrupt the wire transfer records."

Padilla grinned and said, "Certainly."

In three days, $115,000,000.00 was transferred from Panama to the account in the designated National Bank of Berne.

From there the funds were transferred twice more by wire until they landed finally in a special numbered account in the National Bank of Zurich. All wire records out of Panama were corrupted making the funds untraceable even by the most sophisticated law enforcement methods.

Chapter 47

Zurich, Switzerland
Baur au Lac Hotel
Thursday, May 6, 2004
1:30 p.m.

Jonesy smiled and thought to herself that her experience in having been married to a banker had paid off. She did not like keeping her scheme from Sam. But she knew it was best for now, especially since Sam had inadvertently provided the information to her about the secret bank account kept by some Alabama crooks in Panama.

As soon as she saw the sheet of paper in Sam's kitchen, and then heard what he said, she figured it out. Jonesy had done a quick study of the information and wrote it down when she was leaving the liquid love recipe.

Assets were in the "B.B" or Bank of Brazil. Panama was the perfect place for holding bearer share corporations and secret offshore accounts. She also knew about the sometimes-secret pass and password procedures for safety deposit boxes from her discussions with her husband and his business associates prior to his death. The fraternity password procedure was easy to find in some books at the local public library. A telephone call to a friendly librarian was all it took.

After her treatments were over, and after she had gotten a little of her strength back, she headed straight to Panama. There she got a cheap blue tattoo and had a special key made to certain specifications. She knew she had to act quickly, as others would soon figure it out also.

Jonesy had paid the Panamanian lawyer a small fortune, but she now controlled a large fortune. If only her cancer treatments would be ultimately successful. Her doctors had been cautiously optimistic, and she tried to be.

Jonesy had also learned a good deal from her banker husband about international money holdings, and now she planned to put that knowledge to use.

She was having lunch at the Baur au Lac hotel where she had rented a suite of rooms overlooking the lake. Her young female account manager, Heidi Basel, from the National Bank of Zurich, and a middle aged male attorney from Vaduz, Liechtenstein, joined Jonesy. The attorney had come highly recommended by Ms. Basel. His name was Norbert Planken.

Planken asked as they sat down for lunch, "Where did you hear of the Liechtenstein foundation laws?"

"From my deceased husband who was an international banker. He told me that many rich families in South America, and in other parts of the world, had set up family foundations to provide security for themselves and their heirs. I would like to do something similar but with a charitable feature, which I understand is available."

He said, "That is correct. Let me explain. Liechtenstein's laws on foundations are some of the most liberal but stable in the world. One can use a foundation for private and/or public charitable purposes, all without any approval procedures or official supervision."

"What about taxes?" asked Jonesy.

"There are no wealth, business, or income taxes. There is only a small 0.1 per cent capital tax on declared assets calculated on a diminishing scale. There is a small stamp duty on the original capital, but proper planning makes it fairly insignificant. Payments to beneficiaries in foreign countries are tax free, and there are no estate or inheritance taxes when or if the foundation is wound up."

"Can I operate commercial activities out of the foundation?"

Planken replied, "No. Commercial activities are generally excluded, but some forms of commercial trade can be conducted in the necessary pursuit of foundation charitable purposes. Most founders use the foundation vehicle to hold assets and promote the purposes of the foundation."

"So exactly how should all this work?" asked Jonesy.

"You would be an entirely anonymous founder, and you would define the beneficiaries and purposes of the foundation. A Liechtenstein trust would actually form the foundation for you in order to keep your identity out of the public records."

Ms. Basel said, "We at the bank would coordinate the deposit of assets, accounting, management, distributions and any investment or financial matters that would come up."

Jonesy asked, "What about succession?"

Planken replied, "That is taken care of in the foundation documents. The usual estate and gift laws have no application. We use the foundation device for what is commonly called 'unrestricted estate planning'."

"What about creditors?"

Planken smiled and said, "We recognize the 'bankruptcy privilege' in Liechtenstein law, and so long as the foundation document says so, creditors cannot get at the assets of any beneficiaries."

Jonesy thought for a moment and asked, "Can I appoint an U.S. citizen as an administrator, director, custodian or whatever without undue tax consequences to him or her in the United States?"

Planken looked around slowly and replied, "I am not a U.S. tax lawyer, and I am not technically competent to give legal advice in this area, but I would say this."

He coughed slightly, and then continued. "If the U.S. citizen is a beneficiary of lifetime foreign gifts, or inheritances upon your death, as defined in the foundation's document, there would be no U.S. estate or gift tax consequences to the U.S. citizen. However, if the amounts were large enough, there could be an enormous U.S. tax consequence to his or her estate when the U.S. person died, assuming all the accumulations had not been spent."

"What about involving a U.S. citizen in the foundation's charitable decisions, would there be any adverse U.S. tax law consequences?" asked Jonesy.

Planken replied, "Again, I am not a U.S. tax lawyer, but so long as the person was let's say, a 'recommending director' of the foundation's charitable functions with no interest in, signature rights, or authority over the foundation's assets or foreign bank accounts, then there should be no adverse U.S. tax law consequences. You would want to say in the foundation document that such a 'recommending director' is not entitled to any powers, authorities or distributions. The questions about foreign bank accounts and trusts on the U.S. Internal Revenue Form 1040 could then be checked 'no' by the person."

"So how would this aspect work?" asked Jonesy.

"The U.S. citizen could simply participate by making recommendations which a board, made up of yourself, could approve or disapprove. Upon your death, the U.S. citizen could inherit as much as you want to leave. During your life you can give the U.S citizen as much as you want. All this should be without any adverse tax considerations to you or the U.S. citizen."

Jonesy thought for a moment, and said, "Good. Let's set up a mixed family foundation. Please keep my name anonymous. I wish to be the board, and I would like to have the bankruptcy privilege for any beneficiaries. I would also like to have the authority to appoint a recommending director."

Ms. Basel said, "It only takes a deposit of 30,000 Swiss Francs to set up one of these foundations. I recommend that amount to start with for tax and other purposes. You can transfer the bulk of your assets later if you wish."

Jonesy said, "I want to pay off medical bills in the U.S and a large mortgage in Brazil in a total that amounts to about $1.5 million. The remainder will all then go eventually into the Liechtenstein foundation. I assume that I can manage it from any location in the world that I choose, correct?"

"That's right," said Planken. "By the way, how much to you estimate that the eventual transfer of assets will be?"

Jonesy glanced at Ms. Basel and said, "Close to $110 million in cash."

Planken turned pale and said, "I had no idea. I assure you that I am at your complete disposal day or night. Here is my personal international toll free cell phone number that only my wife and daughters know. Now you have it also."

Jonesy said, "Thank you. After the foundation is set up, I want you to have someone discreetly contact a certain U.S. citizen about becoming a 'recommending director.' Can you do that?"

"Certainly," said Planken. "There is a Washington, D.C. law firm that is most discreet which I use from time to time for similar assignments in the United States. Just give me the name and address of the person. It will be taken care of."

Chapter 48

Washington, D.C.
Ireland's Four Provinces Bar
Friday, May 21, 2004
9:30 p.m.

The Irish music was about to start as Sam entered the 'Four P's', as Ireland's Four Provinces bar in Northwest Washington was called by the locals. Each time Sam was in Washington, he tried to drop in to have a beer and listen to the folk and Celtic music. Some band or group, usually from Ireland, played traditional music there most nights, especially on Fridays and Saturdays.

Sam ordered a draft Smithwick's Irish beer along with a corn beef dinner special as he sat at the bar contemplating the extraordinary events of the day.

It had all started with a call from a District of Columbia law firm named Henry, Levin & Mayfield two days before. A lawyer in the firm by the name of Sherman R. Prescott, III, had telephoned him in Birmingham and asked if it would be possible to meet in DC on Friday at 9:30 a.m.

According to Prescott, a foundation had nominated Sam for an advisory position that had strictly charitable purposes, and the interview would take less than 2 hours on Friday morning. Assuming reciprocal approvals, some paperwork memorializing an agreement with the foundation would be signed before the close of afternoon business. In the words of Prescott, "an unprecedented honor and privilege was in the making" for Sam.

Prescott told Sam that everything was above board and that the nomination and advisory position would not adversely affect him or his career as an Assistant U.S. Attorney.

A first class round trip ticket on Delta had been purchased for Sam already so that he could fly up to DC on Thursday night. A room had been reserved for him at the Hay-Adams Hotel for Thursday and Friday evenings, with Sam's return to Birmingham expected on Saturday. Reasonable expenses would covered by the $500.00 per day per diem that would be given to him on arrival which would cover three days in all.

Sam consented, and then just to make sure, he looked the firm up on the Internet. It had one of the most impressive websites that Sam had ever seen. Partners and "of counsel" members ranked among the country's most influential former Senators, Congressmen, and federal judges. Sam also called the U.S. Attorney's Office in DC and spoke to the Civil Chief. The firm had unquestionably the best reputation in town with the Assistant U.S. Attorneys in the DC office. Many former Assistants left public service to work there.

He was given the names and numbers of three attorneys with the firm that the Civil Chief knew personally from their work for her in the U.S. Attorney's Office as civil Assistants. Sam called each, and was given some degree of comfort by what they said about the firm in general and Sherman R. Prescott, III, in particular. This had to be a legitimate deal, but Sam's curiosity was certainly heightened and he could not allay all suspicions.

The firm was located on K Street near McPherson Square, and Sam had arrived promptly for the interview with Prescott.

In a private wood-paneled conference room, Prescott had indicated that he represented an international foundation, called the International Relief & Charities Organization, or IRCO, of Zurich, Switzerland. It had nominated Sam to a position as a "recommending director" of its international charities program.

This meant that Sam was to recommend charitable projects, including the hiring of administrators, if he saw fit. The board of the foundation would review the recommendations and give approval so long as the board found the recommendations worthy. Sam would not be paid a salary or stipend, but he would be reimbursed for any and all expenses at rates set by the foundation.

The interview explored Sam's education and career. It did not intrude into his personal life, and Sam was glad of that fact. After an hour or so, Prescott said that the interview was complete and that he was prepared to conclude the confirmation of Sam's nomination later in the afternoon. He suggested that Sam find a place for lunch and take in some of the sights in Washington while the paperwork was being finalized. Sam should return at 4:30 in the afternoon.

Sam had lunch at the Old Ebbitt Grill, and finished around 1:30 p.m. He then walked down to Pennsylvania Avenue in the direction of the U.S. Capitol. As he walked by the U.S. Department of Justice's Main Justice Building he remembered that the National Archives building was next door, but that in all his years of coming to Washington, he had never been inside to see the Declaration of Independence, Bill of Rights, and the U.S. Constitution.

He spent the remainder of the afternoon there and in its book and gift shop. Just after 4:00 p.m. he walked outside, and caught a cab back to the offices of Henry, Levin & Mayfield.

At 4:30, Prescott asked Sam into the conference room again, where he directed Sam to sign some papers which indicated that Sam had accepted the position of "recommending director" of the International Relief & Charities Organization.

Sam was then given a notebook with the name of the organization, its mission statement, and reimbursement rates. Special instructions for charitable proposals were included with sample documents and a formatted computer disk for ease of use. All proposals were to be forwarded to Prescott who would in turn provide a legal review and forward the same to the board for approval.

Prescott said that he felt that Sam would have many questions in the future and that he was to call on him at any time for assistance. Sam said that he had only one question. How much money could be devoted to a charitable project's budget? Prescott said that the actual figure was confidential, but that he had been instructed to answer the question, if asked, by stating that no project could exceed $100 million.

Sam felt faint. How and what had he become involved in?

Sam asked Prescott if everything was legitimate, and the reply was the firm would not risk its clients and the firm's reputation if each and every aspect of this matter were not honest and completely above board. Prescott said that while some could view what was happening to Sam as unusual, or even eccentric, it was all ethically and morally correct. The charity and its methods and goals were completely legal and proper.

Sam left the law offices wondering about many things and many possibilities.

He went back to the hotel and took a nap.

When he awoke at 9:00 p.m., he caught the metro to the Cleveland Park stop, and headed back down Connecticut Avenue to the Four P's. After the band's first break, Sam pulled out his cell phone to check his messages in Birmingham.

The only message was garbled. There was an international operator, and some foreign language exchange in the background. It sounded like Portuguese. Sam immediately tried to call the number Jonesy had given him, but there was no answer.

Too much had happened for one day, so Sam went back to his hotel.

As he drifted off to sleep he wondered if Jonesy was financially and medically O.K. Sam would try to contact her as soon as he got back to Birmingham.

Chapter 49

Vail, Colorado
Beaver Creek Lodge
Tuesday, May 25, 2004
4:00 p.m.

Duval started the meeting, without Pickering, who had not been heard from in 30 days. "We have been screwed out of our fortunes. The bankruptcy court in Birmingham has seized the trust and real estate holdings in the Caymans. I can't get a lawyer to touch that case it is so hot."

Wassel said, "I hear that federal grand juries have been cranked up about Pickering and me in Columbus and Birmingham. I've decided to leave the country. We still have our mother load of money in Panama don't we?"

"No, Hell no we don't. I called Padilla, the crooked Panamanian lawyer that helped us get set up and who maintained Alabama Investors, Inc. I was told that he has closed his firm and retired to Spain or some other damned place. His whereabouts are unknown. The secret corporate account has been cleaned out and the corporation wound up. How that happened I have no clue. It's all gone."

Ben Blake asked, "If we were to skip the country, how can we avoid extradition back to the states?"

Robert Nolan replied, "I've been told that if you go to a place like Columbia in South America, get married to a local woman, and have a child, you won't get extradited back to the states even for murder."

"Yeah, but there's a catch. You have to have enough money to pay off the local authorities as necessary or you'll wind up with what they like calling, 'informal extradition'."

"What's that?" asked Blake.

"That's when the local police don't get paid, and they stick your ass on the next non-stop fight to Miami. A call is made to the feds with your fight number and time of arrival," said Duval.

"So what are you going to do?" Blake asked.

"I'm going to stay out of sight and fight," said Duval. "We all have a few stateside assets left. It's not like we are completely broke or helpless. I'd advise ya'll to liquidate everything and start disappearing. You know, like they say in country music, pull a 'Hank Snow.'"

"What's that?" asked Nolan.

"Be a moving on," said Duval. "For me, I believe that a certain Assistant U.S. Attorney has some information on where the Panamanian account moneys went. When I get the chance, I plan to ask him in a very persuasive manner."

"That's not the kind of fight that you should pick," said Nolan.

"Don't worry. It'll be my kind of fight, a knife fight. And the first rule in a knife fight is that there ain't no rules."

Chapter 50

Cambridge, England
Senate House
Tuesday, June 15, 2004
2:30 p.m.

In the Fens, or flat farming country of East Anglia, about 60 miles north of London, lies one of the greatest centers of learning in the world.

The University of Cambridge dates from 1209, when a group of religious scholars from Oxford broke away due to "town versus gown" problems and established themselves in a small farming village by the banks of the River Cam.

Over the years, many greats have been associated with Cambridge, including: Desiderius Erasmus, Geoffrey Chaucer, Francis Bacon, Isaac Newton, Charles Darwin, John Milton, Lord Byron, Samuel Coleridge, William Wordsworth, Alfred Lord Tennyson, Edmund Spenser, Thomas Hardy, Bertrand Russell, Ernest Rutherford, and John Harvard, for whom Harvard University was named.

In more recent times, James Watson and Francis Crick, the discoverers of DNA, and Steven Hawking, the disabled scientist who has promoted the study of cosmology and the universe, have dominated the publicity landscape.

An academic revolution of a sort is taking place nearby with the advent of many new scientific research companies being located around Cambridge. The University's traditional disdain for the commercial realm has been giving way to what has fast become Europe's "Silicon Valley."

Sam and Professor Redmond enjoyed a walk around the Cambridge Colleges prior to their scheduled meeting with University officials at the Senate House on a street called the King's Parade, just across from the St. Mary's Church, which was the center of town.

Sam had never seen such a beautiful college setting. Both had just come from Oxford University the day before, and while it had its scenes and buildings, they did not match those of Cambridge.

Sam's plan to create a special assistance fund for disabled students attending Oxford and Cambridge on Rhodes and Gates' scholarships was more than well received by the respective University administrations. The program was officially called the Oxbridge Scholars' Special Assistance Fund.

Sam's proposal included hiring Professor Redmond away from the Birmingham College of Christ at a salary of $250,000.00 per year, with a $150,000.00 expense account and another $150,000.00 per year for a housing allowance. Professor Redmond was grateful to leave traditional academia and become the Fund's administrator. Sam had been amazed at the speed with which Prescott had gotten approval from the International Relief & Charities Organization for every aspect of Sam's Special assistance Fund proposal.

The stroll around Cambridge included a tour by punt, or flat bottom boat, on the Cam along the "Backs" of the colleges that line the river. The views of the Mathematical Bridge of Queen's College, King's College Chapel, Clare Bridge, Trinity College, the Bridge of Sighs, and St. John's College were breathtaking.

They even climbed to the top of the St. Mary's Church for an all around view of the town and colleges. Sam and Professor Redmond then went from the church across the central market to Sidney Street where, at Sam's insistence, they made a stop at Sidney Sussex College.

Sam told Professor Redmond the story of Judge Crowell and his connection with the Cromwell name. They saw the plaque that indicated that the head of Oliver Cromwell was buried somewhere near by.

Judge Crowell had recently resigned from the federal bench due to alleged health reasons, and he had not been seen in the last three months. Maybe his head would turn up in some strange location someday.

They saw the Round Church, walked by Jesus College, and came back toward town center via Milton's Walk, passing by Emmanuel College, Christ's College, Pembroke College, and Peterhouse, the oldest college, located on Trumpington Street. For lunch they ate at a pub overlooking the Silver Street Bridge and the back of Darwin College.

The official meeting in Cambridge was set to finalize the Fund's availability and obtain official approvals by the University and its officials. The Chancellor, Vice-

Chancellor, three faculty and two student representatives from the Council, and the Treasurer had scheduled a special conference with Sam and Professor Redmond at 2:30 p.m.

As they entered the Senate House, a reception line of University officials greeted both Sam and the Professor. After an hour of discussions and verifications of intentions, the conference was concluded. Prescott, again, apparently had had a heavy hand in making sure that all legal and financial issues were pre-cleared prior to Sam's official meeting.

The Vice-Chancellor asked Sam on the way out of the Senate Building, "When do you think the first funding assistance for a Gates' Scholar will be granted?"

Sam looked her in the eye and said, "As soon as I can get back to Alabama."

Chapter 51

Nashville, Tennessee
Grand Old Opry
Saturday, July 3, 2004
11:30 a.m.

Sam and Professor Redmond came up with a plan for Steven that was quickly approved by Prescott and the foundation, despite some rather unique extra expenses.

Sam started the ball rolling by calling Steven and telling him that a special charity had selected him to see and hear performances by different artists at a bluegrass festival that was to be held at the old Ryman Auditorium in Nashville on the 4th of July week-end. Transportation, food and lodging were included.

From 1943 to 1974, the Ryman had been the home of the Grand Old Opry. It had witnessed much in the way of famous performances over the years. In December of 1945, Earl Scruggs had first played his style of bluegrass banjo with Bill Monroe's band.

The Grand Ole Opry moved to the Opryland complex out from downtown in 1974. The new 4,400 seat auditorium dwarfed the capacity of the old Ryman. In recent years, the owners of the Ryman started bringing in various artists for concerts. These were immensely popular.

Steven consented and was somewhat surprised when a limo picked him up with Sam on Friday at about noon and drove them to a private hanger at the Birmingham airport where they flew to Nashville. Upon arrival, they were again picked up in a limo and taken directly to the Gibson factory, where after a short tour, Sam presented Steven with a new gold plated Mastertone banjo with his name inscribed on a metal plate attached to the inside wooden shell underneath the resonator.

Steven was speechless. His eyesight had improved somewhat, but not enough to see the details of the mother of peal inlays clearly. Sam told him that these pegs would not slip, and that the quirky sounds of his old banjo were a thing of the past.

That evening they enjoyed crowd pleasing performances of bluegrass at it s best at the Ryman.

The next day, Sam had Professor Redmond meet them for lunch at Opryland.

As they sat down, Professor Redmond said, "Steven. I have a new job that I have not told you about."

"I wondered about that. I have not heard from you in over a month," said Steven.

"Well," said Professor Redmond. "I am the administrator for the Oxbridge Scholars' Special Assistance Fund, and as the first official public act, I have been asked to inform you that a special grant has been funded so that you can have all of the support you might need to accept the

Gates Scholarship and attend Cambridge. It has been pre-cleared with the Gates Foundation and the University."

Steven started to tear up with happiness.

"Does my Mom know?" asked Steven.

"Yes," said Sam. "I told her two days ago but asked that she let us surprise you with this trip to Nashville."

After another evening of bluegrass at the Ryman, the next morning they flew back to Birmingham. Upon dropping Steven off, Sam headed home.

When he got there he called Jonesy in Rio. He told her a little about the charity work and the past week-end. She thought his activities were grand. Sam asked if he could see her soon.

She said that her hair had not come back in fully yet, and that she had had to have a small operation on her left leg which had not healed. It required plastic surgery. Sam thought that she was very vague about the medical nature of this operation, but he did not pursue it.

Jonesy said she would let him know when she was healed enough in her body and mind. She estimated it would be October or November. Would he come to Rio? Travel to the states had become a hassle for Brazilians and other foreigners due to recent terrorist concerns. Sam said that he would await her call.

Chapter 52

Birmingham, Alabama
U.S. Attorney's Office
Wednesday, August 11, 2004
2:30 p.m.

The reason Pickering's criminal associates had not seen him in a while was because he had entered the federal witness protection program and was telling all to the two federal grand juries.

In the course of these proceedings, Pickering's lawyer, Ned Able, a noted local white collar defense lawyer ran into Sam on the street outside the old Federal Courthouse building on Fifth Avenue North.

Ned asked, "Sam, have you got a minute? My client Pickering asked me to pass the word to you about something."

Sam replied, "You probably know that I am no longer doing criminal cases. The U.S. Attorney assigned me to the Civil Division. If it has to do with criminal or grand jury matters you might want to direct the information to one of the criminal Assistant U.S. Attorneys."

"This is a little different. It involves you and the U.S. Attorney personally," he said.

Sam was taken aback somewhat and asked, "What is the world are you talking about?"

Ned replied, "According to Pickering there was some funny connection between his old buddy in crime, Tom Wassel, and Linda Lott, the U.S. Attorney."

"Tell me more. Are there any specifics?" queried Sam, who was becoming focused and angry.

"Linda and her father had a secret meeting in New York with Wassel within the past year. Wassel bragged to Pickering that he was 'getting Sam's ex to squeeze Sam's balls.' Wassel also claimed that he got drunk with Linda and painted the town red."

Sam struggled to control his temper and asked, "Would Pickering be willing to testify to all of this under oath?"

Ned replied, "Of course."

"Thanks for the information. I'll put it to good use."

They shook hands and Sam headed straight for his office. Linda had clearly overstepped the bounds of propriety.

Sam immediately called the U.S. Department of Justice's Office of Professional Responsibility. This was the office within the Department that investigated attorney misconduct. He told them the entire story of what had transpired. An investigation was immediately launched, with investigators from Washington flying in the very next morning.

By Friday afternoon Linda had resigned from the U.S. Attorney's Office for "personal and family reasons."

Sam had no remorse about what he had done, and he certainly had no pity for Linda.

Chapter 53

Little River Canyon, Alabama
Rented Log Cabin
Saturday, September 4, 2004
11:30 a.m.

One of the deepest canyons east of the Grand Canyon lies in the middle of Lookout Mountain as it runs through Northeast Alabama in DeKalb and Cherokee Counties. The Little River that passes through the canyon has been designated wild and scenic under special legal protection. In 1992, Congress established the Little River Canyon National Preserve. A few private cabins and summerhouses are scattered along the rim. They were mostly built on lands that owners originally acquired prior to the Preserve. A few new large houses were springing up along parts of the rim on private lands to the alarm of some who wanted to preserve the natural beauty of the entire canyon area.

For the Labor Day weekend Sam rented a log cabin near DeSoto Falls that had been well used over the years. The nearest neighbor was a quarter of a mile, and the place was generally so quiet that the buzzing of dirt daubers, wasps, and billy bees in the late summer were the loudest sounds heard. In the winter, sometimes you could get snowed or iced in, especially in February or March. Alabama's only ski resort was nearby.

Sam had been coming to this area of Alabama since he was a kid. There were terrific camps in the area, and the town of Mentone held plenty of unique characters and charms. Sam recalled his first banjo lessons when he was 16 at Rising Fawn, which was just up the road in Georgia.

Sam planned to take some leave in order to go visit Jonesy. He needed to decide what he was going to do with his life, so his first stop was the canyon area. He did not want to quit his job as an Assistant U.S. Attorney, yet he felt he needed some new direction in life. New opportunities had been opened to him since the foundation had come into being. The cabin area was a good place to relax and reflect.

It was still warm in early September, and the leaves on the hardwood trees had not yet begun to turn. It wasn't like mid-May, Sam's favorite time, when the mountain laurels, wild azaleas, and rhododendrons were in bloom.

Earlier that morning Sam had hauled on his old hiking boots and took Holmes with him on two miles of trails along the canyon rim, stopping at some old Indian caves to take a few pictures with his new digital camera.

The hike also gave Sam a chance to think about many people that had impacted his life in the past year or so.

Steven had just arrived in Cambridge. He was preparing for his studies with full assistance and enjoying every minute. He was now a member of Trinity College, the same college that Sir Isaac Newton had attended. Steven even joined a local folk club where he played his new 5-string banjo. One could not imagine a better place for his new academic life or a learning environment in more beautiful surroundings.

Steven's mother, Karen, would soon be set for life financially when the real estate from the Cayman trust was sold and she and the interim trustee received their fees. She and Lauren planned to visit Steven over the Christmas holidays.

Linda was being investigated by a separate federal grand jury, and she would loose her license to practice at the very least. The ruthless ambitions instilled in her by her mother and crooked father brought her down. Sam was thankful that she had not entangled him in any illegal activities during their marriage.

All of the Cayman trust beneficiaries had been indicted for U.S. income tax violations. There would be superseding indictments for money laundering soon. All of these defendants, except Pickering, had disappeared. Sam figured they had headed for Central or South America, or possibly one of the islands in the Caribbean. He didn't think he would ever see any of them again.

When the FBI turned up at Judge Crowell's mansion on Red Mountain with a search warrant, he had had a severe stroke. The Judge was now in a nursing home with a life expectancy of less than 6 months. He could not walk, talk, or communicate. His major life activities consisted of drooling and soiling himself.

Professor Redmond was having the time of his life in his new position as Administrator of the Oxbridge

Scholars' Special Assistance Fund. He now lived in London and traveled the world.

Yesterday, on his drive up to the cabin from Birmingham, Sam had stopped in Centre for lunch with Uncle John. The night before Sam put a corned beef brisket on the barbecue grill and cooked it slowly for several hours with the mustard based sauce that he had bought from the Smokey Pig Number One. Sam also made some jalapeno cole slaw.

He also brought some vanilla ice cream and Drambuie along with the Viagra tablets. However, when he asked Uncle John about any medications he was taking, Uncle John said that he was using nitroglycerine tablets for his angina. Sam, therefore, kept the Viagra tablets to himself.

He knew from the internet that men taking nitroglycerine or nitrates and Viagra could go into extreme hypotension (low blood pressure) and have complete heart failure. There was a good reason for men to see a doctor in order to get a prescription. Out of an abundance of caution, Sam told Uncle John about potential heart stoppage and death from taking the combination.

Uncle John said that he appreciated the warning and that it was a good thing that Sam had not furnished him with the pills, or else he might have taken the stuff and died. He said he would look for other recreations at his age and condition.

"After all," said Uncle John, "according to Miss Julia, God rest her soul, you have a gray hair for every really good time you've ever had during your life, and I do have a full head of gray hair."

Sam and Uncle John enjoyed the barbecued brisket, cole slaw, and plain liquid love for dessert.

Uncle John like the dessert the best and commented, "I didn't know what my body needed but I believe that was it. Write down that formula for me."

They talked at some length about dogs and fishing, two of Uncle John's favorite topics. Sam left the Drambie, the rest of the ice cream, and the formula. Sam also left with a good feeling. Uncle John was in a fine mood and his health was holding up well.

On his hike, Sam also thought a lot about Jonesy and wondered where he and she were bound.

Sam and Holmes had headed back to the cabin for lunch, where he had made a tomato, cucumber, onion and lettuce sandwich on whole wheat. He washed it down with a Bass Ale.

Sam was sitting on the back porch in a guitar rocking chair picking his Mastertone 5-string, contemplating the worn fret board and its needed replacement. Sam was trying to compose a banjo tune that he wanted to call "Banjo in the Canyon", which experimented with harmonic chimes in an echoing effect. Holmes had wandered off somewhere while he was playing. Sam didn't think that Holmes ever really enjoyed bluegrass, but that was a character trait that was understandable and forgivable in Holmes.

Sam heard a loud thunk and looking to his left he saw a large copperhead snake on the porch floor less than five feet away.

Someone yelled, "Incoming!"

Just then another copperhead came flying through the air and landed almost at Sam's feet. He suddenly realized that someone had tossed these snakes at him.

As Sam stood holding his banjo, Jeff Duval stepped into view from the corner of the cabin. He was waist high to the floor of the porch, just at the base of the six stone steps that went down into the yard. He wore a set of faded bib overalls with no shirt or undershirt. A redneck fashion statement, as Uncle John would have said. Duval also had on long boots, no doubt snake proof.

Duval said, "Howdy *Capitan*, its time we settled some accounts. Hold that banjer out with one hand so I can see it good."

As Sam held out his banjo by the neck with his right hand, Duval put a shot through the resonator with a .38 Smith & Wesson pistol, the impact stinging Sam's hand and causing him to drop the banjo to the porch.

In the meantime, the copperheads appeared to be drowsy and not moving too much, but they were headed in Sam's general direction, advancing very slowly toward his feet.

Sam thought to himself that Duval had probably used gasoline to catch them and dry ice to make them woozy so that he could safely toss the snakes at Sam, as he had obviously done with the packaged copperhead on his apartment doorstep. But Sam wasn't sure. If Duval had gassed and dry iced the one in the package, he would have done the same with these.

Duval said, "I want my share of the Panama money, and you are going to help me get what's mine. Neither you nor that crooked former lawyer of mine, Judge Crowell, are going screw me on this. Did you know that he also had a blue banjo just like mine tattooed on his left knee at one time but that he had it removed before going on the bench?"

Sam started putting many pieces of evidence together, but he had more immediate worries. Sam fully realized that Duval intended to hurt and then kill him. Duval could not afford to let Sam go free at this point.

A plan suddenly started forming in Sam's mind, but he needed to know if the copperheads had been gassed and dry iced. Otherwise they would be quicker than Sam and more dangerous for his idea.

He asked Duval, "Did you send me a copperhead in package to my apartment in Birmingham?"

He said, "Yeah, what of it? I also had your brake lines cut."

Sam had his answer and then some. He tried to remain calm and as still as possible, not wanting to agitate the two copperheads. They were slowly coming around, and they would not be happy with any warm bloodied critters they happened to encounter.

Sam saw his opportunity and asked Duval, "If I help you with the money, will you leave me and my dog alone in peace?"

"What dog?"

Holmes had been sneaking up behind Duval since the gunshot, and Sam shouted, "Get him, Holmes."

Duval's pistol hand was suddenly in the jaws of Holmes.

At the same time Sam's plan was to practice his soccer style kick with the copperheads. Just like Jonesy had taught him years ago, Sam stepped forward and planted his left foot. Then with his right hiking boot turned sideways, he swept both snakes forward towards Duval in one swift movement.

Duval was bent slightly forward trying to deal with Holmes when the first copperhead smacked him in the head and briefly wrapped around his face. He was so stunned and scared that he dropped his pistol.

As Duval was still bent down face forward, the second snake scored a miracle goal because it went sailed down the slack front of Duval's bib overalls.

Sam grabbed his shot-up Mastertone by the neck, yelled for Holmes to move away, and leaping off the porch, swung the heavy wooden rim with its tone ring made of bell brass at Duval's legs. Sam heard a serious crunch in Duval's left knee as he went down on his back yelling and flailing.

Sam picked up the pistol and watched carefully as the two copperheads slithered away from the crying, cursing, and crippled Duval.

Sam told Holmes to watch him while he went inside the cabin for his cell phone. Sam called the FBI duty officer first, making a quick report. Sam also asked him to call 911 in Ft. Payne, and have some deputies from the DeKalb County sheriff's department come to take Duval in.

Finally, Sam told the duty officer that medics should be dispatched immediately, and they should be prepared to treat a prisoner with multiple snakebites.

Copperheads.

Epilogue

Birmingham, Alabama
Sam Stone's Apartment on Southside
Monday, October 11, 2004
5:30 p.m.

After the business with Duval on Labor Day week-end, Sam went back to work at the U.S. Attorney's Office, but things were not the same. The Civil Division cases kept him busy but they weren't as fast paced as criminal ones. He thought about asking for a transfer back to the Criminal Division, but he had had enough of dealing with criminals on a personal basis lately. Within a month or so he decided that, if nothing else, he needed a change.

Sam used the Columbus Day federal holiday to clean his apartment and pack his bags. Karen had agreed to look after Holmes for a while. Sam was not giving up his Assistant U.S. Attorney job yet, but he was thinking about it. He had three weeks of leave that he planned to put to good use.

With his Mastertone shot up and damaged, Sam finally had a good reason to build that custom made banjo that he had always dreamed about. Sam was thinking that he needed an expert consultant on some exotic Brazilian hardwoods which he wanted to incorporate into the custom 5-string's design. Sam knew where he could find her. He was headed for Rio in the morning.

Jonesy had called yesterday and said, "Come on down."

She was ready for him, and Sam could not wait.

Acknowledgments

I would like to acknowledge and thank the following who have given me help, support, or ideas from time to time:

Judges: Marianne B. Bowler; John E. Ott; Cecelia G. Morris; J. Robert Elliott; Morey L. Sear; W. Louis Sands; J. Scott Vowell, Arthur J. Hanes, Jr.; Caryl P. Privett; Robert S. Vance, Jr., David A. Rains, and Randall L. Cole.

Law Professors: Perry R. Sentell, Jr.; Kurt Lipstein; Samuel M. Davis; David E. Shipley; John L. Carroll; Harold S. Lewis, Jr.; Manning G. Warren, III; Guenther Handl; Donald Q. Cochran, Jr.; Rebecca H. White; Jack A. Taylor; and Michelle R. Slack.

Attorneys: Benjamin A. Hardy, Jr.; Georgette Sosa Douglass; Alice H. Martin; J. Michael Shea; Sharon D. Simmons; Carolyn L. Duncan; Herbert H. Henry, III; Vicki R. Crowell; D. Owen Blake; Samuel A. Wilson, Jr.; H. James Lewis, III; Joyce W. Vance; Joe D. Whitley; Samuel W. Jackson; G. Douglas Jones; Leon F. Kelly, Jr.; Robert Joe McLean; E. Ann McMahan; E. Stephen Heninger; S. Greg Burge; C. Paul Cavender; Kenneth E. Vines; H.

Randolph Aderhold, Jr.; Adolph J. Dean, Jr.; Robert L. Coley; Lawrence F. Jones; George B. Mattox; John W. Ragsdale; Hubert J. Bell, Jr.; Joseph W. Popper, Jr.; Al J. Smith, Jr.; Dennis P. Helmreich; Timothy T. Herring; Gregory T. Gronholm; Darrel F. Brown; D. Martin Low; James P. Farwell; Daniel Beck; Curtis A. Thurston, Jr.; Willie J. Huntley, Jr.; E. J. Saad; Donald G. Beebe; James H. Crosby; Richard M. Crump; Bill L. Barnett; John C. Bell; Alison S. Blackwell; Walter Braswell; Ronald R. Brunson; Mary S. Burell; William R. Chambers; Katherine L. Corley; Angela R. Debro; John C. Earnest; John H. England, III; David H. Estes; J. Bradley Felton; James G. Gann; William R. Hankins, Jr.; M. Matt Hart; Laura D. Hodge; James D. Ingram; Robert P. McGregor; George A. Martin; Tamarra Matthews; John Patton Meadows; A. Clark Morris; Richard E. O'Neal; Lloyd C. Peeples, III; Russell E. Penfield; James E. Phillips; Robert O. Posey; Edward Q. Ragland; Michael V. Rasmussen; Frank M. Salter; William G. Simpson; Winfield J. Sinclair; Jenny L. Smith; Carolyn W. Steverson; Sandra J. Stewart; James A. Sullivan; James L. Weil; Michael W. Whisonant; Lane H. Woodke; Michael W. Bailie; R. Wayne Hughes, Jr.; Paula D. Silsby; Robert M. Taylor; James R. Shively; Susan Dein Bricklin; Roger L. McRoberts, Jr., Herbert C. Sundby; Steven E. Obus; Irene Dowdy; Tom Majors; Ronald K. Silver; Jill O. Venezia; Edward M. Robbins, Jr.; Roy D. Atchison, Jr.; Stephen Graben; Frederick E. Martin; Sidney P. Alexander; Debra J. Prillaman; John W. Zavits; Nina L. Hunt; Lawrence B. Lee; Rachel C. Ballow; R. Emery Clark; Beth Drake; Lee Deneke; and John P. Moran.

Brazil Consultants: Diva Gonçalves McCourtney and Ian McCourtney; Luciana Lyra; Marcio Lyra; Lucia

Salanes Lyra; Regina Fontes Foster; Erika Sargent; and John Sargent.

Panama Canal Consultants: Charles R. Lavallee; John D. Nolan; John M. Eberenz; Olga Nance; Ada Favorite; Allen Cotton; Jim Smith; Lynn Rodzianko; Carl Haberland; Mike Rodzianko; Pablo Prieto; and Beverly and Keith Moumblow.

Physicians: Dr. Hugh M. Hood; Dr. John Lockhart; Dr. Michael G. Cromey.

Paralegals: Sue A. Moore and Mary L. Erhart.

Legal Secretaries: Deanna M. Stone and Wanda England.

Economist: Thomas D. Walsh.

Special Consultants: Kate Carr; P.J. Walsh; Jill Coveny Birch; Phyllis R. Cooke; Anne S. Moser; and Doc Lawrence.

Banjo Player, Teacher and Repair Expert: Herb Trotman.

Other Banjo Players: Samuel A. Wilson, Jr.; Lawrence B. Lee; Joe Scarborough; Don Rabon; Horace Green; Gregory T. Gronholm; and Terrence W. Cromey.

Bluegrass Bands: Chiva Bus Bluegrass Band; Habersham County Bluegrass Band; and the Strung Jury.

Organizations and Businesses: The Alabama Historical Association; The Birmingham Inns of Court; The Brazilian-American Cultural Institute; The Cumberland School of Law Library; The Panama Canal Society; The Redemptorists of the Amazon; The University of Alabama Law Library; and Fretted Instruments of Homewood, Alabama.

Wife and Family: Pat Hood, and daughters Sara and Laura, who make my life worthwhile.

This is a work of fiction. Any references to events, locales, businesses, organizations, political structures or legal entities are intended only to give the fiction a sense of reality. The names, characters, places, and incidents are products of my imagination or are used fictitiously and not to be construed as real. Any resemblances to actual events, locations, or persons, living or dead, are entirely coincidental. All mistakes are mine.

Jack B. Hood
Birmingham, Alabama

About The Author

Jack B. Hood was born in Clarksville, Habersham County, Georgia in 1948. He received an A.B. degree in 1969 and a J.D. degree in 1971, from the University of Georgia. In 1972, he received a Diploma in International Law from the University of Cambridge. He has been a JAG Captain in the USAF, a law professor, and a private practitioner.

He worked as an Assistant U.S. Attorney in the Middle District of Georgia and presently works as an Assistant U.S. Attorney in the Northern District of Alabama.

He is a member of the Alabama, District of Columbia, Georgia, Tennessee, and former Canal Zone bars.

He is the author and co-author of several books, primarily legal texts, published currently by Thomson/West.